COOCHIE
Gibran Tariq
©2017

This is a work of fiction. All the characters, incidents,
organizations, and dialogue
In this novel are either the product of the author's imagination or
are used fictitiously.

SOULFIRE BOOKS

Charlotte NC 28206

980 299 0867

ACKNOWLEDGMENTS

Above all else, all praise is due to Allah, the Creator of the heavens, the earth, and all between.

I cannot fathom dedicating this to anyone other than the members of my family: my sisters: Charlotte, Lorraine, Valerie, Jacqueline, Carolyn Denise, Gwendolyn, Angela, and Paula; my brothers, Buddy Cool, Qayyam(Brotha Dave), Butch, and John; my daughters, Latonya, Adrienne, Shameka, and Joy; my grandchildren, and all my wonderful nieces and nephews. I especially thank my son-in-law, Nathan, who powered this whole project through when so many others had tried and failed.

Others I must acknowledge include Mrs. Joan Boudreaux, the very first person to believe in me and who wouldn't permit me to give up. Without her guidance, I would have given up. I also feel compelled to thank my 8th grade teacher at Polk Youth Center, Maurice Baker, who inspired me to study words.

I must also thank Sista Laylah, and Sista Angela Morrow, both of whom have been vital to my survival as a writer.

At every step I've taken during the course of my life, I have enjoyed the luxury of good company, and I feel compelled to salute my comrades and hustling partners with whom I spent many years in the trenches with: RL Morrow, Napoleon "Napo" Melton, James "Flint" Wells, Jafar (Odell Ware), DC Mobley, Malik (Keith Ross), O'Neal "Hard-Times" McGill, Jihad Omar Hasan, Ahmad (Marty Rorie), Hassan (Lenny White), Jamal (Johnell Porter), Abdullah (Leon Funderburke), Turk Maxwell, Larry Manns, James, "JB" Brown, Chris Bailey, Curt Riley, Ronald Brown, Ronald Dixon, Irshad(Buck Cox) and Ray Vanover. Last but not least, I salute two of my hustling mentors, Billy Dykes and Billy Brown.

Big ups to brothas such as Bo Jones, Martin Russell, Askia

Shabazz(Johnny Cherry), Damon Stafford, Eddie Mungo, and Rob Shambor, and all the other comrades struggling to survive on the inside. Fight the good fight!

COOCHIE

Chapter 1

On the afternoon of October 20th, a very sunny, unseasonably warm Tuesday, Neon Ashford, a short, brown-skinned female, shook her ass like she was trying to break it. She had on a pair of tight-fitting, cream-colored jeans whose relationship to her apple-bottomed behind was more like a second skin than a piece of fabric. Even though, at nineteen, she was well aware that black women with phat asses were part of the urban culture, she also recognized that the man eyeing her down from behind the wheel of a badly battered, black Ford Escort had probably never seen that much ass-shaking going on in one pair of jeans. She allowed herself a faint trace of a smile. The man had one hand on the steering wheel. She instinctively knew where the other one was, and exactly what it was doing.

By the time she was two and a half steps away from the corner of Hyde Drive and Craighead Street in northeast Charlotte, her strutting was strictly a "come buy this pussy" advertisement. After all, the same way she could make her hips move in her jeans, she could move them like that between the sheets.

"You need a ride?"

4

Neon stopped her 5'2" body abruptly, staring casually out of her dark brown eyes at the driver of the Escort. "Depends on which way you going." She licked her painted lips seductively. "Which way you going?"

"Get in," the driver muttered. "I'm going your way." Lazily reaching over to unlock the car door for her, the tall, thin, dark-skinned, dreadlocked driver drove down Craighead towards North Tryon Street. "What's your name?"

"Neon."

"Boo's friend?!"

Neon took a deep breath, wondering what Boo might have said about her, hoping it wouldn't ruin her plans. "I haven't seen that bitch in a minute. Plus, we wasn't all that to begin with."

The driver smiled as he neared Mike's, the neighborhood store run by a well-liked Asian couple. "Want something outta there?"

"No, but I need to make me some money."

Supreme nodded knowingly, not having to think about what the young girl meant, yet the concept of buying pussy outright was new to him. The situation at hand made him pause, knowing full well that in a matter of seconds he had reached the crossroads, where in the hood, he was about to become a trick.

In the hood, tricking was as real as slanging dope or sticking up, but to an ol' G like Supreme, it was not an option. At least, not while he still had trap skills.

"Where you want me to drop you off at?" Supreme cracked coolly.

"I thought I was going with you?"

"Something just came up."

"What?"

"I ain't no trick."

"Then why you stop me, nigga?"

Supreme privately studied the pretty, young girl. She was tempting, almost worth tricking with. He understood that tricking wasn't the ultimate weakness hustlers had made it out to be and as far as he could tell, tricking hadn't traumatized any of the niggas who participated fully in the ritual of buying pussy. In fact, it was the existence of tricking that had paved the way for strip clubs where wannabe and has-been gangstas threw money away like it grew on trees.

"Got anything that's free?" Supreme half-teased.

"Free? Nigga, please."

"How I know them titties real? Suppose you wearing butt pads or something?" Supreme grinned. "When I go to the store, I be squeezing shit like crazy, be feeling on them crackers' shit so I know what the fuck I'm spending my money on."

When Neon looked at Supreme, she wasn't amused. "Let me off at the corner, if you don't mind. Ain't nobody got no damn time to waste."

Struggling mentally with the girl's irrefutable sexual appeal, Supreme gave way to his desire, and took the path countless men before him had taken. "Let's go to my place." He slowly drove towards his one-bedroom apartment in Cedar Greene.

The apartment was a refuge for Supreme and he never usually brought people where he laid his head so when he opened the door, he took a long breath and graciously invited Neon in. "Ain't much," he remarked casually, "but it's home."

Ignoring the remark, Neon expertly appraised the apartment's impressive interior, and instantly the price for her services, whether hips, lips, or fingertips skyrocketed. This nigga could pay! She sat on the edge of the expensive Italian leather sofa. "Good pussy ain't cheap."

"And good money ain't easy to come by," Supreme argued, "but I'm willing to splurge if the price is right."

"I need a hundred dollars," Neon snapped. "Be the best damn money you ever spent."

Like her mother before her, Neon was personally opposed to giving pussy away, and she took great pride in making men pay dearly for the privilege of fucking her.

"Good pussy is the greatest sensation known to exist," Neon's mother, Stella, had taught her, "so don't never ever come home with nuthin' but a wet ass to show for it." No lesson, either from church or from school, had had a bigger or more lasting impact on Neon than that one.

Beginning her sexual career at fifteen, Neon was determined to gain more than her rightful share of the profits that "pussy money" made available, but unlike the common ho whose career was usually ruined early, Neon planned to elevate the selling of pussy to new heights. She felt like an evil genius, but she wanted bitches in the hood to idolize her as their sex hero like young niggas looked up to Wilt Chamberlain, who claimed to have fucked ten thousand women in his life-time.

Neon felt good about her chances because her sexual credentials were impeccable, and she could fuck like a bitch twice her age. Her mother had taught her well, had schooled her intensively in the fine art of making a trick out of even the hardest male on the block.

"They ain't really tricks when you turn 'em out yourself, girl," Neon's mother had proudly proclaimed on Neon's fifteenth birthday. "They providers. A trick's money is available to any bitch who can get his dick hard. A provider's dick belongs to you, but always keep in mind that it ain't the dick you after, it's the finances."

Neon had known that this talk was her birthday present so she had listened attentively as her mother had explained that somewhere in the world some bitch was probably getting the keys to a new car for her birthday, that some ho might even be getting the keys to a new house, but that wasn't shit. She was giving Neon the keys to life.

"When a bitch got good pussy, she can invent the kind of man she wants. Good pussy can transform a zero into a hero, can turn a stressed motherfucka into a blessed motherfucka, and the way you do it is one nut at a time!"

So far, Neon's career as a sexual predator was perfect. She was fine, phat, and gifted; a triple threat bitch who could get a man off with her pussy, her mouth, or her hands. Undoubtedly, being a Triple Crown ho upped her sexual value tremendously.

Neon took immense pride in being at the forefront of a new movement of young bitches who used sex not merely to make money, but to make themselves wealthy. What this meant for

Neon was that if she desired to possess total control, she had to get inside a man's head before he got inside her panties. The belief that good pussy was the best thing in the world was so powerful and so profound to Neon that when she had inherited the notion from her mother, she had become so emotionally attached to it that it was like second nature to her. Good pussy carried its own rewards, and Neon cursed and despised silly bitches who didn't recognize the stupendous value of what nestled between their thighs.

"From time to time, every bitch on the planet has gone to bed dreaming about dick," Stella remarked bluntly one rainy afternoon, "but it would be a violation of everything a good bitch should be about if she let it get the best of her. This is the real world where money is the yardstick by which everything is measured. Dick can make you cum, but only money can make you come up."

Neon and her mother sat in the kitchen, the most prestigious place in the world for training and advice on how to become a gold-digger. It was around this table that many young girls had discovered Stella's secret formula to escape the harsh reality of the hood.

"Your pussy is an ATM machine," Stella had declared on countless occasions like a sex prophetess. "You can let it grow cobwebs or you can let it make money for you. The damn choice is yours!"

This encouraged Neon.

"You gotta have sexual pride," Stella warned her oldest daughter, "or else your ass will go down in history as being a sexual hypocrite. You get your shit together and you can change a nigga's taste when it comes to bitches. All you gotta remember is that the motherfucka ain't getting with yo' ass 'cause he got money to throw away. He getting with you 'cause yo' pussy good."

Evasive about her own sexual upbringing, Stella had made her way into the ho game as a teenager on West Trade Street. She had been (and still was) a stunningly attractive, brown-skinned female with plenty of titties and ass.

Suffering an untimely stroke while still young, Stella had been sidelined, but was determined to use her sexual genius so that her two daughters, under her direction, would become the First Ladies of the ho game in Charlotte.

"I got me a big fish on the line," Neon bragged. "Nigga write books."

"Hmmph, a writer." Stella attempted to act uninterested. "Nigga probably ain't never wrote shit that nobody be wanting to read."

"All I know is that the nigga ain't starving. You should see his crib, bitch laid out real fabulous. Plus, this his third book, so that means somebody buying his shit." Neon knew that her answer robbed her mother of a quick reply, and the last thing she wanted to do was to appear to be acting sassy. "Wanna see him? I took a picture of him without him knowing it." Neon touched her cell phone, bringing it to a startling burst of color, and then scrolled through her photos. "Here he is, Mama." She handed the phone to her mother. "My new fish."

Stella stared at the picture, started to say something, stopped, looked away, blinking her eyes as if they were deceiving her. She looked once more. "Girl, that ain't no fish. That's Jaws. Leave that nigga alone."

"You-you know him?"

"Hell yeah, I know his motherfucking ass. That's Slim Green, one of the original gangstas in this town. Nigga ain't to be fucked with."

Neon cut her eyes at her mother defiantly. "I don't care who he is or was. I'm turning his ass out."

"Young bitch----"

"You said that any nigga could be flipped." Neon's voice was still defiant. "And you also said that there were no exceptions. Said that any motherfucka with a dick could be made a slave to a bitch with good pussy, and my pussy the best there is." Neon put her hands on her hips. "This my test, Mama. Too bad, he know you or we could double-team his ass. Anyway, I gotta do this more than ever now."

"Go 'head on, girl," Stella said with a hushed sigh. "Just

remember that this nigga ain't no trick."

"He done already told me that, Mama, but he still wanting to fuck me. That gives me the upper hand."

"He yours, then." When the first signs of joy appeared on Neon's pretty face, Stella embraced her oldest daughter. "As far as I know, ain't nobody ever tricked Slim Green out of shit, and lived to see the sun shine the next day."

Chapter 2

Later in the evening when a smooth, easterly breeze blew in from the mountains of Tennessee, warming up the Charlotte atmosphere, Neon made her way towards Dare Drive. She stopped at the corner store to give her young sister some last minute instructions.

"Let me do all the talking."

Brianna frowned. "I know what to do better than you. You should let me pull him."

"This my trick, not yours. Anyway, you ain't ready, probably not even able to turn nobody out." Neon laughed. "Yo' young ass still wet behind the ears. You ain't but sixteen."

Brianna ignored the remark about her age. "Ain't you forgetting what Mama said? She said don't be looking at that ol' G like he no trick. Nigga a gangsta."

"I remember what I want to remember. Anyway, Mama at home, so don't be telling or re-telling me shit she done said. I'm my own bitch, so lissen and learn, okay?"

Brianna was already moist between her legs although her role would be small. That frustrated her since she was much prettier than her sister and though younger, had more ass and titties. Plus, she was red. "I still think Mama should have let me put on something to show my shit off ." She ran her hands over her hips. "How I'm gonna do you any good if I'm dressed like a bitch going to church? Can I put on some of your lipstick?"

"No, and stop acting like you ain't got no sense or I'll tell Mama you giving away pussy for free."

Neon's anger was gone as quickly as it had come. She

11

loved her baby sister in a way she never thought possible, but the girl was a bit too womanish for her age. At first, Neon had been naturally resentful as she had jealously witnessed Brianna go from flat to phat so fast. Watching Brianna develop was perhaps one of the most unnerving experiences of her life, but to her credit, Neon didn't let it get in the way of her devotion to her sister. Brianna's blossoming would be good for the family business.

A few minutes later when the sisters arrived at their destination, it was clear that both girls were excited. Neon knocked. The white wood door was open so Neon could look through the screen door and see Supreme seated at his computer terminal. He turned slowly at the knock as if he was not expecting company or wanting to be disturbed, but a smile lit up his face when he recognized who the visitor was. He sprang from his chair.

"Neon!" He unfastened the latch on the screen door, and for the first time saw Brianna who was standing demurely at the bottom of the four steps that led to the front porch. "Come on in."

"Whatcha doing?"

"Nothing much. Just checking my email. What's up with you?" Supreme's eyes zeroed in on Neon as she took a seat on the sofa. She wore a pair of tight-fitting white pants with an equally snug top. Her hair was still fixed the same way it had been the day they had met, but today it was streaked with plum highlights.

"This my sister, Brianna, and we need a favor." When Neon scooted to the edge of the sofa, she parted her legs slightly so that Supreme could get a clear view between her thighs. She then leaned forward to allow him a peek at her breasts. "We were wondering if you could loan us some money to catch the bus over to our grandmama's house. Brianna locked the key inside the house and we can't get in until our Mama comes home from work tonight, so we need to go to West Boulevard to chill for a while."

"Y'all can chill out here if you want to, watch a movie or something."

Neon looked to be considering the offer, but glanced at Brianna who sat timidly in the far corner of the sofa. "My sista scared, that's the only reason why we can't."

Deflated, Supreme muttered. "That ain't being scared,

that's being smart."

"So can we get bus fare?"

Hitting upon another idea to keep the young girls close to him, Supreme blurted. "Why don't I drive y'all over to West Boulevard and then we can use the bus fare money to buy something to eat. I ain't got nothing to do."

When Brianna asked to use the bathroom, Neon used her absence to explain to Supreme that Brianna was uncomfortable around men, and if it was okay with him that they would rather have the money, and be on their way since their grandmother was expecting them shortly.

Accepting the news with his characteristic calm, Supreme gave Neon ten one dollar bills. "That should get you there and back."

With that, Neon smiled. "Give me your phone number. I'll call you later and you can come pick me up. I wanna come back heah and get on yo' computer."Neon smiled even more, but her eyes were question marks. "You not expecting any company tonight, are you?"

Supreme shook his head.

"I'll see you tonight then."

"What time you gonna call?" There was anticipation and excitement in Supreme's voice.

"Around nine," Neon purred, "when it's good and dark."

The very next morning.

When it came to dealing with her mother, rolling her eyes was the most offensive gesture Neon could get away with. This morning, she had done it twice.

"Girl, you keep rolling your damn eyes like that, they might get stuck to the back of your damn head."

"But Mama," Neon replied stubbornly, "I don't see where I made any progress."

"You got paid. It might not have been but ten dollars, but it's money." Stella pinched Neon's cheeks playfully. "That dime is the first fruits of your labors, baby."

"But I still think you should've let me go by myself. Brianna ain't ready yet."

"Yes, I am too," Brianna protested. "I played my role."

"That wasn't no damn role, you sitting yo' ass on the couch."

As usual at the onset of an argument between her daughters, Stella intervened. "Both of you hush. Now, listen. I did what I did for a reason, figuring this was the best way to play it right now. I wanted to introduce Brianna early. Guess why?"

"Why?" Neon was truly curious.

"As an insurance policy, that's why." Stella nodded her head knowingly. "The nigga got loot."

"Tole you," Neon remarked triumphantly. "Tole you he was holding, had plenty of cheese."

"Yeah, you tole me right, but his money ain't from no books like he wanting everybody to believe. That fool still got dope money. I did some checking and the word is that the feds didn't break him when they locked his black ass up. Yeah, they took some shit from him, but the nigga was smart, stashed 'bout a quarter mil. Now, he back on rich, but he playing that square Joe shit. Why you think he living on this side of town?"

"Trying to stay out of the way?"

"Right."

"Think he hiding from somebody?" Brianna quizzed.

Stella shook her head without delay. "Naw, that ain't Slim's style. Nigga ain't no scared nigga. Don't nobody put no fear in a nigga like that. The nigga just trying to stay under the radar. He just finished doing ten years in the feds so all he trying to do now is to chill---"

"And spend all that money."

"Well, that's about to change if we play our cards right. We don't fuck up and we'll be the ones chilling and spending money." Stella's mood turned thoughtful. "And that's why I sent Brianna with you. Brianna is a baby---"

"Ma!" Brianna protested as though her age was a curse. "I ain't no baby."

"Just the same you ain't legal yet, so what we need to do is to put Slim in a compromising position with you and then blackmail his ass. He just got out of jail and ain't wanting to go back for no statutory rape bullshit."

"Last time we talked," Neon howled, "it was all about me. You said I could do him, now some kind of way, it looks like Brianna gonna be the bitch who gets the glory. That's not fair."

Stella shook her head disapprovingly. "What difference it make who gets what as long as we get-the-fuck- paid?"

Neon pouted, glaring at her baby sister as if she was a wicked witch. "I found him."

Stella sighed in resignation. "And the nigga yours, so put your lips back in. My strategy ain't to take nothing from you, but to give us all something. Brianna ain't nothing but bait, you gonna be the one pulling all the strings so yo' selfish ass better not fuck up. You hear me?"

Not quite sure how to react without appearing to gloat, Neon simply whispered. "I hear you, Mama."

"Don't sit there with your black ass talking that I hear you Mama shit, and then not be listening to a word I said 'cause if you do, you gonna end up like them other silly bitches who be dead wrong about how shit go in life." Stella turned up her nose in disgust. "Dumb hoes be thinking the white man gonna rescue they ass. It ain't happening. White man tired of that party."

"I don't do white men," Brianna said. "Not me."

Stella threw up her hands in exasperation, glaring at her daughters. "See, that's the shit I'm talking 'bout. Y'all asses don't be listening to shit I say, so I'm gonna have to repeat my-damn-self." She sighed wearily. "I ain't talking 'bout no ordinary white man. I'm talking 'bout the big Three, the three white men that black bitches can't get enough of. Hoes be thinking they saviors."

"What they names?"

"To the young sista, it's Santa Claus. To the sista in the church, it's Jesus, and to the bitch on the block, it's Uncle Sam with his welfare check. Motherfuckas ain't no saviors, motherfuckas pimp. Y'all can fall for that bullshit if you want to, but this ain't the movies where some goody-two-shoes cracker coming to the rescue. This the hood where a motherfucka too damn busy trying to save himself to be worried 'bout rescuing somebody else."

The next time Supreme saw Neon was during the middle of the week just before Halloween and the girl's sex appeal was so pronounced that Supreme experienced a bout of sexual delirium that practically drove him insane. He had to have this female, but also found that he was glad that Brianna was along. He didn't want to pressure himself into making a move too soon. Today, he felt safe.

As the girls fed the neighborhood cats that always gathered at Supreme's backdoor, he kept his distance, eyeing Neon down, studying her every move. He also discovered something else that stunned him. Brianna was also phat! Until now, he had never really paid her any attention as Neon was always the focal point of his unresolved lust, but he had to confess that Brianna was very attractive as well.

"Since the cats have been fed, why don't we go out and get something to eat?"

"Where?" Neon asked

"Anywhere you want. The choice is yours."

"Chinese?"

"If that's what you want. Today is your day."

"Since today is our day," Neon said casually, "can we get some green?"

"Where we gonna get it from?"

"The weed man stay down the street from where we live. His weed be fire."

Supreme gave both girls a crisp twenty dollar bill and took a special delight when he saw how their eyes lit up. "Let's go. I know a Chinese spot up on Beatties Ford Road."

"We ain't got to go that far," Brianna offered, "because there a place on Graham and Atando that's closer."

Going to the car, Neon realized that Supreme had been checking Brianna out, so she knew she had to reclaim his attention. Her strategy would depend on how much Brianna went out of her way to get the spotlight, but she also knew that their jockeying for position could make this outing less successful than it should be. She made a mental note to have a meeting with her sister in the ladies' room at the earliest possible convenience.

While Neon was at the counter at the Chinese restaurant, Supreme exploited his first chance to speak with Brianna privately. They sat in a small booth as Neon ordered.

"How old are you?"

"Sixteen, but I'll be seventeen in February." Brianna smiled sweetly. "I know I'm young, but you can think of me as a woman in a school-girl's body."

Supreme groaned. "A nigga can go to jail for fucking around with you."

"How they gonna know what goes on behind closed doors?" Brianna giggled mischievously. "I don't put my business out in the street like that. I know how to play my position."

In response to her perception that Brianna was attempting to undermine her, Neon stormed to the table and demanded that they leave. She had ordered take-out.

"I thought we were eating here."

"I changed my mind," Neon huffed, struggling to contain her anger. "I want to go."

Supreme and Brianna looked at each other in surprise, but they both scrambled to get up and to follow Neon as she quickly strutted to and out of the front door. In the parking lot, she impatiently patted her foot as she waited on Supreme to unlock the car door so she could get in.

"Take me to get some green." Even before the car was started, Neon was giving Supreme driving directions. "Go back towards your house but make a right at the next street once you go pass the school. Better yet, pull into the Burger King parking lot and let me make a phone call."

Dismissing the theory that he had done something wrong, Supreme simply said nothing and did as he was told. He pulled into the Burger King parking lot where a Burgundy Acura soon pulled in, stopping alongside his car. The transaction was swift and Neon jumped back into the Escort.

"Let's go," she ordered.

The short drive back to his apartment was quiet, but no sooner had they arrived than Neon was back to her usual bubbly persona, and once the front door was opened, she burst into the apartment, singing cheerfully. Supreme shrugged it off. He just wanted to get close to the girl and to enjoy the scent of her perfume.

"You sure you don't want none?"

"Naw, I'm good," Supreme explained. "I'm on paper and my P.O. might piss me at any time."

Curiously, he watched as Neon ripped open the cheap, cellophane bag and emptied the contents on a brown cutting board she had found in the kitchen. She poked around in the pile of reefer with her fingernail, raking through it to remove any unwanted stems, but the weed was clean. Pleased, Neon turned oddly silent as she went to work putting together the fixings of a blunt.

Like a scientist, Neon cautiously extracted the Dutch green cigarillo from its wrapping, studying it as if it was a fine jewel before expertly turning it on its side to slit it open like it was the catch of the day. She then dumped the contents of the leaf into a white napkin which she ceremoniously handed to Brianna to be discarded.

Out of the corner of his eye, Supreme could see the evening sun glistening through the branches of the trees in the front yard. It was a beautiful day. Blinking once before shifting his gaze back to Neon, he noticed that the girl was going to great lengths to make the blunt perfect. She obviously enjoyed the ritual because when she was finished, she smiled. This was a piece of work, and Supreme gave himself credit for giving her props on a job well done.

Sweeping her brown eyes over the blunt, Neon studied each lump and curve, admiring their form, but after a second was ready to get down to business.

"Fire it up." She handed the blunt to Brianna.

Although he had no clue how the weed would shape Neon's sexual behavior, he was hopeful that the weed would end all of her pent-up frustration and help her keep her demons at bay long enough to help him defeat his own private demons. He knew nothing would happen this evening, but the prospect of getting some young pussy thrilled him endlessly. He, suddenly, felt very lucky.

Chapter 3

Supreme looked in the mirror and laughed so hard that snot flew out of his nose. His life was so fucked up that it would take a miracle, a blessing, and some outrageous good luck to straighten it out. Supreme laughed again. Motherfuckas thought he had money. That was bullshit because he was broker than a motherfucka. Ain't had shit.

Ever since he had been out, he had bounced between jobs and the only way he had survived so far was because his best friend, Ice, was lacing him up with cash. Ice had promised to look out until he could support himself, but good hustles were hard to come by with the economy in the shape it was in. And now he was out of paper again.

"I'm tired of begging."

"So what you saying, nigga," Ice cracked. "You want in?"

The two friends sat at the counter at The Rock Bottom Brewery, a local uptown establishment.

"How I'm gonna be in when you ain't never told me what I was getting into." Supreme grinned. "All you keep saying is that you done stumbled upon the hustle of a lifetime, which, though it sounds good, ain't telling a nigga shit." Supreme laughed. "Let you tell it, that last caper we went on was
supposed to have been sweeter than pussy, and I be damn if our black asses didn't end up locked up."

"Man, don't remind me of that bullshit 'cause we damn sho' overplayed our hand that time. Anyway, I ain't lying 'bout the game I'm playing now. Can't beat it."

"Man," Supreme whispered, "I need another drink."

When the waitress returned with the shot of Hennessey, Ice watched patiently as Supreme nursed the drink in his hands, occasionally swirling the smooth brown liquor around and around in the thick glass. "In a minute, you keep doing that, shit gonna get warm and taste like you drinking piss."

Supreme smiled wearily. "Betcha the crew in the cellblock got 'em five gallons of hooch cooking in the back of the showers right now, especially--------."

"Man, fuck them niggas. Them locked-up fools got they own cross to bear. What we---me and you---need to do is to discuss how you gonna roll."

"What choice I got?"

Ice could understand Supreme's reluctance, but why bullshit. They both knew that living well was the perfect reward for a nigga who had just spent time in the trenches. There was nothing fascinating or brave about being broke, and any motherfucka on the bricks who wasn't in search of a dollar might as well step out in front of an oncoming bus. "Legend has always had it that there was a hustle sweeter than the ho game."

"And I suppose you done found it?"

Ice grinned devilishly. "Naw, it found me." Ice shrugged his shoulders nonchalantly. "Hard to say when or how it happened, but one day just like it was meant to be, I was reborn in the game."

"Now, you're scaring me, getting all religious and shit, especially since you a nigga that ain't never even went to Sunday school."

"Dig that," Ice cracked irreverently, "but what I done found for a hustle is like what a sinner feels when he finds Jesus." Still amazed at his own good fortune, Ice sat back, gushing excitedly. "And ain't nuthin' like it in the whole, wide world."

At that moment, Supreme wasn't sure what happened, but he knew he wanted in. "So today is my lucky day?"

"Lucky?!" Ice scoffed. "Today could become a glorious day for you, and since I now see you interested, I'm gonna let you ride with me." Ice grinned, standing. "C'mon, nigga and check out my world."

Parking his Aston Martin by the softball field, Ice felt his heart flutter as he stepped outside the vehicle. It was a beautiful day. Not a cloud in the sky.

If nothing else, he had picked a good day for his friend to die if it came down to it, but in a very personal way, Ice hoped it wouldn't go that far. He loved Supreme liked a blood brother; however the plan had already been mapped out so there was no mystery as to what would go down if Supreme bumped his gums wrong.

The fact that he had been chosen to run the nuts-and-bolts operation of such an international organization puffed Ice up with pride, but he took his responsibilities seriously. His superiors depended on him, but he knew that one error would seal his fate, and he had personally witnessed the brutal manner by which his bosses dispensed justice. The thought made Ice shiver, but that was only a small part of what he felt when he thought of Ivan Gugarin, the Russian.

Crossing the small bridge, Ice and Supreme walked up a twisting path that led to the rear of the main shelter at Freedom Park located on the top of the hill. They didn't stop there. They veered right, skirting the ass-end of the shelter, now moving onto the concrete sidewalk that was filled with walkers and joggers. Out of the corner of his eye, Ice caught Supreme's curious gaze.

"Nigga, where the fuck we going?"

Maintaining a leisurely pace, Ice ignored the question. "I don't think they let motherfuckas feed the ducks no mo'. Po' birds gotta get down for theirs, gotta grind just like a nigga on the block. That is if he wants to eat."

Having assumed Ice wasn't going to answer his question, Supreme made it a point to become more alert, to watch everything, everyone. Suddenly, something didn't feel right, and although he trusted Ice, he wanted to be prepared for the unexpected.

At the band shell, the two men slowed down and from their vantage point, it was obvious when Ice spotted whomever it was he was supposed to meet here. He carefully guided Supreme away from the pavilion, and Supreme got the surprise of his life when Ice gingerly pushed back the sleeve of his shirt and spoke into a hidden microphone attached to his gold nugget bracelet.

"I got you in view. Give me a few minutes and I'm there."

Supreme looked away as if a nigga with some James Bond

type shit was nothing new to him, but he also knew this was his friend's golden opportunity to explain what was going on.

The path they were following led uphill, but all of a sudden Ice abruptly grabbed Supreme by the elbow, steering him towards a wooden park bench. "We've got a minute, so let's talk."

"You talk, I'll listen. What up?"

Ice's mind raced, knowing that a lot hinged on Supreme's decision so he wanted to be clear when he spoke, yet he sputtered. "I-I….damn, nigga, I love you like you blood. We go back to being shorties together, so this ain't about getting a new hustling partner." Ice, a 6'2", 220 pound, brown-skinned, bald-headed hustler averted his eyes. "This about love."

"I can feel that so no matter what, we always gonna be people. You my peeps for life." Supreme smiled. "Go 'head on and spit it out."

"What do you see when you look at me, Supreme?"

"Shit, nigga, I see Ice."

"Then you ain't looking deep enough 'cause when you look at me what you seeing is a millionaire."

Supreme's jaw dropped. "Say what?!"

"I'm a millionaire, Supreme. Excuse me, make that a multi-millionaire, and I want for you what I want for myself. What I'm saying is this. I want to make you a millionaire too. And that's my good word." Ice expelled air from his lungs. "I hope you ain't got no problem with stacking real paper."

"Man, stop playing. It's every nigga's dream to be rich". Even now, Supreme was counting money in his head, but he remained cool. "Who I gotta kill?"

Ice laughed. "Nobody."

"Then what------?"

"Just talk to my man, the Russian, and if you feel you can handle the work, then you rich. If not, no hard feelings." Ice spoke into his microphone once more. "We're on our way."

A moment later Supreme was dropped off on a park bench where a man spoke with him, and the news was so mind-blowing that Supreme stuck his hands into the pockets of his jeans in an effort to prevent Ivan, the Russian, from seeing how much they were trembling. In addition, his mouth was as dry as cotton. He coughed.

Despite the clarity of what he was hearing, Supreme was finding the news increasingly difficult to decipher although his best guess was that his ears were deceiving him, but he stopped wondering about that when Ivan swiveled his bald head around on the hairy stump of his neck and resumed speaking.

"This is the sex trade on a global level. We traffick women, young girls actually, all of whom make us, the players, very rich." Ivan spoke as if he were a business consultant, lecturing about iPods. "Every year 600,000 to 800,000 girls are trafficked across international borders." Ivan shrugged. "Personally, I don't give a damn about those numbers and neither should you, that is, if you decide to tag along with our organization. However, the numbers I prefer, and which I think you will like as well, is that these girls bring in about thirty billion dollars each and every year. And in case you're interested in statistics, only weapons and drugs are more profitable than sex trafficking."

Unlike anything he had ever heard, Supreme was completely lost in the enormity of what Ice had gotten himself involved with, but there was no ignoring those numbers. Thirty billion dollars. No wonder Ice was a millionaire.

Supreme watched Ivan's pale face as he spoke, enunciating each word carefully. "Don't be afraid to dream," Ivan chuckled. "Have you ever seen Ice any happier?"

Supreme struggled to find an answer to that question, but already he knew that his friend had scaled the mountain and was now firmly on top. "I'm happy for him."

"And I can make you as happy as he is." Ivan's tone lacked emotion, but his phasing left a space designed to grant Supreme the opportunity to be awed by the exceptional offer, but after the silence, the voice shifted to its strong baritone where the spare words were mingled with a blunt exclamation point. "The logic of it all is terrifyingly simple. We want to extend the market into the United States. Los Angeles was basically our initial stronghold, but we've discovered that focus much too narrow." Ivan paused. "Any idea why?"

23

"I can't say that I do," Supreme responded truthfully.

"Over the last half decade or so, legitimate global business has increased tremendously, and this expansion has brought businessmen to this country who have never been here before. I speak of Eastern Europeans. These men get lonely over here, and they long for Eastern European women with whom they are familiar. It's nothing against American women, but these men like what they like, and being the wonderful social service we are, we supply the women, but sometimes it is not so easy smuggling girls from such faraway places as Russia, Romania, or the Ukraine." Ivan chuckled. "But that is not your concern. It is mine. I have something for you that is oh so easy." Ivan shrugged. "I think you'll love it."

Every now and then as Ivan spoke of the financial rewards of the adventure, Supreme sometimes felt as though he had planned all this himself. He had always told himself that he was going to be fabulously wealthy one day, and now the chance was within his reach. All he had to do would be to embrace the opportunity at hand.

"It's all right on the money," Ivan muttered. "Nothing else in your life will be any easier. I honor that with my word of bond."

Supreme knew the conversation was drawing to a close, and it now did because without saying another word, Ivan abruptly left Supreme sitting alone on the hard wooden bench to soak up the sun and to think. Within a few seconds, Ice was sitting beside him, a look of anxiety on his face.

"He didn't wait for an answer."

"That's what I'm here for," Ice announced, looking Supreme directly in the eyes. "Millions, nigga."

Supreme smiled.

Ice smiled back. "You in?"

'Man-----."

"It would mean a lot to me and I'll do everything I can to make sure that you move up the ladder where there will be more and more millions." Ice gripped Supreme's arm. "Nigga, please, say yes."

"Yes, motherfucka, yes!"

Chapter 4

Lonnie McKay was the principal at Myers Park High School. He was a thin, brown-skinned man who favored Cornel West, minus the wild afro and Clark Kent glasses. He also had an eye for young girls so his position at the school was ideally suited to his job in Ivan's organization.

Supreme met him for drinks at a titty bar Ice owned in Monroe on a Thursday night when the black sky appeared to be over a thousand miles away, and the twinkle of the stars were nothing more than a dim blinking.

"Do you understand what you're getting into?"

"School's out, Principal. Plus, I wouldn't be here if I didn't know what was up."

McKay smiled. "Just checking." A moment later his voice hardened. "The last thing I need is to be dealing with a scrub. Too much money is involved and I don't want my cash flow disturbed, so I hope that a word to the wise is sufficient."

"I'm not your responsibility, brotha," Supreme rasped.

"But there's so much I need to teach you and if you're not a quick learner, it will make life a little more difficult for everyone concerned."

"Anything else?"

"Yes, there is. If you think you're going to have any guilty feelings over what we do, then now is the time for a reality check. It's like you said, school's out." McKay accepted it as a positive sign when Supreme didn't respond. "You got any children?"

"No."

25

McKay leaned over as though ready to impart some great pearl of wisdom, then smirked disdainfully. "And if I were you, I'd be glad." He sipped from his drink. "Especially girls. Now is not a good time to be a female, especially a black one."

"If you hate what you're doing so much, why do it?"

"Who said I hated it, first of all?"

"Your voice."

"Must be the liquor you hear because I enjoy doing what I'm doing. It pays too damned good not to."

Moments later the counselor from West Charlotte arrived, and slid quietly into the booth beside McKay who immediately called for a drink.

"Surprised?" McKay teased as he watched Supreme watch the counselor.

"I'm pleased to meet you." The counselor extended her hand. "My name is Eve." The beautiful, light-skinned woman smiled politely. "I understand that you're the new kid on the block."

Supreme nodded, wondering what other surprises lay in store for him. Eve Chambers was certainly a big one, but what immediately came to mind was the warning not to trust a big butt and a smile.

After a few moments of social chatter, Eve reached into her purse and extracted a computer disc. "Guard this with your life, honey. It contains all the names and contact info on everyone in our little group. We have sources, be they teachers, principals, coaches at every high school in Mecklenburg County who funnel us data on potential Hoochie-Mamas. We then filter this info into our pipeline to assess precisely what we're working with." Eve smiled sweetly. "I took the liberty of having a domestic bank account set up for you. There's already some courtesy money in it." She handed Supreme a slip of paper.

"Cool."

After a few seconds of total silence, McKay solved the problem of what to say next. "In the sex trade business, Supreme, we are a close-knit community even though we're light years away from the real action and the real money, but financially, we survive quite well indeed."

"But what happens------?"

"To whom, the young bitches we turn out?' Eve's eyes were cold. "Look, I'm not saying we're total angels, but I do call what we're doing an act of mercy."

"I'll drink to that," McKay said pointedly.

"Maybe you done had enough of that already." Supreme nodded at the bottle of Grand Marnier. "An act of mercy?"

"Consider how many young, black girls presently in high school in this city can make it in the real world using their brains. A very damned few," Eve hissed, "but how many of these same bitches do you think can make it using their bodies? Just judging from the size of some of their asses, shit, these bitches are sitting on a fucking goldmine."

"All we do," McKay added, "is to put them on the fast track to financial security. I see bitches every day with brains the size of a peanut, but with asses and titties that would make a grown man cry. Left to their own devices, they'll either end up as unwed mothers or on crack. The only other choices are jail or welfare. Some life, but that's it for a lot of young sistas. We offer an option."

Supreme poured himself a drink. "Whatever you say," he conceded. "Just tell me what to do to make me some money. Fuck everything else."

McKay cleared his throat. "I don't want you to assume anything, so here it is. The Organization has a string of strip clubs scattered throughout the country, and our job basically is to stock them with young dancers. The school system provides us with a virtually inexhaustible selection so that problem solves itself." McKay shifted his weight in the plush VIP room chair, pausing as he finished off the remains of his drink. "Throughout the country, we operate a series of very exclusive underground clubs that feature the nude dancing of underage girls, some as young as thirteen."

"It's an adventure for the selected girls," Eve gushed excitely. "They are treated to the best of everything because our accommodations are top-notch."

"And how do you get pass the mothers?" Supreme wanted to know.

"Easy," Eve confessed. "We sponsor trips through our Big Sisters program. The parents believe we're whisking the girls off for a weekend at camp. My favorite time is summer when we have the girls for the whole school break." Eve's smile lit up the room. "The little tramps come home loaded with free shit. We provide them spending money, well actually, it's their own earnings. We give them a debit card that they can use, but they can only withdraw one hundred dollars a day. I think that's good for a bitch that doesn't even have hair around her pussy yet."

"We've thought of everything, Supreme."

McKay's statement turned out to be accurate. In addition to operating its own club, The Organization, it seemed, was preoccupied with providing legal, eighteen year old dancers to strip clubs across the country. In fact, it was an iron-clad policy of Ivan's that every strip club in America employ his girls or else. The agreement was that 20% of the strippers in any club had to be hired from him.

"We don't bullshit," Eve commented "and we all get paid well for our services."

"Behold!" McKay pointed dramatically at the stage. "Look at them. It's their physical assets, Supreme, that keeps them from starving. Men are in awe of such bodily perfection and will never tire of watching them dance and sweat." McKay's eyes drooped. He sighed wearily. "So many bitches, so little time."

Then Eve talked of how their group was ahead of the sexual curve, providing sistas who had zero chances of making it with a fresh perspective on success. "This is the Ass Era so this is a triumph for well-endowed young girls. Why study when bitches with degrees are working at Wendy's? What that means is that for the first time in history, ass trumps education."

"Thank God," McKay whispered. "Amen."

Chapter 5

The phone rang. It was Ice. "Get up, nigga, and meet me outside."

Supreme stepped outside of his apartment, a copy of The Charlotte Observer tucked under his arm.

Ice chuckled. "Nigga, you job hunting?"

Supreme eased into the gold Maserati. "The world will fall on a motherfucka who don't know what the fuck is going on in it.'

"Well, Mr. Philosopher, don't none of that bullshit you talking apply to you no mo'."

"Why?"

"'Cause you just entering a world don't nobody know nuthin' about, and to top it all off, a nigga ain't never gotta worry 'bout the sky falling on his ass. This is one game, my nigga, that's trump tight."

Supreme gazed at Ice. "I might need another place to stay."

"No, you don't, dawg. It's handled." Ice handed Supreme a ring with two keys on it. "One is the key to your new crib. The other one is to your new ride, a Beemer. I picked the motherfucka out myself."

"What color is it?" Supreme blurted in excitement.

"Midnight black, just like your old one, but with ten more years of technology. Bitch is fly." Ice paused. "Oh yeah, look into the glove compartment. That envelope got ten grand in it. It's yours, compliments of Ivan." Ice grinned. "Shit, everything is from Ivan."

"Yo-you mean all this shit is on the house; free."

Ice shrugged. "That's how we roll, partner."

It was during the ride across town that Supreme knew his life had changed forever. He also knew that he had just been bought. He'd be bossed around later, and he realized that everything he would be told to do would never allow him to lead a normal life, but what a way for the cookie to crumble. He tried to enjoy the music booming through the car's stereo, but he found he was much too restless to concentrate on Melanie Fiona's new song. It made him think of Neon who loved the song.

"Does it ever bother you what you do?"

"Naw," Ice retorted bluntly, "pimping gave me the stomach for it." Ice turned down the music. "Man, don't sweat the small stuff. There are bitches out here, half of 'em ain't shit nohow, so it ain't like we stopping they trifling asses from going to college or something like that. Gold-digging hoes ain't good enough for nuthin' but getting turned out. Pimps on top, my nigga. Hoes on the bottom."

"Kidnapping bitches is deep though."

"That ain't your cross to bear, Supreme, so don't sweat it. That end of the game is handled by professional snatch artists. Plus, they ain't snatching sistas. They snatching bitches in Europe and bringing they white asses over here."

Supreme was not surprised at his friend's casual reaction, but he remained silent on the issue as he was weighed down over his own unyielding desire to fuck Neon, a yearning from which he couldn't free himself. He turned the stereo back up.

"Everything cool?"

"Nuthin' I can't handle," Supreme remarked.

"You sho' don't sound too happy for a motherfucka on the verge of becoming a millionaire."

Suddenly, Supreme was defensive. "Ain't no thang, big brer. I just gotta learn how to live with treating black women like shit."

"A million motherfucking dollars should help yo' ass survive it just fine. It did me."

"But you was already a pimp. I ain't."

"Your black ass broke which is as good a reason as any to say fuck them hoes, and to climb up to the top of the world on they motherfucking backs. What, you weak for young bitches?"

"How the fuck I know, I ain't had one yet."

"Nigga, what you waiting on? Bitches out here fucking out of both draw legs. Man, you done been out long enough to be done got yo' nuts out of the sand. Yo' dick will still get hard, won't it?'

Supreme broke out laughing, but he was crying inside.

Chapter 6

Ivan sipped his Grey Goose, then sat the drink down. "New YIvan sipped his Grey Goose, then sat the drink down. "New York and Los Angeles are no longer our hub for black girls. Charlotte is."

The news, unexpected, startled Uri, who poured himself a double. "But those cities have been good to us, and we've been doing business there ever since we started a North American operation. Why the shift?"

"I just think that Charlotte is better. Plus, southern, black girls have the biggest asses it seems."

"You'd hardly move for that reason alone," Uri protested mildly, "so there has to be more, especially with all the money currently coming from our West Coast set-up. A new operation would take years to generate that kind of income."

"Maybe. Maybe not."

"I don't like it."

Ivan said. "I'm not desperate for anyone's approval. I think we could bring in more girls via Charlotte."

"Are there problems?" Uri persisted.

"Nothing." Ivan winked. "Everything is cool."

It had been a simple question, but Uri knew that things were far from normal in the sex trade. Years ago, everything was, as Ivan had so casually mentioned, cool. However, some things had changed and sometimes change was not good. Ten years ago, no one knew what they did. Now, they did. Back then, it was such a simple thing to snatch young girls from Eastern European countries and to sneak them across transnational borders.

Uri had loved it then even though they had decimated the female population of some of the poorer countries in Europe. At the time, the Soviet Union had been the chief export country, and America had been the chief import country, taking in some 10,000 young girls a year where most ended up in strip bars in Jersey, or in massage parlors in San Francisco. Uri missed the good old days.

But all of a sudden Ivan had turned his attention to the desperately poor, black girls of America. He foresaw them as a new start in the sex trafficking business, but first he had to create a demand for them, a demand so voracious that he could traffick them internationally. And he would. Outside of Nigeria, black girls represented only a small fraction of the girls working in the global sex trade, but Uri knew that with the right advertising and marketing, the demand could change overnight. In the twinkling of an eye, young, black girls from America would become the sweethearts of the sex slavery market.

"So you still think black girls are the new black gold?" Uri was one of the few people brave enough to question Ivan, but despite the fact that they were brothers, Uri knew better than to be recklessly bold.

"And you still don't understand it?" Ivan flashed a sly grin. "You need to get out more. Ass is the rage nowadays and no one has more of it than black girls." Ivan laughed. "In any men's magazine, look at how they pose the white girls. They always try to get the shots that flatters their asses, that will have their asses look bigger. With black girls, you don't need any trick photography. Ass just pokes out naturally." Ivan shrugged. "I have to admit that a big ass has a striking effect."

"And now we're ready to sell the concept to the rest of the world?"

"Not sell it, Uri, but to capitalize on it. The genie is already out of the bottle. For years, the sexual fantasy has been for women with big breasts. Well, now it's ass."

"But these are American girls, Ivan."

Ivan brushed aside the concern. "A poor bitch is a poor

bitch, and the one thing that all poor bitches have in common is that they want to escape being poor. They dream of a way out. We offer a way out." A scholarly glint appeared in Ivan's cold eyes. "What do you suppose the difference is between a starving girl in the Ukraine and a starving girl in the hood? Nothing. And do you know what that means, Uri? It means that black girls in America are as vulnerable and as desperate as any bitch we have smuggled out of Russia, Thailand, China, or Germany." Ivan smiled. "What helps in America is the videos, the movies, and MTV cribs. These young girls are tired of living in run-down neighborhoods, tired of dodging bullets. They pray for the good life."

Uri stared blankly at his brother in an attempt to sort out why Ivan was so irresistibly drawn to this new enterprise, and wondered what he would do next. It was one thing to topple New York and L.A. as hubs for black girls, yet quite another to begin smuggling black girls out of the country. The FBI would not be as easily mocked as corrupt police in Moldova or Laos, but he was in no mood to quarrel which would only make Ivan more fiercely resolved to carry out his plans.

"Listen to this," Ivan growled, "and tell me what you think."

"Alright, my brother, I am listening."

As Ivan talked his way through the planned operation, Uri found it to be a nasty piece of business and his bottom lip trembled involuntarily, astonished that his brother believed the scheme was doable. Uri instantly recognized flaws. The hood was no bleak European outpost where girls could be lured away or kidnapped without any consequences, and there were no reliable indicators that law officials could be easily bought or corrupted. Uri imagined how hard it would be to get the girls out of the country, or how they could hide from aerial observation if they were detected. Unlike Eastern Europe, there were no vast mountainous terrain or windswept passes here through which their cargo could be whisked. Urban cities lacked inaccessible gorges or canyons that offered natural hideaways.

Intoxicated by his plans to traffick in black girls, Ivan had already presumed that the girls were sufficiently demoralized by the conditions in the hood that they would be eager to leave America freely to work in a wealthy nation like Moscow, Tokyo, or Dubai. Uri knew that those who didn't choose to go willingly would be forced to go unwillingly.

"We know little about black girls," Uri said finally.

Ivan's reaction was predictable. "Well", he snapped, "we'll simply find someone who does."

Uri knew that Ivan had already laid out his plans to his black friend, Ice, who, no doubt, had provided strong evidence that the mission had no possibility of failure. In all probability, Uri reasoned that Ice knew a lot less about black girls than he suspected.

"You do know that America is the home of the free, don't you?"

Ivan hooted in derision. "So what. I say now is the time for us to go shopping. Only we don't shop at Macy's or Saks Fifth Avenue. We shop in the hood."

Sunday night.

Even in the dark, Supreme knew where she was. The push inward, at first, was tentative; probing, then he felt the warmth of her invitation, letting him come in…slowly. They would not rush. The soft caress of skin touching skin, enveloped by darkness turned on the red-hot flames of their all-consuming sensuality, bathing them both in the nectar of pleasure. This give and take, the knowing ebb and flow of two bodies, completely submerged in oneness transformed this act into art, painting the night with bright-colored passion.

He moved teasingly slow, in gentle circles, revolving and rotating at the core of his essence, spinning out wave upon wave of golden contentment. He fell down deep into the grasping abyss of her being, and then delicately extricated himself only to repeat this joyous rise and fall of nature over and over again.

At length, when he had had coaxed a thousand thrills from her body, he deftly shifted the angle of his thrust, an almost imperceptive move, then delightfully introduced Neon to the virgin within herself. Once acquainted, she applauded this heightened sense of sexuality, greeting it with oohs and aahs of ecstatic welcome.

They strained toward heaven; earth-bound genies performing delirious magic upon each other's bodies. She would get lost, playing hide-and-seek in the shadows of her impending orgasm. He would find her, carrying her home on the crest of his overpowering virility. All at once, when nothing else mattered, when the universe was hushed, when the stars stood still and spelled out her name across the sky, he granted her the reward of blissful satisfaction.

Neon went to sleep.

Supreme cried in celebration.

Chapter 7

Ice was the most powerful man in the Charlotte arm of Ivan's international organization, and on Thanksgiving Day announced the formation of a stripper's school. And he wasn't elusive about his aims. He fully intended to turn out a crew of truly professional strippers as young as fifteen. Sure, it may have been cute to watch fifteen year old girls cavorting onstage nude, but this was not good enough for Ice because his plan was to push these young girls past the threshold of cuteness into full-fledged professional dancers.

The south was fast becoming a stripper's paradise, and Ice hoped to have a stable of trained girls large enough to meet the demands, and in the process to transform Charlotte into the hub for exotic dancers.

This strategy wasn't merely to be confined to dancing because there would be the understanding that the young bitches who couldn't develop the talent for dancing and stripping would be used in the escort service as teenaged call girls. This way it was a win/win situation for both him and the girls and no money would be missed.

All over the country, "Miss Independence" fever was running high among teenaged girls who felt that the notion of waiting on a man to provide for them was old-fashioned. These bitches were willing to do it for themselves and Ice knew a good thing when he saw it. God bless America, he sang.

The announcement of the Stripper's School almost got to Supreme, especially after he discovered that he had been put in charge of this operation, and as soon as he got the news, he set out to find Ice. While he didn't have any problem dealing with the more experienced, older girls, he did have qualms about driving innocent thirteen year olds into a life of sexual depravity.

"Nigga, stop bugging. Them young bitches ain't innocent, done already starting fucking, and they too busy being grown-assed women. They ain't thinking 'bout being no lil' ol' schoolgirls. Hoes be ready to get some paper."

In a cozy Caribbean café where Bob Marley blasted from the sound system, Ice filled Supreme in on his plans, amazed that his friend had reservations about turning teenaged girls out. "Man, this the best damn game going on and a motherfucka would have to be sillier than Peter Griffin on Family Guy not to want to ride this gravy train. Plus when has there ever been any danger involved in a ho taking off her clothes and shaking her ass?" Ice drummed his fingers on the table impatiently, waiting for a response. "Can't think of shit to say 'cause there ain't shit to say." Ice slouched down in his seat, pulled out a blunt, lit it up and toked deeply.

"Nigga, is you crazy?" Supreme babbled, looking over his shoulder, "you can't be blasting no weed up in heah."

"You can," Ice laughed, "if you own the joint." Ice hit the weed again, then passed the blunt to the next table. "Alright, nigga," Ice teased, "tell me you don't want to hit some of that tender, young coochie?"

The argument went back and forth for a few minutes until Supreme admitted he would fuck a fifteen year old, provided she had enough ass and titties even though he wasn't sure someone that young would truly understand real affection. To most men, it wouldn't matter as long as they got a nut. Supreme thought of Brianna and quickly pushed the thought out of his mind.

"Let me tell you something, dawg, and this ain't no bullshit. There has been a definite shift in sexual taste. Men likes 'em younger." Ice sipped from his Red Stripe beer, guzzling noisily. "And this bitter earth ain't gonna stop turning because of it. For sho' there will always be them sassy-assed, older bitches for niggas who want to fuck with 'em, but why risk some baby Mama drama when you can have a tenderoni?"

The scheduled 'quick lunch' ended up lasting ninety minutes, but by the time he left, Supreme's initial concerns were gone. In fact, he was now thrilled to get started. Maybe his thinking had been primitive. Maybe young pussy was the best pussy.

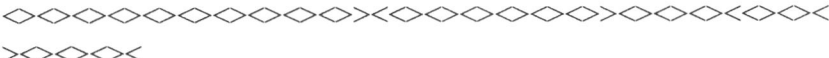

24 hours later.

Since he would be needing a lot of girls quickly, Supreme put the squeeze on McKay and Eve to up the quota from the high schools. Both were scornful.

"Brotha," McKay rasped, "we're not General Motors and we sure as hell don't have an assembly line where we mass produce these young bitches. It's a process to turning them out, a time-honored process that's tried and true, one that can't be rushed."

"That's right," Eve chimed, "we fuck around and put a ho out there before she's ready and we got the police, DSS, welfare motherfuckas, and the Mayor in our faces."

"But I thought it was all about making money?"

"Can't spend it if your ass in jail," Eve complained. "Why tamper with a fool-proof system?"

"Because what I found out," Supreme countered , "is that a fourth of these young girls live below the poverty level, that half come from single-parent homes, and that all of 'em have big asses."

McKay laughed coldly. "And the damned Justice Department has a 100% conviction rate. While you were doing your so-called homework, did you research that because if you had, you would have known that all sex trade cases tried since 2001 have resulted in a conviction."

"Business is good, Supreme," Eve added, "and the key to our success has been to do only what was required which means being extra careful and choosy. You may think I'm lying, but I choose my girls with as much care as I choose who I let fuck me, and you can believe that it's not a lot of motherfuckas hitting this pussy."

Supreme had no answer for that except to tell the duo to shed their illusions. He pointed out that a business, no matter what goods it dealt in, had to grow, and he ended the discussion with a challenge for everyone to step up their quota. "Fuck New York. Fuck LA. We got the best teenage bitches in the world right here in the Queen City, and now is the time to take this shit all the way to the top of the mountain." He stared at McKay and Eve. "This ain't no bullshit talk and no, I ain't on no power trip. I'm simply following orders so I gotta dance to the music just like y'all do so why not do the damn thang right?"

In actuality, neither Eve nor McKay were baffled by any of this because Ice had predicted some time ago that he was pondering a move that would force Charlotte into the limelight of the sex trade, and even though Supreme gave his assurances that much thought had gone into the planning of this new venture, McKay still saw warning signs everywhere. Still, he remained obediently silent. He'd simply do what he had to do until it was every man for himself, and McKay instinctively understood that that day could come rather swiftly if either Ice or Supreme thought they could fight the clock and win.

As for Supreme, he was not surprised at how small a fight the two had put up so he sighed in relief when it appeared that neither McKay nor Eve felt their beloved system would cave in from the additional pressure.

"Supreme?"

"What's up, Eve?"

"Just how much time do we have before Ice expects us to get with this new program?"

"Immediately," Supreme cracked. "That's you timetable. And right-motherfucking-now wouldn't be a motherfucking minute too soon."

Eve seemed concerned. "Again, that could be dangerous and personally I would feel much better if things remained the way they are now."

"Sista," Supreme said with polished courtesy. "You have your instructions. Now, do your job."

"Then you had better talk to The Diva," Eve huffed angrily.

◇◇◇◇◇◇◇◇◇◇◇◇◇◇◇◇◇◇◇◇◇◇◇◇◇◇◇◇◇◇<
>◇◇◇

24 hours later. The weekend. Early.

The day scheduled for his first meeting with The Diva was an unseasonably warm Sunday morning. He would not normally be awake at this time of the morning, but the young girl had insisted on brunch and oddly enough, he hadn't argued.

Supreme arrived early and when The Diva popped up, he was in for the shock of his life. He couldn't believe his eyes.

"Brianna!"

"Surprised?"

Sitting across from the young girl, Supreme tried to concentrate on the food on his plate, but his mind was elsewhere. He felt that every eye in the place was on him, and that the one thought in their minds was if Brianna was his daughter although it was very obvious she wasn't. "Is it me or are people actually staring at us."

Brianna giggled slyly. "They probably wondering if you fucking me."

"That's what I thought."

"No problem," Brianna shrugged, "maybe one day we'll give them something to talk about." She winked her eye. "That will be your lucky day……or night."

"You're sixteen, right," Supreme countered dryly.

"And?"

"You're still a little girl."

"Man, you just don't know." Brianna laughed amicably. "I look like a little girl this morning 'cause that's how I wanted to look this morning. I approached you like a lil ol' schoolgirl 'cause I felt like it."

"And why was that?"

"Because this is a business meeting and I didn't want you to forget it. If I would have shown up in all my womanly glory, then business would have been the last thing on your mind, nigga. I wanted you to concentrate on business, not me."

Supreme laughed. "So you looking out for me?"

"Umm-hmm. Heard you new to the game, so I don't want you fucking up on my account." Brianna cut into her pancakes. "I know what kind of effect I have on niggas."

Brianna's arrogance amused Supreme, but he did respect her knowledge of herself for she definitely possessed the power to enchant men, and without further hesitation, he studied the girl. Simply put, she was magnificently beautiful and to his surprise, he could vividly see a woman in her finely chiseled features. He peered intently.

"Really, you haven't seen nothing yet," Brianna bragged. "I can easily pass for twenty-two when I'm done up and dressed, and stop staring at me like you want to eat me up, but that's nothing new. Most men do want to eat me up."

Supreme smiled, delighted.

After a few more minutes of casual conversation, Supreme guessed that it wasn't the girl's fault that she was so beautiful, and neither could she be blamed for using this tremendous gift in any fashion that suited her. He was also intrigued by how smart she sounded and talked, a far cry from the language she used when with Neon.

"What about your sister?"

"What about that ho?!"

The venom in Brianna's voice left Supreme breathless. "I just thought----"

"Neon has no idea. Neither does our mother."

"But how can you keep what you're doing a secret from them?"

"It's as easy to fool stupid bitches as it is to trick stupid men." Brianna laughed. "Confused?"

Supreme confessed that he was.

"I don't live with Neon and our Mama. I live with my daddy down in Hidden Valley which gives me the chance to do as I damn well please."

"So you're The Diva?" Supreme shook his head in disbelief.

"Have you heard a lot about me?"

"Enough to know that a young bitch like you could never

be my woman."

Brianna's face fell.

"But that don't mean I wouldn't put dick up in yo' young ass."

Pretending not to be hurt, Brianna finished eating. "Let's talk business, nigga, but first here's some shit you need to listen to and I ain't never gonna repeat myself. Stay away from Neon because the bitch crazy. She's bi-polar and subject to violent mood swings. The doctors have her on meds, but the bitch won't take 'em, so that's why she is the way she is. Don't tell me you ain't never noticed how she flips?"

"Thank you, lil Miss Sunshine, but for your information, ain't a bitch alive that I can't handle, bi-polar, bi-sexual, or bi-racial." Supreme leaned forward, speaking softly. "Stay the fuck out of my personal business."

"Kiss my ass, nigga."

Quick to notice he had angered the young girl, Supreme felt guilty although he did not let it show. "To pull this off, I'm gonna need a bigger consignment of young hoes, the phatter the ass, the better."

"I can pull 'em," Brianna replied smugly, "that ain't no problem. The problem is the extra work which means extra money."

"I got you."

"Good, 'cause I ain't never had a problem with turning bitches out to the life."

It had never occurred to Supreme to believe otherwise because from all accounts, Brianna's influence on the other girls at school was legendary. "You must enjoy corrupting----"

"What I do to other people is none of your personal business. It's my business, what I get paid to do." Brianna paused. "Anyway, it's like Miss Eve taught me a long time ago. Black women are the mules of the world, and if we don't look out for each other, ain't no-damn-body else gonna do it. Miss Eve say white bitches set the standard for beauty and we can't measure up 'cause we ain't got no blonde hair and no blue eyes, so it would be stupid for us to think we can make it in the cracker world no matter how many damned degrees we got. And do you know why?"

Supreme shook his head. "No. Why?"

"Y'all niggas, that's why."

"Bullshit."

"Let me school you then, my brotha. Crackers hate y'all niggas with a passion. Kill y'all asses every chance they get, and what's left that ain't scared gets put in jail. To the white folks, niggas is the scourge of the earth. Y'all motherfuckas lazy, y'all steal, and y'all got big dicks. White man ain't having it. He hate y'all."

"But what that got to do with black women?"

"We produce y'all black motherfuckas." Brianna paused to let that thought linger. "So do you think it's possible for crackers to hate the product and love the producers?! White man hate us too. He hate us because we give birth to what he hates most------y'all." Brianna's voice cracked and fear showed in her eyes. "One day", she rasped, "the white man is gonna come after us. I guess that will be when he through dealing with y'all, but he's coming for us just like he's gunning for y'all now." Brianna's voice grew stronger. "But we ain't going down easy. Hell no."

Supreme laughed uncomfortably. "And Eve tole' you that fairytale bullshit?"

"Ain't no fairytale. I see it happening, and every day I see what he's doing to y'all. We a burden to these white motherfuckas and one day they gonna wipe us all out, so bitches in the know better be ready to travel when the shit hit the fan, or else her ass will be stuck here just like the poor people that got stuck in New Orleans when Katrina came through."

Supreme was glad when Brianna's anger had run its course. It was the first time he had actually considered her feelings although he felt that Eve had laid down one helluva game. It was a lot like the lie the old pimps told the new, green pimps about the name of the game being cop-and-blow. Curiously, enough, the new pimps went for it so it made them comfortable when a ho he had turned out left him. Usually, it was the old, wise pimp who would then catch the ho. In essence, the old pimp was pimping the young pimp, letting him do all the hard work of catching a ho and turning her out, only to lose her a short time later. Cop-and-blow. This piece of trickery made life a lot easier for the old pimp who knew the name of the game was actually "cop-lock-and block" which meant that once you copped a ho, you locked her down, and then you blocked other pimps from trying to steal her.

Supreme grinned. Damn, that bitch Eve was good.

The next evening.

It took Brianna only a second to recognize that the young girl was ripe fruit. It felt like Brianna had been especially bred for this calling, given her ability to decipher when one of her schoolgirl acquaintances was ready to be introduced to a brand new way of life. Eve had always told her that it was bad form to act in any way superior to the other girls who were deaf, dumb, and blind to the game, but it couldn't be helped. Brianna felt powerful and she cherished the feeling.

Brianna seemed to understand teenagers. As a young girl, she had heard the hushed talk about how fast her body was maturing, and about how her ass was going to make men cry, but best of all for her was that she wouldn't have to wait until she was grown to realize what fine messengers a phat ass and juicy titties were. And that had pleased her immensely.

At thirteen, her physical assets had brought her to the attention of Eve who had thought it quite incomprehensible that a child that young could be so well-endowed.

To Brianna that all seemed like a long time ago, and as she stared across the bed at Rena Evans, she knew she couldn't be careless or hasty. At the moment, she knew she had the girl under her spell, but one false move could take all the mystery out of what she was doing, and that would be a terrible mistake.

Discounting the fact that Eve had given her the authority to turn out more girls, Brianna didn't feet compelled to implement any new work scheme. Her usual "trap game" would have to do.

"So what do you think?" Brianna asked. "You like it?"

Rena held the red thong up, inspecting it. "Yes," she said honestly.

"Put it on and it will make you feel sexy."

"Y-you wear 'em?"

"Hell yeah, all the time." Brianna stood up and yanked down her jeans. "See."

"Damn, girl, all your ass is out," Rena giggled. "And I thought my butt was big. Yours is huge."

Brianna narrowed her eyes. "Put the thong on and look at your ass in the mirror. It'll look phatter."

In a second, Rena was out of her clothes, but as she was slipping off her panties, she stopped. "Have the courtesy to turn around. You're not a boy."

"You ain't got nuthin' that I ain't got and I see pussy every day because my big sister loves to walk around naked. Thinks her pussy got a gold ring around it or something."

Rena laughed. "Mine must have gold 'round it the way my boyfriend be acting, like his ass can't get enough of it, be wanting to fuck all the damn time." Rena slipped on the thong and pranced over to the full-length mirror on the bedroom door. She squealed. "Oh my God!" she gasped. "My ass does look phatter. Oh shit!"

"Tole you."

While Rena continued to study herself in the mirror, Brianna walked over to a console, slipped in a CD, then pressed play.

"Who's that?"

"Never mind," Brianna cracked. "Now move your ass."

"Huh?"

"Dance, Rena. I want to see if you know how to operate all that ass. I hope you move it better when you dance than you do when you walk. To have such a nice ass, your walk is wack."

"How you know?"

"I been checking you out."

Rena looked unhappy. "Don't tell me yo' ass gay?"

"Hell no, I ain't gay."

Rena sighed in relief. "For a minute there----"

"Sit down, girl, and watch me dance." Brianna licked her lips suggestively as she disrobed. "By the time I'm finished, you gonna wish you was gay." Strolling casually over to her bedroom door, she locked it. She then put her hands on her voluptuous hips, smiling at Rena. "Now, watch me."

By the time Brianna had decided to quit dancing, Rena was visibly aroused, and would have licked the sweat from Brianna's thighs had she been asked, but Brianna's plan was to move the girl one step closer to accepting The Life. "It wouldn't be a bad idea if you let me teach you how to dance like that," Brianna said softly.

"Why?" Rena was curious.

Brianna walked over to a chest of drawers, pulled out a stack of glossy photographs, and handed the bunch to Rena. Afterwards, she sat down on the bed, not saying anything as the girl shuffled through the photos.

"Girl!" Rena gushed, "that girl in that fur coat looks just like you."

"That is me, Rena." Brianna took the photos out of the startled girl's hand. "And so is this. And this." She flipped through a few more. "Oh yeah, that's my PT Cruiser."

"You-you got a car?"

"Of course. I just don't drive it at home."

"Wow, Brianna, you look so beautiful, so grown-up. You got a Sugar-Daddy?" When Brianna shook her head, Rena's voice grew firm. "What's up?"

"I dance, Rena."

"Like what you just got through doing?"

"Look at these pictures and see."

Rena flickered through the photos without delay. "Ohh, girl, you so nasty. You busting it open."

Brianna saw this as an opportunity not to be modest. "I do good work, Rena. I'm a professional so I don't be playing when I dance."

In a later photo when Rena spotted money and flowers strewn across the stage where Brianna danced, she had an envious look on her face. "They must really love you."

"They do, and they'll show you the same kind of love. All you gotta do is to take it to the stage."

"And bust it open," Rena giggled.

"It's a business, but it's fun. Whether you know it or not, there's a price on phat ass these days. Sistas ain't got to sell pussy no mo'. Dancing and stripping are better. The price of pussy may go up or down, but in the adult club scene, money is plentiful and it's been my bread and butter since I was thirteen."

"W-what?"

"Ain't no big deal."

"To me, it is," Rena huffed.

"Why?'

"'Cause you waited so damn long to tell me about it. I was just as ready to flash pussy then as I am now." Rena cursed. "Shit, I could have already had a car. Damn, bitch, next time don't wait so long, okay?"

Chapter 8

On the late night flight back to Charlotte, Ice did his math. What it would amount to, he figured, was a couple of thousand girls over the next three years. Those were the numbers he intended his school to accommodate and after some initial skepticism, he found more and more to like about his Charlotte operation. He felt that teenage girls, especially black ones, were underappreciated. This made them unreasonably vulnerable, and he had every intention of taking full advantage of this most gracious psychological gimme.

The report Eve had prepared went on about what it was like to be a black teenaged female in America, and it fired off some obvious technical moves that could be used to lure them into a career of dancing and stripping. It all made perfect sense because black girls thought of themselves as unloved, abandoned by absentee fathers which only added to their enthusiasm to please men. Ice grinned widely. The momentum was definitely in his favor, and he would manipulate these dreary statistics into a victory for his stripper's school.

But his school would do more than merely train dancers. He'd be damned if he would be that one-dimensional when there were so many other angles he could tap into. In fact, what he had in mind was more of an academy where hoes were taught to be gung-ho about everything The Life represented. He would train these young hoes to be the ultimate bitch. It was long overdue.

As early as last week, Supreme had phoned him to advance the concept that the school, The Ho Academy, be modeled after a real academy where the girls would wear uniforms, practice the latest strip-club dance moves, and be taught all the skills of the profession. In short, they would be fully indoctrinated into the ways of how to manipulate men with their bodies.

The notion intrigued Ice. He could easily envision strip club owners from all over the world flocking to his academy to compete with one another to buy dancers from him. The price would be steep, but there would be no complaints as he would have the best strippers the world had ever seen.

Flipping open his laptop, Ice spent twenty minutes studying every aspect of his school's concept: dance, dress, presence, and after-hour entertainment. Everything was in place except the precise location in Charlotte.

He called Supreme. "Where we gonna put down at? You know we just can't stick The Academy anywhere."

Supreme broke in. "I got a spot in mind, but I wanna check it out a lil' mo.'"

"Well get back at me 'cause shit 'bout ready to pop off."

By the time his flight touched down at Douglass International, Ice was familiar with every aspect of the Academy's design and intent. Everything was tight.

Monday. A week later.

After school, Supreme picked Brianna up and drove her across town in his new Beemer.

"Where we going, the hotel?"

Supreme gazed at Brianna sullenly. "And what would make yo' lil', fast ass think some shit like that?"

"'Cause, nigga, I know you want to fuck me."

"Correction. I want to fuck yo' sister."

"So you don't want to fuck me?"

"Girl, listen, we don't have time for none of yo' high school games. This is business, not nonsense."

Brianna fiddled with the CD player. "And so your ass will know, good pussy ain't no nonsense." She stared directly into Supreme's eyes. "At least, mine ain't."

After a few minutes, Supreme arrived in front of a newly abandoned, two-story building. He sat, watching it for a brief second, then turned to Brianna. "This is it."

Brianna stared at the red-brick structure. "This is what? The school?"

Supreme nodded nervously. "What do you think?"

Brianna didn't think long. "The building don't mean shit. It's what goes on inside the damn place that gonna count."

"You don't worry 'bout what goes on inside, dammit," Supreme snapped. "Your job is to recruit the bitches. They'll get schooled, so don't trip."

"I ain't tripping," Brianna snapped back, "but knowing niggas like I do, this just might turn into a ho house. Bitches might not get taught nuthin' but how to suck dick or slang pussy out of both draw legs."

Supreme exhaled. "Damn, girl, what's up with you? You got a problem with men or something? I hope not."

"I just don't want no whole lot of shit on my conscience, that's all."

"Yeah, right," Supreme laughed, teasing Brianna. "And when did you get a conscience? If you getting soft---"

"Pardon me," Brianna gasped, "but ain't shit soft about me."

Supreme stepped out of the BMW. "Let's go in and see what the joint looks like on the inside."

Brianna slammed the car door closed. "I want to be in charge of the decorating."

"You got it, Miss Thang. Now, stop fussing. It's gonna be all good." Supreme kissed Brianna on the top of her head. "I promise."

On the top floor of the building, Supreme paused and pointed out of a window. "My dad used to live right over there a long time ago."

Brianna acted as though she hadn't heard Supreme. She was too busy talking to herself, decorating the place in her head.

"You like it?"

"Yeah, it's straight." Brianna snapped out of her reverie. "This spot cool. I like it."

"Well, let me call Ice now that I have your approval."

Brianna's eyes sparkled. "My opinion meant that much?"

"You The Diva," Supreme bragged, "and if you say it's right, then it's right."

"Now, take your dick out."

"For what?"

"So I can treat it real good."

When Brianna reached for Supreme's zipper, he stopped her. "Hold up, girl. I got that nigga Ice on the line. Let me handle my business."

"Then can I handle mine?"

Supreme moved away. "Yo, dawg, I got the location and Brianna gives it her stamp of approval."

"That's good money, my nigga, but you got to remember that we got a database full of young, high school hoes, junior high hoes too, all of 'em qualified candidates for The Academy, so how we gonna narrow it down to the cream of the crop. I want to give all them bitches a shot at performing so they can get they asses out the hood."

"Ain't no biggie. We work 'em all."

"I feel you, soldier, but how we gonna front? I mean what kinda image the motherfuckas in the community gonna get if they see a bunch of young bitches running in and out of that spot. Police would be all over the spot quicker than they would a dope house, see what I'm saying? We gotta think of a good front, come up with a good okey-doke so we can operate in peace. Think of something, but be careful it ain't nuthin' the police can see through. Motherfuckas get suspicious real quick they think the spot an all-girl after-school hang-out. Nosey people sho' gonna think we putting dick in those young bitches. And speaking of young bitches, you done popped Brianna yet?"

"Naw, not yet."

"You sho'?"

"It's 'bout to happen soon,"

"Don't know what you waiting on. Young bitch a star. She--

-"

"I got it," Supreme blurted excitedly.

"Got what?"

"Our front for The Academy, but I gotta make a phone call first. Hold on while I three-way this ho."

When the call went unanswered, Ice commented. "Leave the ho a message. Tell her to holla back."

After Supreme had hung up, he rubbed Brianna's ass. "Let's roll." He placed the young girl's hand on the front of his pants and let her caress his dick, but moved her hand away quickly when it got hard. "Don't you love it," he said, "when a good plan comes together.'

"But you'll love what I wanna do to your dick even mo' and I don't need no damn plan for that."

"Business before pleasure."

Chapter 9

Neon knew that when she took a long, hard look at her personal history, the one thing she would be forced to contend with was the fact that what she was doing right now would be her legacy, a piece of work that would outlive her. So she wanted to do the damn thang, to set it off, to give motherfuckas in years to come something to talk about. She wanted to be certain that the world remembered who Neon Ashford was.

She didn't give much of a damn about what some preacher would say in his tired-assed eulogy because church people would be the last ones to get her drift since she would never be no Goody-Two-Shoes bitch. What she wanted instead was for her deeds to testify to just how bad a bitch she had been, but right now she had a lot of work to do. She smiled. Although good pussy was not the admission fare to heaven, it sure as hell helped pay bills on earth.

"You been clocking lately?"

Neon stared at her mother. "Hate to think I ain't."

Stella plopped down on the plush sofa, her eyes twinkling. "Fill me in." She loved to hear her daughter's reports about how she was working Supreme. "Where you at now?"

Neon sat down next to her mother. "I'm on it. I might not be at the point where he ready to buy me a car, but he spending. You saw them shopping bags I brought home last week. We be busting the door down at all them top-notch shops that be selling fly shit for bitches." Neon hugged herself as if she was cold. "Guess who gonna be wearing a full length mink this winter?"

"Go on, girl", Stella gushed proudly. "You sho' as hell my daughter alright. I remember when I got my first fur coat, took me 21 years. You done beat me by two years. I'm proud of yo' sneaky ass. Jealous too."

"Jealous."

"Bitch, pleeze. You got a real gangsta." Nigga used to terrorize these city streets. Back in the days, all the motherfucka had to do was to pull his dick out, and a half-dozen bitches would be fighting over who would put in they mouth first. Nigga was like that."

Neon shrugged. "Nigga done fell off then 'cause I don't recognize his swagger. I mean I wouldn't just totally disrespect him or nuthin', but I ain't scared of him. Plus, I got his black ass so pussy-whupped, the nigga would kill for me."

"Hmmph", Stella snorted, "don't get carried away."

"Don't worry, Mama, I'm gonna stay on top of my game. Oh yeah, I let him fuck Freda----"

"Girl, you know I know all about it. Freda called me no sooner than the nigga finished busting a nut up in her skinny ass."

"Shit was funny. That nigga was the first nigga to put Freda's skinny ass in the buck and to long dick her." Neon laughed. "She was calling out Supreme's name like he was her man" Just as suddenly as the laughter had started, it abruptly stopped. Neon turned serious. "I don't want Brianna's trifling ass nowhere 'round that nigga no mo'. I'm thinking she might try to make a play for him. Nigga already be looking at her."

"Disregard her," Stella huffed, "if she don't get mo' serious about the pussy game, she gonna be as useless as two left shoes, and I hate to have to say that 'bout my own flesh and blood. I'm giving her the game same as you, and I don't see where she making any progress. Just because she ain't legal yet don't mean shit. Ho supposed to be clocking, supposed to be playing all them dumb teachers at her school. I remember when you was in school---"

"But I was a quick learner," Neon interceded. "Ain't nuthin' feel better to me than making a full-grown man do what I wanted him to do. A'int nuthin' and I mean nuthin' mo' satisfying than having that kind of power."

55

Stella beamed proudly. "We trainers," she bragged. "The same motherfucking way that that man on television can come to yo' house and train yo' dog, a bitch who knows how to work her shit should be able to walk into any house in America and do the same thang, only she won't be training no stupid dog. She'll be training the nigga." Stella giggled. "Works on white motherfuckas too."

Neon turned her nose up. "Brianna think she so pretty that her shit don't stank. Mama, she don't wanna do the work that gonna make her a real star like me. When you get right down to it, she ain't no better that Kim or Candy. Bitches got good pussy, but they can't think."

Stella pouted. "Just 'cause that bitch fine don't mean shit unless she capable of catching a nigga who can bring home the motherfucking bacon each and every motherfucking day." Stella winced painfully. "It ain't cute when a ho depending on a nigga and the nigga fall off, leaving the bitch on empty. Wanna know something else? It ain't enough for a ho to merely appreciate the game, she gots to be able to appreciate what the game can do for her."

Neon offered a big Amen to these assertions. "I'm committed to my duty to elevate the game until it's bitches on top and bustas on the bottom." Neon smiled. "You started the revolution. I'm gonna finish it."

"That's what you say now. You probably gonna get lazy once you get what's left of that quarter million from Slim. Money will spoil a bitch."

"Shit, I done paid too many dues, been in the storm too long. What I do with Supreme is for me. What I do with the game is for other bitches."

During the next series of exchanges, Brianna walked in.

"You make any money today?" Neon quizzed.

"For your information, I was in school. Thank you very much."

"You got a fish on the line yet?'

Brianna rolled her eyes. "No, Mama. Not yet."

"What the fuck you waiting on, girl? I know all them

damn teachers at your school ain't gay. Your ass need to start clocking----"

"Please, Mama," Brianna squealed, "not that again. Imma be on it."

"When? I know we done had this conversation before----"

"Last week to be exact," Brianna huffed, "and like I tole you then, it's all good."

"As your Mama, I'm concerned, that's all. It's just that I feel like you ain't living up to yo' potential. Lately, you been preoccupied with other shit. School can't be that important 'cause they ain't teaching nuthin'. School nowadays ain't nuthin' but on-the-job training for thugs. Shit, a motherfucka safer in Grier Town than at West Charlotte High School."

For a second, Brianna wasn't going to respond, but when she saw the smug look on Neon's face, she blurted. "I'm sorry, Mama, if I'm not the ho my sister is, but just give me a lil mo' time and I'll be reeling in so many fish that it's gonna make Neon wanna borrow my pussy to fuck niggas with." Quite by purpose, Brianna couldn't resist a parting shot. "Plus, by this time two years from now, Neon's pussy gonna be wore out."

Stella went upstairs, laughing.

"So cracking motherfucking jokes is the thanks I get for not telling Mama on yo' ass, 'bout how you sucked Lucky's dick . I try to push it out my mind 'bout how you be disrespecting Mama by giving away free pussy when you know she done taught you better than that."

Much of what scared Brianna about this moment could be traced back to the fact that she hated her sister and wanted to tell her what was really up. She was sick and tired of bending the truth out of proportion, but knew she had to continue to suspend reality until the right moment.

"Let me hear tell of you----"

Brianna got up in her sister's face. "Stay out my personal biz'ness." To reinforce how angry she was, Brianna pointed her finger at Neon. " Bitch, you don't know shit 'bout me."

Neon struck her sister. The painful intensity of the slap jolted both sisters. Brianna went limp as Neon walked to a far corner of the room.

"Maybe you should go home," Neon said softly. "I think that might be a good idea."

"No, I got a better damn idea. Why don't you apologize for hitting me."

"I-I can't."

"What the hell you mean, you can't?"

"'Cause I ain't sorry, that's why," Neon hissed. "It's the best thang I could've done for yo' ass. From now on, I ain't playing no games with yo' ass. You slanging pussy like a grown-assed woman so that's how I'm gonna treat you. So, woman to woman, I'm warning you to stay away from Supreme. He mine." Neon's voice went emotionally flat. "If I ever want you to have some of the dick, I'll arrange a three-way."

"Thank you, but I don't need no help in doing something for my pussy. I'm highly capable."

"Listen, Brianna, I ain't wanting to fight with you, but I'm serious. My warning about Supreme goes into effect starting now." Feeling she had made her point, Neon walked out of the house, slamming the door on her way out.

Brianna rubbed her cheek where she had been struck. Neon had just made herself a problem, and just like that the hunt was on to find the perfect solution to the problem. Brianna knew she couldn't let her ego or her emotions get the best of her although it would be hard not to.

Her first reaction was to have her sister killed, but she knew she would have a hard time looking her mother in the face if she chose that option. She also knew Supreme would have a hard time understanding what had happened.

So here she was with a problem, but when her street instincts kicked in, she made the one phone call she knew would end the problem.

Forty-five minutes later.

Arriving at the hotel room dressed in some thugged-out designer gear, Ice knocked on the door. Brianna opened it.

"What up, pretty girl? Here I am."

"Come in, Ice."

Both parties, while paying utmost attention to the pretense of civility, had the look of the hunter on their faces, and though the vibe between them didn't evoke outright hostility, it sure didn't approach friendliness either. Both were suspicious of the other.

After a brief instant, Ice stepped into the room, and his breath caught in his throat when he saw that Brianna was dressed in only a long t-shirt. It was anybody's guess if she wore panties underneath..

"What up?" Ice repeated, staring at Brianna's legs. "What can ol' Ice do for you?"

Brianna sat on the edge of the bed, leaning back slightly. "Do you still want to fuck me?"

"You giving it up?"

Feeling annoyed, Brianna sat up. "I need a favor and if you will help me, yeah, I'm gonna give it up." Brianna indicated a spot next to her on the bed which Ice immediately occupied. He rubbed Brianna's thigh. "This has got to stay between us. Nobody can ever know."

Ice stared at Brianna. "You mean I gotta keep it quiet that I done sampled some of the best young pussy in Charlotte. Damn."

Brianna waved away that idea dismissively. " I ain't talking 'bout that. If you want to tell motherfuckas that you put dick in me, do it. I mean it can't be no talk 'bout what you did to get the pussy, okay?"

"Look, Bree, once the fucking is over with, whatever I had to do to get the pussy over with too, and that's my good word. I ain't saying shit."

Brianna felt she could trust Ice. "And I'm expecting you to keep your word."

"Obviously, you don't know ol' Ice like you think you know him. Ask yo' boy, Supreme 'bout me. He know me better than anybody. Nigga will tell you that my word bond." Ice kissed the young girl on her neck. "If I tell you that whatever I do for you is gonna be dead just as soon as it's done, then there ain't nuthin' or nobody that can resurrect the deed." Ice shoved his hand under the t-shirt and fondled Brianna's breasts. "Give up the booty and see what kind of nigga I am."

"You got a condom?"

"Stop playing. I got a whole box. Now, what you want me to do 'cause my dick hard already. Ol' Ice ready to skeet. Call it, Bree. Call it so I can hurry up and put dick in you." Ice rubbed his dick.

Brianna smiled. "Let me help you with that." She pulled Ice's dick out and licked it once, twice…..then took the whole organ in her mouth. When she looked at Ice, she knew she had him. "And that was just a teaser."

"Don't tease me," Ice groaned, "please me."

"You gonna give me what I want?" Brianna stroked Ice's dick.

"Hell, yeah, you got it. Call it, Bree. I done tole you that. Call it."

"Okay, this is what I want……" Brianna paused, thinking about the after-effects of her particular request. She stalled for a second longer, then blurted. "I want you make my sister's ass come up missing. I want you to sell her to one of your Russian friends who kidnap bitches." Brianna pushed Ice back on the bed and straddled him, easing down on his dick. "Can you make that happen for me?"

Ice thrust up in the young girl. "It's a damn done deed. Now, pop that pussy, young bitch."

Chapter 10

A week and a half later a short, light-skinned girl about fourteen years old approached Supreme's BMW, knocked on the window, and stood impatiently, hands on hips, smacking her gum loudly until she was acknowledged.

"Next time," she snapped sassily, "don't let it take you so long." Before Supreme could respond, she thrust an envelope through the open window. "Here you go, nigga."

Then she was gone.

On impulse, Supreme hollered down the street. "Sassy-assed------"

"Yo' Mama!"

Just as the young girl reached the end of the block, she stopped, planted her legs together, and flipped up the very short skirt she was wearing. Then she patted her bare ass at Supreme before dashing around the corner.

"Bitch ain't got no draws on," Supreme muttered to himself, a pleasant smile creasing his face. "Damn!" Sitting there listening to Nicki Minaj's new CD, he wondered what that little exhibition would add up to when he popped the seal on the envelope. "Fuck it," he mumbled, ripping the pink paper apart. He extracted the contents, reading the card first.

"Nigga," the note began, "I'm calling your bluff. I am dancing in Richmond Virginia this weekend and I want you to be there. These are first-class plane tickets, nigga, so enjoy your flight. I'm setting it out for you and I expect you to show up. The name at the bottom is the one the hotel room is registered in, and the key will be waiting at the desk for you. Love and kisses."

Supreme slowly and quietly re-read Brianna's invitation. The young girl was extraordinarily bold, but that appealed to him. The bitch was mature beyond her years and although he felt that fucking an under-aged teenager would not crown his sexual achievements, he did not see where it would hurt any. He'd take her up on her offer, and allow himself the pleasure of enjoying the weekend.

The weekend.

Too excited to eat, Supreme drove directly to the hotel in downtown Richmond. He was thinking about what he was going to do to Brianna, and the mere thought of that sexcapade quickened his pulse. He could scarcely wait. Tonight couldn't get here soon enough.

At the desk, he was surprised to discover he didn't need the key as Brianna was in the room. Supreme wasn't expecting that. He figured she would be out, at least that is what she had led him to believe. Supreme grinned appreciatively, realizing that the girl possessed a remarkable capacity for surprises. He had drifted into this one, it seemed, and he was open to whatever would happen next.

Per Brianna's verbal instructions, he was escorted to the room and when the bellhop dramatically opened the door of the suite, Brianna sat at a table set up in the middle of the floor.

Almost at once, she rose, gracefully walking across the room until she stood before him. Rising on her tip-toes, she planted a delicate kiss on the lips of a very startled Supreme.

"Brianna?!" Supreme blurted in dazzled awe. "Wow!"

The young girl he had met at his apartment with her sister was not the girl who now stood in front of him. This Brianna was elegant, a far cry from a high schooler. This Brianna, dressed in an expensive red gown, sparkled with the mannerisms of royalty, a true Nubian Queen.

Overwrought with emotion, Supreme again blurted. "Wow!"

"Welcome, my king," Brianna purred, "come let's eat." Gripping his hand, she led Supreme across the floor to the dining table where everything was exquisitely laid out. "I hope you like the idea of being with me." She stared hard into his eyes. "You haven't said much."

Supreme's only response was a weak smile. Talking was the last thing on his mind so he simply eyed the vision Brianna presented. Even though his heart beat rapidly, a devilish grin appeared on his face. "Damn, girl, you fine."

"Am I, really?" Brianna teased. "Or do you believe you're looking at a lil' high school girl from Charlotte?"

Supreme pulled Brianna close. "All I see---and feel---is 100% woman."

Brianna snuggled into his embrace. "And make no mistake about that. I'm all woman as you'll soon find out, but for the time being, let's eat."

It was a light meal complete with a bottle of champagne. Neither ate much as both allowed themselves to get lost in the moment, listening to the smooth jazz Brianna had selected for the occasion.

"Tell me," asked Supreme, "where did you learn to put a man under your spell?"

Without saying a word, Brianna abruptly got up and cut the music off. "Listen, nigga," she angrily snapped, "if you think I'm out to trick you with some of the shit I learned from my Mama, then you can leave 'cause I ain't got no time for no games." She was close to tears. "I invited you here 'cause I'm feeling you and want to be with you, but yo' ass acting like it's some kind of damn game. You must think I'm Neon or something?"

"Girl, you got it all wrong."

"Okay, then, what you saying?"

"I'm just surprised, that's all. This is the first time I seen this side of you and it kinda fucked me up to see you go from a lil' girl to a grown-assed woman."

Putting her hands on her hips, Brianna pouted. "So which me do you like most?"

Supreme approached Brianna coolly. "What, you mean, I

gotta choose? I like both sides of you 'cause it's like I'm getting two females in one." Supreme kissed Brianna tenderly. "You forgive me?"

"Kiss me again and I'll think about it."

Midnight.

And then there was Brianna number three. His eyes, wide in disbelief behind his sunglasses, Supreme took all of Brianna in as she danced onstage. It was the first time he had seen her naked, and it was like he was seeing her for the only time.

Watching Brianna lick her lips suggestively, Supreme noticed how large and soft her painted mouth was, how full of expression her beautiful green eyes were. Her smooth, red complexion glistened with flawless perfection and her hair, long and straight, swayed gently across her shoulders as she moved to the beat.

No one was bored watching her. She was like a wonderful work of art come to life. Her large breasts blossomed from her upper torso like a pair of succulent, ripe melons while her taut, smooth belly tapered into a waist so tiny Supreme was almost certain he could encircle it with both his hands. And there were her legs, classically sculpted and impossibly long. But it was her ass that was the real show stopper.

"Oh shit!" a male patron near Supreme shrieked when Brianna gave the audience the first glimpse of her booty.

"My goodness, look at that ass!" another satisfied patron roared. "I feel sorry for all the other bitches in the world 'cause ain't none of them holding like Shawty up there."

"You got that right," someone else heartily agreed.

Supreme listened to these giddy exchanges, his chest puffed up with pride at Brianna's erotic brilliance, and the men's appreciation of it. Supreme knew that most of the men in the club were playas and womanizers, but by the time Brianna had concluded her number, she had everyone completely tamed as dollars of every denomination flooded the stage. Everyone wanted more of her. She had fascinated the crowd and for a moment, Supreme wondered if anyone knew---or cared---that she was an under-aged high school student.

"I told you they had the finest bitches up in heah!"

Hearing that boast, Supreme knew that Brianna's age didn't matter. She had ass and that was all that counted. Thinking back on the dance, Supreme had no objections about what he had witnessed Brianna doing onstage. In fact, it was a masterful performance, a work of subtle genius. It showed that Brianna had gotten into the right profession and regarding her age, Supreme calculated that she would only get better with time.

Staying to see another one of the girls from Charlotte dance, it suddenly occurred to Supreme that the young bitches had been taught well. They danced with a potent mix of youthful innocence and grown-up passion, a combination intoxicating enough to make a man nut in his pants.

After a second, Brianna was at his side. "You okay?' she whispered.

Supreme kissed Brianna hard. "Baby, you were fantastic."

"And you haven't even seen what I will do in private---just for you."

Instantly Supreme experienced a twinge of jealousy at the other men who had enjoyed Brianna privately, but when she saw the look on his face, she squeezed his shoulder.

"Relax, big boy," she offered reassuringly. "I ain't no ho."

"I didn't say you were."

"But you were thinking it, so don't trip."

"H-how----?'

"'Cause, nigga, I got mental skills to match my physical ones. Now, let's go back to the hotel."

"I'm ready. You ain't said nuthin' but a word."

Brianna smiled happily. "Remember that morning when we ate brunch and I explained to you that if me and you ever got together that it would be your lucky night?" Brianna put her arms around Supreme. "Now, you gonna see that I wasn't lying."

EPISODE 2

Chapter 11

"Now, do you take my word for it!?"

Detective Sally Walker just looked at the speaker, saying nothing.

The Silver Dollar Bar was a fancy after-hours dance spot where under-aged girls performed way past their bedtimes. And tonight the place was packed. Delighted patrons stood or sat in every nook and cranny of the open space while loud bass-laden music scrubbed their ears with pounding thunder.

Detective Tommy Larsen was good at bearing the noise, but felt sympathy for his partner, a New-Jack. "You might want to stick your earplugs in. That's why I gave them to you. They weigh almost zero and they help block out the loud music."

The short, stacked black woman shook her head. "I can handle it."

Larsen shrugged. "Suit yourself." He gripped Detective Walker by her elbow. "Follow me."

Not knowing the exact intent of the white detective's interest, Walker tried subtly to show that she didn't like to be touched, especially in a sleazy bar that reeked with the aroma of open sex.

Seemingly unaware of the tenseness in Walker's body, Larsen led her down a narrow opening, moving her closer to the stage, positioning her at an angle where she could clearly watch the action.

Walker looked at the nude girl, then away, but when she glanced at Larsen she was quick to notice the glow of fascination in his eyes as he boldly studied the girl.

"This is business, remember," Walker half-shouted over the music, nudging her partner in his side with her elbow, the same one he had grabbed earlier.

Larsen laughed. "If you don't mind, I'm trying to make a

positive identification."

"Then look at her face," Walker complained.

"Listen, detective, and that's what you are a detective and not the morals police, so back off. I'm trying to do a job here, if you don't mind."

"I saw you staring at that girl's---"

"Tattoos, detective." Larsen's voice rumbled. "Always check for tattoos. Some girls have them done secretly so we can recognize that they are Natashas."

"Natashas?"

Once more Larsen gripped the black woman's elbow. "I think you've seen enough. Let's go. You've seen what we came for." Moving away from the stage, Larsen spied a glassy-eyed waitress heading in their direction. He stopped, watched and waited until the girl was in front of them. Having gone past, he gave Walker's arm a painful squeeze. "Fifteen."

Walker gasped audibly. "She looks twice that."

"I know. This business ages them overnight." Larsen glared at the black detective. "I know, I know," Larsen growled, "about how gracefully black women age." He pushed Walker towards the exit. "But I'm curious to see how that myth holds up once the body snatchers starts grabbing them."

For no particular reason, Walker didn't enjoy the silent ride out of Jersey City back into Manhattan so she decided to clear the air. "I apologize for my unfounded assumption back at the club. It was unprofessional, uncalled for. I'm sorry."

"Don't sweat it, detective. It's water under the bridge."

Walker hesitated a moment before she spoke. "Back there, you mentioned something about Natashas. What is a Natasha?"

"A Natasha," Larsen utterly wearily, "is a trafficked girl. It started out as a brand name, sort of, for all the young females exported from Russia to be used as prostitutes. Now, Natashas are everywhere, but the name kinda stuck."

"But you said---"

"Hear me out." Larsen glowered at the detective. "When the smugglers finally began to arrive in New York with Natashas, we had no defensive strategy so our most ambitious plan was to get word inside to them---"

"So you infiltrated one of the dance clubs and had the girls get a tattoo which would be a signal that they were a Natasha."

"Some plan, huh?"

"Beats no plan at all." There was a measure of consolation in Walker's voice. "What type of tattoo is it?"

"A cartoon, you know, Mickey Mouse. Most of these girls are still only a few years removed from the age of watching cartoons so a Disney figure would be appropriate." Larsen crossed over into New York with a sigh. He laughed bitterly. "And then this new thing?"

"Which is?"

Glancing cautiously at the female detective before turning his focus back to his driving, Larsen almost mumbled. "Rumor has it that young, underage, black females are being used as exotic dancers."

"That's what this assignment is all about? Black girls?"

"You'll find out more tomorrow, but yeah, that's what it was all about." Larsen took a deep breath. "I'm speaking off the record here, you know."

"Of course."

"No one had been able to persuade the State Department to move forcefully on this sex trafficking activity until they learned of the black angle. If you remember, not long ago, law enforcement got its face dragged in the mud over the Amber Alert program. Any time a white girl came up missing, all the stops were pulled to locate her, but whenever a black girl was missing, there was no national attention." Larsen stopped for a red light. "Trust me, the feds don't intend to drag their feet on this one."

"But—"

"Tomorrow, Detective Walker, tomorrow." Larsen pulled into the police parking lot where he stopped the car. "I have never been known to give good counsel, so my advice is this. Don't get eaten by hungry sharks."

Walker felt momentary panic, but pushed it back with a smile. She stepped out of the car. "Sharks don't like dark meat," she replied.

The following morning, Walker found herself in her supervisor's office watching a ray of sunshine cut a slant through a slit in the blinds. She thought suddenly of Rosa Parks and Coretta Scott King, both of whom she had admired. Then she remembered the current threat against young, black females. Had the Civil Rights Movement failed? Had the demands of the movement to bridge the gap between the haves and the have-nots been lost on this generation of young, black girls who had brazenly left the halls of academia for the stripper's pole? What Walker did know was that it would be awful if the tradition of struggle among black women was replaced by sistas who had learned the craft of submissive surrender. How tragic would that be?

After plopping his long, lanky body into his chair, the Chief of Detectives, Al Dennis, resumed talking, his pasty-white face pinched and drawn. "This will be no holiday, no easy egg to crack, I grant you that. We may not realize it for years to come but everything the other guys are doing is shrewdly calculated, and it's like they're hitting us with a double-edged sword. On the one hand, they're smuggling these girls inside the country from Eastern Europe and housing them in boarding houses and such in Jersey and Connecticut. Other states too." A pallor spread across the Chief's face. "Only recently did it dawn on us what else was going down."

"You mean, with the black girls?"

"Based on what's being heard, Russian gangsters are either building or financing the building of a strip club empire that will rival the ones in Vegas. That much we know. What we don't know is where it will be, but word has it that the location will be southern."

"Atlanta? Memphis?"

"For the moment, your guess is as good as mine, but we don't have the luxury to be second-guessing each other because things are set to happen in the near future."

"What's the plan?"

"To somehow anticipate where this nude dance haven is going to be and to get someone---you---on the inside."

"So that explains why I'm here." Walker's tone was flat.

"For the last six months, our sources have indicated a gearing up for something separate from the smuggling of Eastern European girls into the country."

"Black girls?" Walker repeated.

"Yes, detective, black girls."

"But how does that fall under sex trafficking. I thought---"

"I know what you thought," Dennis explained, "but the landscape is quickly changing. Did you know that a recent law makes it illegal to force minors to perform commercial sexual activity? Hell, a person can get up to twenty-five years by even a threat to make underage girls perform. An added bonus is that with this new law, a victim doesn't have to cross international borders or be an immigrant to be a trafficked person." Dennis smiled. "There is even a fifteen year penalty for labor recruiters who deliver under-aged girls to employers, knowing these girls will be forced into servitude."

"Servitude?"

"Making them dance against their will is a form of servitude. These are young, very impressionable girls, detective, many of whom falsely believe they may one day be stars of the stage or of film. The reality is that most will eventually be forced into prostitution."

Walker almost burst out laughing because the connection was not lost on her. She knew instinctively that after seeing the girls dance, men would want to know how well they could fuck. That was always the ultimate question: Can this bitch fuck as good as she dances? And they would pay dearly to solve that sexual riddle.

"Barring any unforeseen development," Dennis continued, "everyone involved with this on our end is convinced that the build-up towards a black strip club empire will continue. We just don't know where."

"Like I said, Atlanta and Memphis are good bets."

"Well, it's your job to add it all up." Dennis slid a manila folder across his desk. "Here's everything about Ivan Gugarin's operation here in the States. Your job is to destroy his domestic

71

scheme to lure young, black girls into a life of stripping and prostitution."

"Sounds like fun," Walker muttered.

"A good place to start," Dennis lectured, "would be to take a long look at the map I've given you to see if you can spot any---."

"I think I may have a better idea, Chief."

A quizzical look crossed Dennis' face. "You do?"

"In light of what I've heard, we can reasonably expect a mass movement of young, black girls, if not from one city to another, but within a particular city, and for that there will have to be a front. Other than school, a large gathering of girls is bound to draw suspicion." Walker paused. "Yeah, they will need a good front to pull it off."

"So what is it you'll be looking for, detective?"

Walker shrugged reflexively. "Don't exactly know, but what I will look for is any new program or project that targets young, black girls."

"Good idea," Dennis mused, pondering the concept. "Good idea."

"It might be an after-school program. Could even be disguised as a church project, but whatever it is, I'll find it."

Dennis sat back, impressed and awed. He folded his long arms behind his head. "I know you were the right one for this assignment. Now, go kick some butt."

Chapter 12

"Most impressive."

Supreme smiled brightly at Ice's approval.

"No need to be modest, dawg," Ice continued happily. "Go 'head and admit it, you did the damn thang with your bad-ass self."

Having a seat at the conference table, Supreme refrained from any over-the-top self-congratulatory remarks although he knew that what he had done with The Academy was indeed most impressive. The school was a pretty sight, and there was nothing either passé or blasé about it, and for the hand-picked hoes that would study here, it would be the urban equivalent of the famed Taj Mahal. The bitches would be awed.

"Since my boy, Supreme, ain't going to give up the trade secrets of how he got this joint ready for class in so short a time, I say we get on down to our biz'ness." Ice stared at Supreme. "Again, dawg, you hooked this motherfucka up."

"Thank Brianna," Supreme said humbly. "Most of the ideas were hers."

"Should have known it all along," Eve teased, "a woman's work. And like they say, behind every great man is a woman." Eve laughed. "And if things don't get any better, there's going to be a woman behind every great woman."

"Yeah," Ice groaned, "y'all females need to stop all that freaking with each other and get a thug in your life, but that's a topic for another day 'cause this morning we needs to deal with a few thangs." Ice glanced around the table filled with the core of the

73

Charlotte operation. All studied or pretended to study the colorful printout in front of them. It was a small group, but each member was dedicated, willing to perform whatever duty was assigned them.

"So far," Ice commented proudly, "we have demonstrated our relevance to the Organization. Needless to say, Ivan is pleased." Ice smiled cordially. "There will be bonuses for everyone's past and recent performances. These were his exact words, people. Mine are, keep up the good work." Turning more businesslike, he continued. "Assuming everyone has had time to peek at the proposal, I think it's safe to say that Charlotte has just entered a new era in the adult entertainment world. Due to our magnificent work ethic, Ivan has granted us full range to develop our own night clubs, our own brand of nude photographs, and our own X-rated videos."

A hush fell over the room. None of them had expected that, but none failed to sniff out the profit quotient involved. This, they knew, was their chance to become real players in the "sex sells" sweepstakes. Just like that, they had taken a giant step.

"Hope you don't mind me proposing a toast?" Ice got up and deftly splashed a shot of champagne into everyone's glass. After the toast, Ice pushed his glass aside. "This is no bullshit. Once we get this machine up and running on all cylinders, none of us will ever hurt for money again." He paused. "Like you been doing bad before now," he teased. "If you remember, a long time ago I made a prediction. I said that if you stuck with me and remained loyal that I would bring you untold wealth. That prediction has just come true. New York and Los Angeles would love to be sitting in the position you guys are in right now, but Ivan said fuck 'em. And you know why? When he saw y'all's devotion, y'all's dedication to the future goals of the Organization, he knew Charlotte was the shit. We getting ready to blow up," Ice bragged.

Feeling it would be rash to mention it aloud, Supreme did have a problem with child pornography. He knew Ice would laugh at his insecurity and immediately point to the fact of him fucking Brianna. Although Supreme realized there was no way he could minimize the wrong of having sex with a minor, he still wasn't ready for the full-fledged exploitation of young, black girls in such an unforgiving fashion. Hip-hop videos already cast sistas in the worst light imaginable, but to depict underage girls in porno flicks would or could traumatize them.

"I don't have to exaggerate the possibilities that kiddie porn will open up for us," Ice said, staring at Supreme as though he had read his friend's mind. "We'll be playing in the big leagues where a million dollars ain't nuthin' but chump change. Take my word for it, everybody in this room is getting ready to get paid in full, and you can quote me on that."

That comment prompted Ice to briefly disclose bits and pieces of the entertainment package Ivan expected them to put together.

"We ain't gonna have no competition 'cause our shit gonna be so risqué that motherfuckas gonna be thrilled outta they rabbit-assed minds." Ice spoke with gleeful delight. "Our girls gonna be famous in the kiddie porn world, gonna be able to retire by the time they ass legal. We gonna have these hoes performing all kinds of sexual acts, doing stunts that will make a priest's dick as hard as Chinese arithmetic."

Supreme listened closely as Ice sold the idea of a black kiddie porn mecca in Charlotte, but he had recently read an article on the crackdown of kiddie porn in the United States. He raised his hand.

"Damn, nigga," Ice joked, "this ain't no classroom. You got yo' hand up like you a student at Myers Park or something who know the right answer. What up, dawg?"

"Man, that shit you kicking sound gooder than a motherfucka, but the feds trying to shut down child porno rings. I just read the article. The feds ain't bullshitting when it comes to children."

"First, I don't consider none of our girls children. Look at Brianna, and that's how most of 'em look. Hoes trapped inside a school-girl's body. Secondly, the police coming down on them rooty-toot motherfuckas who doing second-rate amateur work. We ain't going that route where we can get clocked."

"How we rolling, then?"

"Good question," Ice grinned, "damn good question. How we rolling? Well, I'm gonna tell you . We gonna play the Internet with our shit. Motherfuckas won't even know the videos and pictures are even being made in Charlotte 'cause our distributor will be a company in Russia. Ivan got it set up where our customers will pay seventy-five dollars a month to access our site. They'll pay by credit card which will be processed through a company in New Mexico. They keep 10% and the rest of the money will flow through accounts at Morgan Stanley. You see, by releasing our shit over the net, we safe 'cause there's little risk of detection this way, so let the downloading begin." When Ice saw that many in the room, including Supreme, seemed uncomfortable with the idea of kiddie porn, he exhaled wearily. "Look, we won't get into no rough stuff with them. Our shit just gonna be natural stuff, just ordinary fucking and sucking, normal stuff like them bitches be doing on they damn own."

"I just wanted to be sure what it was we getting into."

"And I hope I explained it." Ice looked at Supreme. "Man, we got a hook-up with collectors all over the world who deal in underground nude photos of teenage girls. We shoot the flicks, they sell the motherfuckas. This is a goldmine, I'm telling you. They got perverts out there who want calendars, who buy the hell out of table top kid porn books with lots and lots of glossy pictures. All we do is pay the 10% commission to our distributors, kick Ivan 40%, and the other 50% belongs to us."

"Can you get any more specific than that," McKay quizzed. "I'm speaking in terms of actual dollars going into my pockets."

"Now that's what I'm talking 'bout, a man with his mind on his money and his money on his mind." Ice grinned. "Since we a start-up, it has been estimated that this arm of our entertainment empire should net millions in the first year of operation so all of us should pocket over fifty thousand a month."

The room erupted in a loud gasp.

"Y'all like them numbers, huh. Tole you, I got you." Ice refilled everyone's drinking glasses. "Not only is it sweet, but it's safe. We will have software experts handling production so our product will be professional and the images done in high resolution. And since our company will be doing biz'ness in Belarus, Uncle Sam can't fuck with 'em if something did go wrong 'cause America ain't got no extradition treaty with Belarus. That means they can't get arrested for making porn for distribution in this country, and if they know they can't be touched, ain't no need for them to give us up. This shit tighter than virgin pussy," Ice roared. "Man, we in the money."

Monday 10:45pm

Later than night, Detective Walker felt troubled. Like most black women, she could not yet take the idea of underage girls, especially African-American ones, being exploited and used in explicit pornographic movies. Urban girls were already demoralized, and this would only damage them much more. Sometimes she felt that someone high up wanted to put an end to black people, and since their early attempts at destroying the male had not been overly successful, they were now going to work on destroying the sistas. Could she stop whatever was getting ready to go down?

The initial phase of her hunt for the trouble had turned the spotlight on schools in major urban markets where, to her total lack of surprise, she had discovered that The No Child Left Behind law was indeed leaving black children behind. That did not, in the least, surprise her.

She dismissed magnet schools, private schools, and above all, Muslim and Christian schools. These programs would hardly produce the large volume of accessible girls the bad guys would target in their search for Hoochie-Mamas-in-waiting, so her plan would be to zero in on inner city schools.

With the help of Google, she accumulated enough of a 'report card' on certain school districts where young girls could truly be at risk. She tagged these locations for further attention.

Returning to her internet search, she went for output on advocate groups, hoping that if one was posing as a front, there would be enough red flags so that she would be able to recognize it.

It took her hours to search through all of the countless hits and matches she had Googled up, but after repeated filtering she decided to first concentrate on the ones that kept showing up time and time again. She'd monitor these after a short 'vacation' to the bathroom where she would soak in a tub of bubbles.

But less than forty-five minutes later she was back at her desk, seated at her work station. Clearing her mind of all distractions, she gave herself a pep talk. She realized how easy it would be for her to jump to conclusions, so she charged herself with the responsibility of not going into this looking for evil. That, she knew, would be a dangerous mistake which could doom her experiment before it was even started. Plus she felt that if someone was trying to cover up something as big as the sex ring she was looking for, they would be smart enough not to telegraph it. She instantly got to work.

The first three school programs she probed were deemed as straightforward learning opportunities for school children. They were all started by community activists or educators who desired to raise schools in their area out of the rut most had fallen into. After hours of research, she sleepily accepted that these programs were bonafide. She was tired now, but in the morning would get around to profiling a program called GirlSmart. Tonight, she was just too damned tired.

Chapter 14

Neon could barely hear the conversation through the thick, wood door, but the little she heard filled her with dread, and the nearer she moved to the front of the room, the clearer the voices became. She imagined them plotting her death in their thick Russian accents.

Thankfully she could understand what was being said as her kidnappers openly discussed her plight, but unfortunately, to her dismay, there appeared to be no debate as neither of the men seemed split over the plan they were going to adopt.

"We leave on Tuesday," Vladimir said," and initiate the sale in New York. They have a better conduit out of the country there than in Boston. Besides it would seem more natural to move a black girl via that route because on one of the exotic routes, she'd stick out like a sore thumb."

"Let the gypsies worry about that," Boris grumbled. "She would be their problem then."

"Still this could get pretty interesting," Vladimir offered candidly. Although he had heard rumors of how hard it was for independent operators to get a deal with the gypsies who smuggled girls across international borders, he was still enticed by the prospect of the mission. He also knew they faced steep odds when it came to pulling it off without Ivan somehow finding out about it, and it didn't take him long to figure out what would happen then. "Why don't we enlist Uri's help? That would be much better than just walking into this like some dizzy blonde bimbo setting out to Hollywood to be an actress when she has no idea of what's out there for her."

Boris broke in. "There is a better way than involving Uri who would keep most of the money for himself. There are maverick buyers in New Jersey, but they are in a mystery location. We find them, be specific about what we have to sale, then make the deal. No problem."

Vladimir snorted derisively. "The people you speak of, they are wholesalers. They would never deal with us when we only have one girl."

"If we tell them how sexy she is---"

"It won't work. They deal in plenty."

Boris managed a slight smile. "Then we kidnap more girls."

Neon shrank away from the door, shrieking audibly. Suddenly it was quite certain what her kidnappers' objective was, and they were already celebrating as if the deed was a done deal.

"Help me dear Jesus," she gasped in prayer. "Don't let them do this to me. Please."

When Neon moved back to the door to listen, the vodka the men drank had slurred their speech so much it sounded like they were speaking pidgin English, but still this was adequate enough for her to understand what was ahead for her. None of it was reassuring.

What she learned was that she would be sold like a modern-day slave and smuggled to key points in dozens of cities in Europe until they decided where to settle her. Altogether she would be forced to travel thousands of miles, possibly even to China, where one of her kidnappers had said there was a booming sex-tourism trade which employed 2.8 million prostitutes.

Neon shivered uncontrollably as she envisioned herself cloaked in rags, riding on a train with men called gypsies who would cut off her hands if she yelled out or screamed. And what would she do in a strange country where she knew no one and where she had no money?

After praying feverishly some more, Neon put her ear back to the door, but nothing had changed. The men still were resolved to sell her. That much was increasingly evident. There was no talk among the men to reassess their position which meant they were fully committed to carrying out their plans in spite of its horrible consequences.

Neon wept. Of all that had happened to her and would happen to her in the days ahead, perhaps what frightened her most was that she failed to comprehend why any of this had happened to her in the first place.

Checking back on everything that had gone on in her life, she could put her finger on nothing that would have suggested that she would be kidnapped, held hostage, and then sold. Even though she was no angel and had played the hand life had dealt her like a pro, she felt she had committed no act in her existence that was so unkind that this would be her payback.

How in the world had this happened?

Who had brought this evil down upon her?

After she had cried herself to sleep, her kidnappers talked long and hard into the night. Each thought they saw the future clearly, and was ready to drop everything to breathe life into their scheme while still staying above suspicion.

"I have heard talk of a three man crew of independent operators who are capable of smuggling girls across international borders by using fake identification documents." Boris paused. "It might be worth it to invest a few days in trying to track them down."

"And you believe---"

"I can find them, yes," Boris replied, "but my prayer is that they will take this one girl. To kidnap more without knowing what we are going to do with them would be stupid. After all, we would need money to feed them. Too much trouble," he protested vehemently. "One girl, then many."

Boris had been driving up the New Jersey TurnPike for what seemed like days and then he spied his exit. According to his crudely drawn map, he should reach his destination within the half-hour. He had been told to get there today or otherwise it might be another three days before someone would be available to see him. Boris stepped on the gas. He wanted to be long gone by then.

Burlington County didn't emit the type of vibes that made him feel welcome, and he didn't emit the type of vibes that would make people feel he was a tourist.

Driving down Grant Street, Boris found Rancocas Drive and drove steadily away from the Courthouse towards a more nondescript point of Mount Holly. Although he had grown more comfortable, he still felt like an invader which made him desire to get this business over with as soon as possible. No delays.

Glancing at his watch, he realized he should almost be there, and for several seconds he wondered if the three men would still be willing to talk shop. He felt vulnerable having just one girl to deal, knowing that their business ethics would be to take advantage of him, to cheat him if they could. This was a common practice among criminals, so he knew better than to expect a deal that would be mutually beneficial. Not this time anyway. The next time when he came with more beautiful black girls, it would become obvious then that he was the more unscrupulous crook.

Less than twenty minutes later, he bore west, approaching his rendezvous point. He parked on the shoulder of the road, got out of the rental car, and popped the hood as a pre-arranged signal.

Another car instantly drove up. "Car problems, comrade?"

Boris squinted at the heavy, compact stranger. "Yeah, this car is acting like a woman."

"You interested in selling her?"

"That's why I'm here," Boris said. "You know a buyer?"

Following that exchange, Boris could instantly feel the man's attitude relax, changing from one of suspicion to one of manipulation. He approached the car smugly, his selfish objective clear. He leaned under the raised hood, fingering the engine with an intimacy that proved he appreciated machinery.

"Good," he muttered, "let's have a look."

"What do you think?" Boris asked

"Depends on what you have."

"What if I have a whole lot of woman and I want to get rid of her?"

"Why, only one?"

"Because that's how it is."

"Oh," the man replied coolly, "I see. It must be such an amazing feat to have only one girl."

Boris knew that an argument would turn up little that would be to his advantage, so he brushed the remark off. "Maybe when my corral is bigger, we won't have to meet out here on the road to nowhere."

The man smiled, stroking his beard. "This girl, is she pretty?"

Boris handed over a photo. "See for yourself."

"No good", the man hissed through clenched teeth.

"What do you mean, no good?"

"This chick is black, that's what I mean. No good."

Wondering if this was a ploy to reduce the buying price, Boris sighed wearily. "How long have you been doing this?"

"Fucking long enough to know that black girls are not easy to move out. In, yes, Out, big problem."

"Well, answer one question for me."

"Which is?'

"Are you willing to try?"

The man grinned widely. "I'm willing to try anything for the right price."

"Makes sense to me," Boris replied. "Let's work something out."

Chapter 15

When Ice threw a party celebrating the opening of The Academy, the site of the affair was a residence owned by Ivan in South Charlotte not far from the home owned by Fantasia.

The interior of the house was filled with very expensive furniture and the walls adorned with exquisite artwork. Everyone, including McKay, was visibly impressed by the décor. So was Eve.

"So living well is actually the best revenge," she quipped, tongue-in-cheek. "And they say crime doesn't pay."

"Oh yes, it pays," McKay countered, "especially when you're the teacher's pet." He nodded his head in the direction of Ice and Supreme who stood apart from everyone talking privately. "Wonder what they're yapping about?"

"Probably about how they suckered all the rest of us. I think that conversation would be plenty interesting, but it looks like they're having a disagreement of some sort, more of an argument than a discussion."

McKay studied the pair more closely. "I see what you mean." He nudged Eve politely. "Why don't you mosey on over there and see what's going on."

Raising her eyebrows delicately, Eve smirked. "I think I'll do just that, thank you; however, I'll have you know that such information comes with a price." With that, she sashayed off, the elegant dress clinging seductively to the curves of her voluptuous body. She left a trail of intoxicating perfume in her wake.

In less than a minute, Eve had pushed her way through the crowd and now stood near the two men. She coughed politely.

"Make yourself useful and bring us a drink."

A slight amused smile played across Eve's painted lips. "I didn't know I was invited here to serve drinks to the guests."

"You weren't," Ice snapped, "but get the damn drinks anyway if you don't fucking mind."

Eve stormed off.

Returning with the drink tray, Eve noticed that the mood of the conversation Ice and Supreme were having had darkened considerably. Both men deftly removed a drink, but visibly ignored Eve until Ice stopped talking, sipped his Hennessey, savored its aroma, and then dismissed her.

"See ya later, sista," Ice rasped grimly, "but holla at me before you get missing, okay?"

"That dress looks nice on you." Supreme smiled, winking at Eve.

"Check this out," Ice continued once the two were alone. "It don't get no better than us, dawg. We the shit. We way ahead of the rest of the motherfuckas who trying to get paper. Man, we two niggas who living the American dream."

"I can feel you, but---"

"Nigga, you need to put that shit out of your head 'bout what happens to them hoes. They girl dawgs, dawg."

Meanwhile from across the room, McKay and Eve were having their own conversation.

"That discussion looks like something is up. What do you think?"

"I don't know," Eve confessed, "but I do feel we should stay on our toes. Something's not right and whatever it is, Supreme doesn't like it one bit."

"Supreme is soft, but in the meantime, why don't you pull up on him, and try to find out what's really going on. Give the ol' boy a shot of pussy. Betcha he'll spill his guts then."

"And what will your scheming ass be doing while I got my legs spread?"

"Taking notes," McKay laughed, "and watching your back, of course."

On Wednesday, Eve made it her business to call Supreme.

"You okay, friend?" she purred into the phone. "The last time I saw you, you didn't look so good."

Supreme knew Eve was referring to the night of the party at Ivan's house. "It's a mad, mad, mad world, Charlie Brown."

"A full grown woman can make it less mad, and I'm not Charlie Brown."

"My bad, Miss Black America."

"Now, back to my original question. Are you okay?"

"That depends."

"On what, nigga?"

"If you any good at sexual healing."

"Your place or mine?" Eve cooed. "Call it."

"Why don't we meet on neutral ground?"

"That's fine with me because I'll whip this pussy on you anywhere, anytime. Nigga, we can fuck in the dirt like two mad dogs or go up on the roof under the stars. I don't give a damn. Let's just get it started."

"Go to The Radisson and meet me in the lobby."

"I'm on the way, but I've got one piece of advice for you. You might want to stop somewhere before you get to the hotel to take a crash course in the female anatomy. I'm a helluva lot more woman than you-know-who and I don't want you getting lost in all this flesh. Bye, nigga."

Less than an hour and a half later, something made Supreme want to hold nothing back. He lay in bed snuggled up close to Eve's naked body.

"Still wanting on your second wind?" Eve teased. "Better catch it soon or I'm taking the dick, and I know you don't want me to get rough, do you?"

"No, that's alright. No rough stuff," Supreme joked.

"Well, why don't we talk then?"

"'Bout what?"

"About whatever is on your mind. If my good pussy can't solve a man's problem, I do possess a superior mind. Sometimes brain power works better than pussy juice." Eve kissed Supreme's cheek. "Want to stimulate the other end of my body?"

Supreme sighed. "Okay, let's see what you think about

this."

Eve's pulse sped up at the prospect of learning what was really about to go down at The Academy, but she acted nonchalant.

A voice of warning echoed inside Supreme's head, but he ignored it, choosing instead to believe he would feel better if he got everything off his chest, and the only way he could do that was by talking to someone. Eve, for the moment, would do.

Gently massaging Supreme's shoulder, Eve didn't disturb him as he softly spoke although occasionally she would offer a smile of encouragement. She knew it would take a moment before he revealed anything substantial, and she was willing to wait.

"The world really is a ghetto." When Eve said nothing, Supreme exhaled deeply. "First of all, young sistas grow up in urban, inner city, hell-holes, and society expects them to make their lives out of scratch, like it's as easy as baking biscuits. Then you pit these same young girls against niggas who have been told to make bricks out of straw, and their chances for success drops that much more."

"That could be a problem."

"It's more of a nightmare."

"So now you feel guilty because you're with us?"

Supreme nodded.

Eve stopped her work on Supreme's shoulder. She now faced him. "Okay, let me ask you something. You've been to prison, right? What did you go for?"

"I took money from the white man, his companies. I been hustling all my life and I ain't never took shit from a brotha or did anything to disrespect a sista."

"A noble crook," Eve cracked.

"There's still a few of us left," Supreme cracked back.

"Well how noble is it to fuck a tenderoni who's not legal yet?"

Supreme sighed. "It ain't something I'm proud of. Shit just happened."

"And kept on happening, but there's no need to explain. I know the very tempting Miss Brianna well, taught her myself so you're excused when it comes to her. You could refuse Brianna no more than you could refuse me." Eve stroked Supreme's face. "In a very short period of time, you have had two sexual experiences most men would die for."

"True, but does it ever bother you that some of the other girls may not have such good experiences? It may be fun now, but what about in the future?"

"I can't answer that. I'm no fortune teller."

Supreme sucked in air. "I wish somehow I could stop it."

"Why don't you relax," Eve said softly, fluffing up a pillow for Supreme's head, "and tell Mama all about it."

After school. The next evening.

"Goddamn, Eve!" McKay barked, "your pussy that good it made that nigga tell you all that?"

Eve laughed, feeling good. "Told you my coochie was the bomb."

"Well keep it away from me because I like my secrets well kept. I need for all my skeletons to stay in the damn closet where they belong."

"You had your chance and blew it."

"And that was probably the luckiest day of my life," McKay laughed. "Damn, that nigga spilled his guts." McKay shook his head in disbelief. "Now, run that pass me again."

Pleased that she had come through, Eve repeated the info with a satisfied air of contentment, not the least bit amazed at how easily she had pulled Supreme off his square. She giggled, glad that McKay was so patient since it afforded her the chance to recount what she called the next episode in the saga of The Academy.

The information was well organized, adorned with tidbits of secrecy that would either get her killed or promoted, dependent upon how enthusiastic Ivan would be in knowing that his beloved organization had a weak link. Eve had certainly picked up a lot, and given the complexity of what she had been told, she was sure she could launch a good deal for herself. In her mind, she was absolutely convinced she would be comfortable with betraying Supreme, but deep down she knew she should help him in destroying The Academy. Then, beyond this, she also knew that the killings would start, and her instincts told her that she could be among the casualties.

Suddenly she wished she had never discussed this with Supreme. Moreover, she began to despise herself for not suppressing this bitter data, but she hadn't and now McKay knew all about how The Academy, under the guise of GirlSmart, was going to be used not only as a front for child pornography, money laundering, but also the eventual kidnapping of young, black girls to be smuggled out of the country into Europe.

"Congratulations," McKay said excitedly once Eve had completed her story for the second time. "We have just hit the jackpot."

Or maybe the end of the road, Eve thought. Nevertheless, she smiled openly.

Chapter 16

There was a numbing silence as Brianna strolled through an Academy classroom, peering into the anxious faces of the girls seated at their desks.

"So you think that because you got a phat ass, you gonna automatically rule the world?" Brianna scowled impatiently. "I guess that every one of you silly bitches dream of catching the eye of a neighborhood baller who gonna put your ass in diamonds and furs. Well, let me run it down about how it goes with most of these so-called playas. Basically, they'll fuck you until they tired of you, and then they'll kick your trifling ass to the curb and nobody but a broke-assed nigga wants trash." Brianna shrugged. "I can't apologize for the brothas 'cause if I was a man, I'd do the same shit. I'd keep my dick stuck down a dumb ho's throat or up her ass." There were a few snickers in the room, but they quickly died down. "Y'all think this shit funny. We at war," she raged, "and some of y'all don't even know what the fuck going on, but I ain't gonna lie. I don't feel sorry for no ignorant ho 'cause that's one less ho in my way."

Brianna continued in this vein for another ten minutes, telling the girls, aged twelve to seventeen, about what wonderful news it must have been for them when they learned they were blessed with genes that would make their butts sprout like their backs were growing basketballs.

"You got the blessing already," she preached. "Now, I want you to let me and The Academy teach you how not to interfere with the blessings your blessing can bring you."

Every girl in the class was intrigued. They listened raptly

90

as Brianna resumed their orientation. The fact that none of them had any experience was downplayed. Rookies today. Professionals tomorrow. When Brianna told the group that this was The Academy's motto, each girl accepted it as fact that she could take the world of adult entertainment by storm.

As Brianna spoke of the riches to be had, there were no signs of exaggeration which made it sound all the more like a black Cinderella dream come true. In fact, the more imaginative Brianna did become, the more the girls believed, not one of them daring to doubt that she couldn't challenge destiny and win.

"We live so close to the wealth of this city." She pointed out the window in the direction of the skyline. "Those big-assed skyscrapers should make all of you mad and you know why? Bitches like you should be living uptown, enjoying the motherfucking good life. It's bitches like y'all who deserve to know what it's like to be pampered, to be waited on and fussed over; to have a chauffeur drive your ride, a pretty nigga to suck your pussy, and to have your own damn money!" The girls shrieked in delight.

A few minutes later when Brianna showed a DVD of herself traveling across country, flying first class, being escorted to the hottest strip clubs in the hottest cities where she would wow audiences with her dancing, the mouths of all the girls hung wide open in awe.

"Any questions?" Brianna asked once the viewing was finished.

One girl timidly raised her hand.

"Yes, Danisha."

The girl cleared her throat. "So, it really is true what we done heard 'bout you being a legendary teenage diva?"

Brianna knew she wasn't supposed to brag, but she couldn't resist the temptation. She looked Danisha in the eyes and smiled. "You saw my work. I appreciate your compliment but in the world of exotic dancing, I'm beyond legendary. Shit, girl, I'm on my way to being immortalized."

Tuesday. After school.

"I suppose it's because I like to break the rules as much as anyone else." McKay was talking bad-guy tough. "Why let the other motherfuckas have all the fun? Besides it's called working the system. Anything less and you get eaten alive, my dear. Take it from someone who knows."

"You're right," Eve shrugged, "thanks for the advice."

"Hey, babe, you're not in this alone." McKay's eyes sparkled mischief. "Watch Ice go for it hook, line, and sinker. Supreme is his boy and that's why we go to him instead of Ivan. Ice will pay to hush up what his boy has done, knowing good and damn well that Ivan will kill Supreme's ass if he ever discovered the nigga got loose lips. Plus Ice will look like a fool since he was the one that brought Supreme in, and the last thing Ice would want is for Ivan to call his judgment into account. Trust me, Ice will kick out the money like he's a Las Vegas slot machine."

McKay continued to talk as if he were some sort of smooth operator until Ice's Maserati pulled up in Eve's driveway. Although he pretended that Ice's arrival meant nothing, Eve noticed he had visibly tensed which caused a ripple of anxiety to course through her body.

"You sure we should go through with this?"

"It's too late now not to" McKay said, "so you just as well go open the door and let the nigga in. It's time to play truth or consequences."

Eve didn't find that particularly amusing so she huffed away to answer her door. She stiffened when Ice scanned her face, searching for clues to explain why he had been summoned. Finding nothing, he kissed Eve on both cheeks.

"What up?" Ice's tone was friendly.

"Nothing much, but I need to have a word with you. Come on in," Eve offered warmly. McKay is in the den."

"McKay?"

"Come on, Ice. This is serious."

Initially uncomfortable in Ice's company, Eve began to feel more in control once they reached the den where McKay waited, looking like he didn't have a care in the world. He bumped fists with Ice, then casually sat back down on the sofa, leisurely crossing his right leg over his left knee. He flashed Eve a big smile of reassurance as she sat down beside him.

Ice strode over to a stuffed chair just opposite them. He took a deep breath. "What up, you two?" Then he leaned back, staring at the pair with hard, cold eyes. "I hope y'all ain't wasting my time on some bullshit 'cause I got better thangs to do than to be running 'cross town---"

"It's about your boy Supreme."

"Supreme? What about the nigga?"

"He might need to be checked."

A wave of anger burst through, but Ice contained it so that when he spoke, his voice was not raised. "And just who might you think you are to tell me who needs to be checked in my crew? I feel like I'm quite capable of putting a nigga in check and keeping his ass in check if I personally feel he done fucked up."

"But---"

"Let me finish, nigga," Ice snapped flatly, "before you say shit else. Supreme, like every-fucking-body else in Charlotte takes orders from me, so it ain't like the nigga shot-calling on his own which means he ain't doing shit but what I tole' his motherfucking ass to do." Ice stood. "Now, does that clear up any misunderstanding you might have had."

"No."

"No!?"

The level of tension in the room rose noticeably, but McKay did not appear to be intimidated. "It's like I said in the beginning, you need to step to your boy or else he's going to get checked by Ivan." Pausing long enough to watch the expression on Ice's face change, McKay's silence dared Ice to interrupt. "Supreme has loose lips and if what he said ever gets back to Ivan, there would be real trouble." McKay nodded towards Eve. "He sold his soul for a shot of pussy. Isn't that right, sweetheart?"

Ice glared at Eve with his lips pressed together tightly, his nostrils flared. "Well?"

"It's true. Supreme told me some things that he never should have."

"Was that before or after you sucked the nigga's dick?" Ice

snarled meanly.

"What difference does it make?" McKay interceded brusquely. "And in case you didn't know, pillow talk is the most dangerous conversation there is because in the afterglow of a good nut, men have been known to say shit that has destroyed empires and ruined countries. Your boy is merely another victim."

"Goddamn, Eve," Ice barked, "what did that fool say?"

Ice sat back down and after the initial round of head-shaking and making faces, he became terribly upset. It was evident that Supreme had fucked up. He glared at McKay abruptly. "What do you suggest?" When McKay shrugged, Ice grinned fiendishly. He recognized a bribe when he saw it. "How much?"

Without hesitation, McKay quoted the sum he and Eve had agreed upon earlier and when Ice flinched at the amount, McKay commented in a disinterested voice. "Consider the alternative."

"Still, that's a lot of paper."

"It don't have to cost you a cent being that you could always deduct the money from all the hefty bonuses your boy is sure to get once The Academy reaches full steam. I don't take it that Supreme will complain. He impresses me as one who likes breathing oxygen. Tax his ass for the privilege of living."

"You let me worry about Supreme."

"Cool, my brotha. And now that I've got one less worry, what about the money?"

"It'll be in an account for y'all by the close of the business day tomorrow. How's that?"

"Cool."

Ice stood to leave. "This shit dead, ain't it?"

"Deader than a doorknob," McKay grinned. "Deader than a motherfucka."

Ice was furious, but driving across I-485 he couldn't help feeling depressed. He had to chastise Supreme, a nigga he had pulled up out of the grave. He had given Supreme a free pass, but his dawg had come up limping. Not long ago, he was celebrating the motherfucka. Now, he felt like burying his ass. Man, life was a bitch.

No one knew better than Ice that the key function of The Organization was total secrecy, and he also knew how specific Ivan was about maintaining a monk-like silence when it came to his business affairs. On more times than he could possibly count, Ice recalled how Ivan had stressed that his overall strategy was based on loyalty. Ivan had also confessed to how he would react to any info that pointed towards a breach in the security apparatus, so for Supreme's own good, as well as his own, Ice hoped what had happened never got back to Ivan. All hell would break loose if it did and even though the ultimate sin would be Supreme's, Ice knew that he would be killed also since he was directly responsible for what went on in Charlotte, his sector.

Nervously, he steered his car onto the exit that would take him to the quiet tree-lined residential area where Supreme lived in a three-bedroom home on a corner lot. He hoped to catch his friend by surprise. He also wished to find Supreme home alone, but decided against the chance of that happening since a lot of bitches frequented the premises. Ice wondered if Supreme had mentioned anything to one of the stray hoes about what he truly did for a living. Ice hoped not. Ice arrived just as a phat-to-death brown-skinned woman was coming out of the door.

"Yo, sista, Supreme home?"

"No, he gone."

"Gone where?" Ice was out of the Maserati now. "Did he say?"

"No, and I didn't ask. Why don't you come back later."

Ice grabbed the woman's arm roughly. "Let me tell you something, bitch. Don't ever get fly-out-the-mouth with me again. I just asked your ass a simple question."

"And I gave you a simple answer."

Ice tightened his grip. "Well, it was the wrong one."

"I don't know where Supreme is. Now, will you please let my arm go. You hurting me."

Ice released the woman's arm. "Now, back to Supreme. How long he been gone?"

"Since this morning."

When it was obvious that he had lost the element of

surprise, Ice flipped out his Samsung Galaxy V, but before dialing snarled at the woman. "Yo' ass dismissed."

"And I hope you have a nice day, too" the woman snapped, walking off.

Ignoring her, Ice shouted into the phone. "Nigga, get your ass to yo' crib right now! No, nigga, I ain't wanting to hear shit, and I don't give a fuck 'bout what you doing or fixin' to do. Get here now. I ain't bullshitting, nigga. It's a goddamn matter of life and death."

Because there was a great deal of traffic on South Boulevard, Supreme was not able to make it across town in the time he had predicted which prompted a second angry call.

"Nigga, where you at?"

"I'm coming, Ice. Damn."

"Well, get heah, then."

Ten minutes later when Supreme finally drove up, Ice was at the door of the Beemer, yanking it open almost before the car had come to a complete stop.

"What the fuck up with you, nigga?"

"You 'bout to get both of us killed," Ice screamed. "What you tell that bitch?"

"What bitch!? What you screaming 'bout?"

"So now you gonna play dumb," Ice ranted loudly. "Don't take me for none of them weak bitches you be running game on 'cause now sho' ain't the time."

Supreme stepped out of the car. "Man, you wronger than a motherfucka 'cause I ain't said shit to no ho."

"You ain't, huh? What 'bout Eve? She a ho."

Supreme's face fell. "Ah, man, we was just kicking it, that's all. Plus, I ain't kick shit that she wasn't going to find out anyway. Eve a part of the team, ain't she?"

"Fuck that shit, man. You ain't cut like that. You ain't got the juice to be telling a motherfucka nuthin' unless me or Ivan give you fucking permission." Ice shook his head. "Why you fuck up like that, dawg?"

Ice waved his hands in exasperation. "Let's go inside."

Sensing danger, Supreme hesitated. He patted his pockets,

stalling.

"Don' tell me that you done let that bitch that just left roll out with the only set of keys you had to your own crib?"

Supreme lied. "Seems that way and I ain't expecting her back until---"

"No problem," Ice uttered grimly, pulling out his key ring and heading towards the door of Supreme's crib. "I got my own set."

"Y-you got keys to my crib?"

"Yours and everybody's else in the crew, so don't blow the shit up."

'Who else got keys to my spot?"

"Just me and it will stay that way unless you fuck up again."

"That's some low-down, sneaky shit, and you didn't even tell me about it. If y'all think y'all can run up in my crib whenever you feel the fuck like it, then y'all can have the bitch back. I ain't jiving."

Ice opened the door. "Let's go on in before one of yo' nosey-assed neighbors start looking out they goddamn window."

"How long this gonna take?" Supreme wailed, "'cause you done fucked me up with that stunt you just pulled. Got a key to my crib."

"Nigga, you could be dead right this motherfucking minute," Ice cracked, "and you sweating some small shit. Just think if Eve had went to Ivan instead of coming to me."

"So what I gotta do now, stick my hand on a stack of bibles and swear I ain't gonna do it no mo' That's sucka shit---"

"Nigga, go fix you a drink or roll up a blunt 'cause you 'bout to make me lose it up in heah, and Lord knows I don't want to do nuthin' to you over no stupid shit so let's get some kind of understanding, cool?" Leaning forward to touch Supreme gently on the shoulder, Ice spoke in a voice that showed his true love for his friend. "Please, dawg, don't do nuthin' that will make them make me gun you down. Feel me?"

"Yeah, man, I feel you. I understand where you coming from and I give you my word that it won't happen again. Word."

"Ain't no way I'm gonna let nuthin' happen to you, but you gotta talk to me if you feel the pressure getting to you. You just can't go expressing yourself to people, even people on the team." Ice stuck out his fist for Supreme to bump. "Peace, dawg, I'm out."

Chapter 17

The last day of the month,
Detective Walker greeted the man warmly. "Welcome to the Queen City, Mr. Graham. So glad you could make it. Thanks. Now, if you will come right this way, I have a vehicle waiting right outside."

Smiling politely, the reed-thin, blond man in his J.C. Penney suit followed the black woman through the bustling airport terminal to a parked car just outside the Delta Airlines entrance.

"I trust your flight was enjoyable." Walker let the man in on the passenger side before quickly dashing around to the driver's side. "You did say you enjoyed the flight, didn't you?"

"As long as the landing is safe, I'll call it enjoyable." Graham grinned impishly. "I'm very keen on smooth landings."

"Aren't we all," Walker laughed. "Aren't we all. It's about a half hour from here to headquarters, so why don't you tell me a little something about yourself and please don't be modest. I've read up on you on the Internet, so I'm already impressed."

"Well, in that case, I'd better keep my mouth shut for fear I may ruin your good opinion of me. It's not often that I get some high marks coming in."

"Please indulge me. I'm interested."

"Okay, only since you insist." Graham spoke modestly. "As you know, I'm a college professor turned financial consultant turned financial sleuth."

"Oh, sleuth me, honey," Walker teased playfully. "You sure

know how to turn a girl on. Just think, a man who knows where all the m-o-n-e-y is."

Once Walker had made it into the 4th Street headquarters, she made quick progress in getting Graham to speak specifically about the reason he was in Charlotte.

"Even though it was painstaking to unravel since there's not a lot of a financial information flow between the states and Switzerland, I did come up with something that should pique your interest. What I found was a consortium of basically illegal enterprises supervised by a parent company called T.O.T.I.."

"TOTI?"

"TOTI, yes. T.O.T.I.. Stands for Tip Of The Iceberg which is an entertainment conglomerate owned by one Mr. Isaac Green of this city."

"Isaac Green," the Chief barked. "Detective, do a check, a NCIC."

"Got you, Chief. I'm on it, but I thought this was all about GirlSmart?"

"I'm getting to that in a minute."

"Well, give me a minute here because I don't want to miss a word of this." A short time later, Walker hurried back to her seat with a NCIC printout. "Interesting," she said, nodding at the document. "You may continue now, Dr. Graham."

"From what I've been able to gather, the same person who runs TOTI is the same person that is ultimately responsible for GirlSmart."

"Issac Green, you mean?"

"Precisely, Chief Dennis. Although Green may not be the actual founder of the program, he is the benefactor of it. What else I do know is that funds for the program flow from a Cayman Island account via Basel. I can't get any more specific than that other than to say that at this point my financial surveillance was diverted elsewhere."

"Where?"

"All prime indicators point to Russia as the central artery of money for both TOTI and GirlSmart."

"Russia?" Walker gasped

"Don't be so surprised," Graham cautioned, "because for quite some time now the Russian underworld has been a big wheel in the delivery of illicit finances across the globe to back various business ventures, some legal, some not so legal. So I don't find it that big a coincidence at all to find Russian money behind GirlSmart."

"The question is, what's in it for them?" Walker focused hard on Graham. "Any ideas?"

"Nope. I thought I would leave that part of the investigation up to you." Graham grimaced. "But I'm sure there's a reason why the Russians would have their hands in these two enterprises." Graham's eyes twinkled. "Want me to take a guess?" When there was no reaction from the Chief, Graham pleaded. "Ah, come on, what wrong can there be in an educated guess."

"All right," Chief Dennis conceded, "take your shot."

"Okay, since you ask. The way I see it is like this." Graham rubbed his hands together greedily as though he was preparing to reveal the secrets of the cosmos. "Now, follow this. The Top Of The Iceberg is a conduit for adult entertainment. GirlSmart, well, I imagine, has to do with girls. And when you add to this simple equation the fact that the Russians are the top players in the global sex trade, then I'd say that what you have here is a sure case of all hell getting ready to break loose." Graham was ready to go. "Have a nice day."

Chapter 18

By virtue of the fact that he felt like a fool for accepting the dinner invitation in the first place, it took Supreme almost an hour to drive to the Captain's Galley in Concord, a town just outside of Charlotte. It still wasn't clear why he had agreed to meet Eve there especially after what she had done to him. Supreme grimaced. His last escapade with Eve had almost cost him his life and here he was again off to see her. Was it a fatal attraction or was he just fatal? He didn't know, wasn't at all certain, but the woman had convinced him that her need to see him was urgent. He would find out.

The restaurant was crowded when Supreme entered, but he had spied Eve's car outside so he knew she had already arrived. Looking around, he spotted her seated in a cozy corner, waving him over. Glancing at people enjoying themselves at the tables he passed, it pleased him to find no signs of anyone who knew him. Hopefully, Eve had taken the same precautions.

Eve ordered for them just as soon as Supreme sat down, and then with a look of smug satisfaction on her beautiful face, turned to him. "It's good to see you."

"Alive, you mean?"

"Supreme---"

"You could have got me killed with that stupid shit."

"Look, you have every right to be mad at me, but I just wanted to let you know that I'm not some kind of black widow who gives a man some pussy one minute and then kills him the next."

"You sho' coulda fooled me 'cause that's exactly what the fuck yo' conniving ass did."

"I'm sorry. Believe me."

"What do you want? You said it was important."

"Let's eat first. Then, we'll talk."

Supreme could hardly believe how easily he felt himself melting. It was almost like he was a pat of butter and Eve was the sun because after only a few short minutes in her company, he realized how increasingly difficult it was going to be to motivate himself to remained angry at the woman. Following what had occurred the last time he had trusted her should have made it a natural reaction for him to whip out his gun to pump a minimum of half a clip into her pretty head. Instead he desired to lick her naked body from head to toe.

At one point during the meal, Supreme looked across the table at Eve, his eyes cold and hard. "After that stunt you pulled on me, tell me, what did you expect me to do to you the next time I saw you?"

Eve smiled. "Just what you're doing now, being happy to be with me. I can imagine what you're thinking. Yes, I'm a bitch, but what kind of woman would I be if I wasn't a damned good one?"

Supreme bit into a shrimp, staring at Eve.

"I'm just trying to figure you out. First, you sex me almost to death and then after something as beautiful as that, turn right around and plot to get me knocked off. Now, here your phat ass is again."

"I wasn't out to destroy you, Supreme."

"What do you call it, then?"

"Looking out for number one. Hey, if you catch me slipping, then I expect you to make me pay for the lesson. Life is a dirty business, sweetheart, and sometimes we are forced to compete with the same people we love. That's just how the cookie crumbles." Eve reached across the table, putting her hand inside Supreme's. "I want you to understand that I don't want there to be any hard feelings between us. I don't want there to be any tears in the end, so I had hoped that by us getting together this evening, we could kinda start over." Eve sighed. "I know that you're still fucking baby girl so there's no point in me losing sleep over it. You can have both of us. Me and Brianna."

Supreme's head was spinning. "This shit crazy," he acknowledged, "got me puzzled like a motherfucka."

"Don't you trust you own judgment?"

"Can I trust you," Supreme cracked, "that's the million motherfucking dollar question. No bullshit, Eve. You fine and all that, but you a damn snake in the grass. A motherfucking cobra."

Eve pretended to be hurt. "But I want you to get to know the other side of me."

Supreme looked doubtful. "I don't trust your buddy, McKay, either. That fool is a master double-crosser."

"I'll cut his ass off if that's what you want, if it will help us get along better." Eve leaned forward seductively, lowering her voice to a husky purr. "I know how silly this may sound, but I'm dying to suck your dick again."

"Girl, don't start talking that shit. We a long way from home."

"So what?" Eve giggled. "I got us a hotel room right down the street from here. You ready to go?"

"Hell yeah."

Thirty minutes later.

"Are you going to stay in the game forever?"

Eve raised herself on her elbows to glance over at Supreme. "We don't need to be having any discussions about The Academy ever again. We just went through hell to get over what happened the last time we had this conversation. What are you doing, testing me to see if I'll go tell McKay?"

"Naw, it ain't like that. Plus, I feel like me and you got a good understanding now. I don't believe you would cross me no mo'."

"I won't do that again, Supreme. I promise. You got me sprung."

"I'm feeling you myself."

"Thanks." Eve kissed Supreme's navel. "I needed that."

"You still didn't answer my question though."

"You answer first."

"What, if I'm gonna stay friends with Ice forever?"

"Yeah."

Supreme paused, thinking. "Sometimes when I think about the money and shit, it be like hell yeah, I ain't going nowhere, but when I think about Brianna and what's going to happen to some of those girls, I feel badder than a motherfucka. Shit ain't right what we doing. It's foul as hell."

"I guess the best thing to do if you like money is to forget about all the other shit that goes on."

"How can I not help but think about it when the shit be going on right in front of my fucking face? It ain't like Ice gonna give me a medal for acting like the shit all good when it's turning my damn stomach."

Eve studied Supreme thoughtfully. "I don't think you should make it a habit of talking like this. Jesus knows I hope you never say stuff like this in front of Brianna. I don't care how good the bitch's coochie is."

"Don't worry, Brianna is still a rookie. She's nowhere as good as you in the double-crossing department."

Eve decided not to argue. "Am I ever going to be able to live that one mistake down, or are you going to throw it up in my face any time Brianna's name comes up?"

"I'm sorry, but it fucks me up when I think of all the young girls in The Academy who will never grow up to be special. Some man will never get the chance to tell them the way he feels about them. Sistas, today, are so devalued."

Eve sat up in bed. "You're really serious about wanting to shut down The Academy?" Eve shook her head sadly. "What evidently has not gotten through to you is that Ivan commands and has total control of the sex trade not just here, but all over the world, so thinking locally is not the answer. If you were to strike out at Ivan on such a small scale, you wouldn't last a hot minute. As you know, we are all sworn to secrecy, and while the police in this country are not on his payroll yet, chances still are very good that Ivan would know quite quickly if one of us went to the law on him. I understand that what you're saying sounds clever and all that, but the bottom line is that it won't work. And that's my honest opinion, sweetheart."

Feeling dejected, Supreme groaned miserably. "But there has got to be a way. Ivan is not invincible. There has to be a way to get his ass."

Eve wasn't flattered by the look on Supreme's face because the last thing she needed at the moment was to get caught up in one of his juvenile schemes. After all, she had earned the right to live like a black Queen and she didn't want the embarrassment of trying to explain to either Ice or Ivan why she was sleeping with a man who was stupid. Realizing that friendly advice would not serve as a deterrent, she became more firm. "Ivan will kill you."

"So, what do you suggest?"

"That we leave well enough alone"

The first of the month.

Walker watched in dazed fascination. The woman staring back at her through the mirror behind the polished counter did not look anything at all like a dedicated law enforcement officer because everything from her hair, her face, her clothes were in startling contrast to the way she usually presented herself to the world. And that was precisely the image she sought: a sophisticated Hoochie Mama.

She had been in Charlotte a month now and her investigation of both Isaac Green and GirlSmart were already in progress. Her sources in the local area had provided a lot of info---a lot of it bullshit---but most of what she had learned had been of value and interest to her.

Obviously, a lot of it made perfect sense, and the way the proverbial dots had been connected couldn't be dismissed, so she was not shocked to find out that Green had been a pimp. Who, other than a Mack, would be more finely-suited to betraying black women? With all he had apparently achieved in the ho game, he would not suffer any vulnerabilities, and the harsh treatment of sistas wouldn't bother him in the least.

And on the outside, GirlSmart would not appear to be the

disgusting front it actually was, a way-station for the purpose of converting young black girls into bitches and hoes. To the local community, GirlSmart would seem like a good thing, a blessing. Instead, it was an ugly fraud, and Walker was determined to expose it for what it truly was. Or die trying.

This was her second drink, but that didn't mean shit. She could hold her liquor. Leaving the counter, she decided to walk to the bathroom, not because she had to go, but to provide the male patrons with an opportunity to eye her ass. On her way back to her pretended destination, she noticed that she was about the same age as most of the women in the bar, but none of them had gotten as lucky genetically as she had, First, she was firecracker red, a skin tone that black men found irresistible due to the time-honored color fixation of urban America. Her shoulder length hair was her own as was her fiery attitude, and she had a way of expressing herself that made it clear that she had been to somebody's school.

In the bathroom only long enough to let the men catch their breath, she knew she had emerged victorious when she heard the whispers about the tall, phat, sexy red bitch. She knew it wouldn't take long for the sly stares to turn into open propositions. She took a seat in the rear.

"Don't get me wrong," one suitor said," I'm not usually a nosey person, but please may I ask you a question?"

Walker smiled politely. "Sure."

"Will they let you back in?"

Puzzled, Walker shrugged. "Will who let me back in where?"

"You're an angel, aren't you, so I just wanted to know if you had to be back in heaven at any special time because if not, I'd like to spend the rest of the evening with you."

And that was only the first of the cute and clever lines she heard before Isaac Gordon strolled into the bar. Within minutes, she had succeeded in attracting his attention, and it was only natural that his pimping instincts would bridge the distance between them.

"My name is Ice. You seem familiar."

"I get around," Walker said, "seen some things, done some

things, met a lot of niggas; some fake, some not-so-fake."

"I could be wrong, but you sound like a woman on a mission."

"Could be."

Ice was still standing. "You gonna invite a nigga to sit down or what, or do you want me to keep on standing heah looking down yo' dress at them big ol' titties you got?"

"You can sit or you can stand," Walker cracked sassily, "that's on you, and you can look at my titties all you want to unless you try to touch 'em. Then it'll be on me."

Taking a seat, Ice announced. "I've done pretty well for myself, and I've had a lot of women, but you different and it would cause a damn big blow to my ego if me and you didn't get to know each other better, know what I'm saying?"

"I know you good and damn bold, I know that much."

Ice chuckled. "Then we must be like that soap opera, The Bold and The Beautiful."

"I wouldn't know about that, playa. I'm too busy starring in my own life to get caught up in the phony world of fake bitches on television, you know what I'm saying?"

Ice ignored the comment. "What do you want out of life?" He lit up a Newport, squinting through the smoke. "Fame? Fortune. Great experiences?"

"Shit like that is fair enough for a square ho, but it takes a lot more to turn me on. You see, I get my kicks by living on the edge, running through life just as fast as I can go." Walker's tongue touched her upper lip suggestively. "Being one step away from not knowing what's going to happen next is what makes my panties wet." She stared in Ice's eyes. "I eat soft niggas alive."

Ice held the gaze. "What's your name?"

"Call me Glo."

'Is that short for Gloria?'

"Naw, nigga, I was named after a can of floor wax, Mop-n-Glo."

"Okay, okay, Glo. Damn, my bad."

"Absolutely."

Abruptly, it was as if Ice had let his good humor go too far and his mood changed. "We all grown up. If you ever want to get up with a real nigga, call me." He dropped a business card in front of her. "Whatever does or does not happens, it was nice meeting you. Later."

Chapter 19

Meanwhile

Neon had gotten such a warm welcome in Eastern Europe that her adoration in the dance clubs and the brothels had made her an overnight celebrity. The near riotous sensation she had caused had rippled throughout the tiny country until men in every city and town yearned to touch her, to pay for her. Needless to say, this made Gregor, the gypsy, who owned her extremely happy. And rich.

Although she had been in town for little over a month, Gregor was impressed with the quick progress and the eventual success he had made with the Queen from Black America. He had to admit that what he had achieved in so short a time filled him with immense pride, having every reason to suspect that his accomplishment would become the stuff of legendary lore among the men who broke women like cowboys broke and tamed wild horses. But Gregor had a secret, one which he closely guarded and kept well-hidden from his comrades. Gregor, admittedly, was not that brilliant a woman-tamer, and neither was he willing to uncover the truth of his techniques. He felt he might be challenged, or that others would adopt his training methods and then take the world by storm. Still, his was a simple remedy because the gypsy, Gregor, knew that all that stood between a good woman and a prostitute was to find something she would die for. And Gregor had found it: crack cocaine.

Through his shady deals with his American associates, he had learned of the drug and via contacts in Spanish-speaking countries, he had managed to secure large shipments of the white powder which he then, like a seasoned chemist, would magically convert into crack. Nothing on earth, heroin included, invited total compliance and absolute submission as swiftly, and due to this secret, almost esoteric knowledge, he had emerged as the number one woman-breaker in Eastern Europe. This, however, was cause for an even greater dilemma.

"Shit!" Gregor cursed into his pint of ale.

"What's the matter, Papa?" Nikita stared at his fifty-nine year old father. "Are you not feeling well?"

"I have a problem, I'm afraid."

"What is it, Papa?"

"I need more black queens from the United States and I need them now!"

Nikita listened closely as his father spoke, nodding his head in agreement. "That is true, Papa. In all of my twenty-seven years of living, I have never seen anything quite like the stir your black prostitute has caused. She has mesmerized men and they have no trouble paying for her whereas the same men have problems paying for bread. No one can steer clear of her. I imagine it's her black skin. It's rare here, but it's more than that." Nikita swallowed hard. "She has an ass the likes of which I would never have believed could exist."

Gregor puffed on his cigarette, blew smoke away from his youngest son, then smiled. "Her ass is very magnificent, yes, but I've heard that in black America, women get asses that are forty inches.....or more."

Nikita's eyes stretched wide in amazement. "Forty inches!"

"That's what I've heard, my son."

"Do you believe such a thing, Papa?"

"My black queen leaves me no room for doubt. I am a man who has dealt with the flesh of women most of my life, and I've never seen nothing like her. She is, perhaps, I'd say a thirty-seven, so a forty is not out of the realm of possibility." Gregor took a long, satisfying drag from his cigarette. "I live for the day I get myself a forty inch. That would be nice, eh?"

"Well, what I think I'd better do is to get someone in America to fix you up quick since all the other traders are going to be wanting a forty inch of their own."

Gregor nodded. His son was right. Even now, it almost gave him a complex just to think that one of his competitors would get a forty inch before he did. It sent cold shivers up and down his spine to dare dream that such a creature exited. Such proportions would represent no less than true perfection. He thought of his black queen. If her ass was not close to absolute perfection, then it was not far off. He wondered if there could be a big difference between a thirty-seven inch ass and one that was forty, and after only a bare second of thought reckoned that there was.

"Do you, my son, recall the days when Josef was the arm wrestling champion of all these parts and the surrounding areas?"

"Of course, Papa. Josef was hailed as the strongest man around as well the man with the biggest arms. He had seventeen inch biceps, the largest anyone had ever seen."

"Do you remember what happened some time later?"

Nikita's eyes locked on his father's. "You mean when Pietr came along?"

"Precisely, my son. Exactly. Do you recall?"

"It was sad, Papa. Pietr's twenty inch arms made Josef's seventeen inch ones look like pencils. Humiliated, Josef killed himself."

Gregor sat in painful silence. Josef had been his uncle. That remembrance forced him to come to terms with the knowledge that three inches made a difference. It made no difference if the three inches were arms, ass, or dick, bigger was always ultimately better. These simple calculations of the flesh led him to conclude that he had better get a forty inch first, or else he would be humiliated if someone beat him to it. Suddenly, he had a hunch that while he was sitting around drinking a pint of ale that his competitors were already making plans to acquire the thoroughbred women from America with forty inch asses.

Gregor felt energized. If he was going to get it right, he had better get moving. Fast.

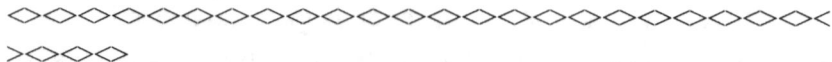

In New York, a day or so later

The office was in total bedlam. Every one of the phones seemed to be ringing at once with the resultant jangling being almost maddening. Everyone's nerves were frayed, except Ivan's. He took it all in with an air of casual stoicism, but he kept his knowing eyes trained on everything that was happening throughout the large communications room.

This was Ivan's New York business tower and he was standing smack dab in the middle of the room where the phone lines were manned by a corps of international salesmen who could converse fluently in a number of languages. Such linguistic proficiency was necessary if they were to remain effective in the sale and trade of women in the global market.

Ivan carefully studied the looks on the faces of his sales personnel as they tallied orders. Most, if not all of them, were veterans at Transworld International Enterprises, and the one thing all of them were used to was being in the thick of things where usually they would perform their duties without so much as a raised eyebrow. But today was totally different. For once, his people were being run ragged.

Ivan smiled. He walked over in a slow, leisurely fashion and tapped one of the salesmen on his shoulder. "What's happening now?"

The man looked up at Ivan with question marks in his blue eyes. "The same thing that has been going on all morning. Orders are pouring in for black girls."

"Where are the calls originating from?"

"From every corner of the globe, sir. It started late yesterday with calls from Eastern Europe, then all hell broke loose. And get this sir, one of the biggest orders I've gotten so far this morning came from, of all places, Africa." The man shook his head in disbelief. "The last time I watched National Geographic, the women of Africa were still black. Go figure."

Ivan walked away, laughing to himself. He didn't need to figure anything out since he knew exactly what was occurring. His multi-million dollar campaign to sell the American black female as the next big thing in the global sex trade business had just caught fire, blazing his new concept of dark sensuality all over the world

113

like nothing had ever done before.

This morning's results were overwhelmingly positive indicators of what a bit of ingenuity could do because single-handedly he had almost, in the wink of an eye, altered the traditional landscape of what constituted beauty. The status quo had been shaken to its core, the root of the once all-prevailing, forever-pervading reality of the Euro-centric model of beauty had been shattered, boldly knocked off its pedestal to be replaced by the image of his choice: the black American woman with a big booty.

The nerve-jangling din of the phones went on and on, but it was music to Ivan's ears who went to stand alone by the Expresso machine. Yet despite his good spirits, he was still a bit upset. All morning he had gotten reports of a queen from black America who had an ass that almost measured forty inches. Rumors of her had started floating in at the beginning of the business day with the bulk of the inquiries originating in an East Europe province where the woman had actually been spotted. Ivan was puzzled over this information since he had not given anyone permission to trade in black flesh from America. This could only mean one thing, that someone was doing some shopping and shipping behind his back. Ivan didn't know whom to call first. Ice, with the good news or Uri, with the bad. His indecision didn't last long. Uri would get the first call.

"Yeah." Uri had been asleep in another time zone, in another country. He was still groggy. "Talk to me."

"We've got a problem."

"Where?"

"In America."

"Can't Ice handle it? You know I don't like the States."

"Too bad, little brother. This requires your immediate attention."

"What went wrong?" Uri growled.

"There is this girl, black American, called Corvette by her many admirers in Eastern Europe."

"Corvette, like the car Corvette. That doesn't ring a bell. Are you sure about this, Ivan?"

"I'm always sure, Uri. Corvette is real."

"That means---."

"Someone is evidently smuggling black girls out of the country without my permission and I want it stopped. You hear me, Uri?"

"Don't worry," Uri snarled, "I'll find out who it is and then teach the bastard a lesson."

"A lesson! I don't want them to be merely taught a lesson. I want them to be made an example of."

"It's the same fucking thing," Uri rumbled. "Go fuck two bitches and call me in the morning."

Next, a call went out to Charlotte.

"Ice, my man, what is happening?"

"You tell me. You sounding mighty chipper this morning. What up?"

"An amazing thing has occurred, Ice. In fact, it's quite a phenomenon, one I'm convinced you will find most interesting, but we have to move without delay in order to remain the early birds we already are."

"Wh-what happened? Tell me, Ivan. I'm curious as a motherfucka."

Ivan laughed his train wreck of a laugh. "I thought you would be, and since you're my most trusted friend, I won't hold you in suspense any longer."

"'Preciate that."

"The blond-haired, blue-eyed image of beauty has just been wiped off the face of the sex-trade and guess who the new 'Miss It' girls are. Well, none other than your American black females." Ivan allowed himself a self-congratulatory chuckle, then resumed talking. "In response to the measures I initiated, black girls have acquired the five-star rating, making them the market's hot-hot-hot commodity. What do you think of that, Mr. Isaac Green?"

"I-I don't know what to say except that you put in mad work."

"I did, didn't I," Ivan bragged, "but until the final tally is in at the close of the trading day, we won't really be able to understand just how huge this is although it already qualifies as tremendous."

"But we're not ready to deal with that kind of volume yet. We just now beginning to get our weight up at the Academy."

"Don't lose sleep over The Academy, Ice. The picture just got bigger, a lot bigger. We can always go back to our original plan for the school, but soon I'm going to need you to get those girls ready for the first exodus out of America."

Air got trapped in Ice's throat. "We'll get plenty of beef from the police if we snatched a whole busload of hoes. I don't believe that will work."

"Well, I'm afraid something will have to be made to work. Like any other business, Ice, we must be able to fill our orders as they come in, that is if we expect to stay in business."

"No doubt about that, but this is so all of a sudden."

"In business, my friend, you have to be able to anticipate events." Ivan's tone remained friendly, but some coldness crept into his voice. "When we first discussed this, I hoped you took me seriously."

"I did. Trust me, I did."

"In that case, you had all the more reason to prepare for this moment. The reason I don't get into your local business is because I trust you to always be on the ball no matter what comes up where. This is the type of understanding we have, isn't it?"

"Yeah, Ivan, it is."

"Good. I knew I could depend on you."

When Ice hung up the phone, there was no euphoria over the prospect of making millions of dollars. Ivan was demanding that he kidnap a whole class of teenage girls, and for the first time in a long time he experienced fear. It gnawed at him like a cat chowing down on a rat. Then a preposterous idea struck him: he could pull it off! He laughed insanely loud, but when the wild laughter died down, he reminded himself that he had to do something fast. This was it. He had to either put up or shut up.

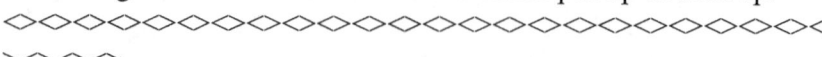

That exact same night

Ice awaited the darkness before he sprang into action,

surprising himself at his own desperation, but it was not until he had gotten into his Jaguar, and had driven down a maze of back streets that he realized what little choice he had. Circumstances compelled him to do what he had to do.

Supreme had agreed to meet Ice at a liquor house on Luther Street in Cherry that was owned by an old hustler they both had known all their lives. Prior to now, something had always held Ice in check when it came to going too far out on a limb, but as the night grew older, he presumably believed that now was as good a time as any to breech the point of no return. After all, where did you go when you had already gone too far?

Killing his engine in front of a wood frame house on Luther Street, Ice felt confident his mission would end successfully. He knew he would have to manipulate Supreme shrewdly, but in the event his begging skills weren't convincing enough, he would make sure Supreme drank his fill of bootleg whiskey. Ice grinned grimly. Booze was such a strong persuader.

Satisfied with his scheme, Ice strolled into Joe Willie's and found Supreme already there.

"Nigga," Ice grinned upon greeting his friend, "where yo' ride at? I ain't see it outside."

"Brianna got it. I had her drop me off, so that means you gotta give me a ride back to the crib whenever we split."

"You know I got you, dawg. Now, let's have a coupla of these ol' drinks our boy, Joe Willie, be serving up heah in this joint."

"Bout time y'all big-time ballers came by to spend some of that paper you niggas got with me. Niggas blow up and forget where they from, don't never come through the hood no mo'."

"Well, Joe Willie, we 'bout to show you some love tonight." Ice flipped two one hundred dollar bills on the counter. "One from me and one from Supreme."

"Don't even try that shit, ol' peanut-head nigga. This heah Joe Willie so I'm gonna put two more Bens with yo' two Bens and then add another Ben."

"Well, since you doing ol' Joe like that, I'm gonna slap a three-pack of Bens down."

Joe Willie's eyes lit up.

"Okay, here's two more of the bitches for you." Supreme winked slyly. "Man, don't let no young girl whup that tenderoni pussy on you and trick you out of that grand."

"Nigga, I don't pay for no pussy. Bitches pay me."

"Let yo' old ass tell it," Ice joked. "Now, give us a bottle of something wet so me and my partner can get our drank on."

After the first round of drinks and some small talk about what was going on down on the block, Ice was ready to immerse himself in his mad-cap scheme, but felt it was his duty to talk away the stream of memories that being in Joe Willie's revived.

"Man, you remember when me and you pulled a train on that crackhead ho over in Earle Village?"

"Hell yeah. Ho name......damn, what that ho name? Shit, I can't remember. Bitch had some good pussy though." Supreme laughed. "Who else was with us?"

"The regulars: Old Pro, Turk, JB. May their souls rest in peace."

Both men were silent for a second out of respect for their dead friends, then went outside to pour out some liquor to honor their names.

Round about midnight, Ice found Supreme sufficiently drunk and after exchanging good nights with Joe Willie, the pair stumbled out of the front door. A few minutes later, Ice had driven to an isolated area in North Charlotte, down the far end of Belmont Avenue.

"Where we at, fool?" Supreme slurred. "This ain't where the hell I live at. We lost or something?"

"Naw, nigga, we ain't lost," Ice said coldly. "We where we need to be at. Get out of the car."

"Get out?! What the fuck for? Oh now I understand. You think I'm gonna piss in your stupid ol' Jag, don't you? Well, motherfucka, I ain't got to piss."

"Fuck you, Supreme."

"Naw, nigga, fuck you."

"Just get out of the car. We need to talk."

"Been talking all goddamn night. What we leave out?"

"This real talk, nigga. I need you to do me a big favor."

"A'ight, fool, damn." Supreme swaggered out of the car. "What is it?"

Ice whipped out his Glock.

"Man, what the fuck wrong with you? Put that piece up. You done had too much to drink."

"Shut the fuck up, nigga."

Looking around, Supreme surveyed his surroundings. They were alone. "So, it's 'bout to go down, huh? You gonna do me 'cause some Russian motherfucka playing yo' black ass. Kill me then, motherfucka. I ain't scared to die."

"Fool-assed nigga, I ain't fixing to do you. I want you to do me."

"What!?"

"Don't kill me. I just want a Suge Knight, you know a bullet in the leg." Ice made the request as if it was a request for a particular haircut or a pair of shoes. "Then you can pistol-whup me and take my shit." Ice handed the gun to Supreme.

"Man, this a motherfucking cannon. It'll blow your motherfucking leg off." Supreme waved the gun in Ice's face. "Get in the ride, homeboy. I'm taking your drunk ass to the crib."

"Stop bullshitting, fool. I can't go home."

"I ain't playing, Ice. Get in the goddamn car."

"I ain't playing neither. I can't go home. This some serious shit I'm talking, dawg. If you don't handle this, Ivan will probably lay both our asses down. That's my good word."

"Talk to me, Ice. What we done got into this time?"

Once Ice had given Supreme the news about what Ivan expected to be done, he spoke with a strain of bitterness in his voice. "I can't just order up a train-load of mud-ducks like they a motherfucking Happy Meal from Mickey D's. Getting shot up, beat down, and put in the hospital might not be the easiest thang to do, but it sho' as hell better than what Ivan will have done to my black ass if I come up short. He'll look at it as an insult."

"Dammit, man," Supreme cursed. "I know this shit was too good to be true. I tried to warn you---"

"Nigga, we ain't got no time for you to be standing out

heah in the dark, preaching no motherfucking sermon. Shit, save sumthin' for the preacher to do on Sunday morning."

"Damn."

"Damn, nothing. You gotta do it."

"Ice, listen to me. You ever seen a nigga get hit with a Glock before? Goddamn bullet tear shit up, break motherfucking bones, knock a nigga's whole back out."

"Okay, okay," Ice grumbled, "I got a .38 automatic in the trunk. What about that?"

"That'll work. Get it. Damn, we shoulda brought some of that drink from Joe Willie's with us. Shit woulda help ease the pain."

"I ain't worrying 'bout no pain. I'm worried 'bout dying."

"And you think this is going to fix shit?"

Ice shuffled back with the other weapon. "Got to. With me in Carolina Medical, Ivan ain't got no choice but to chill the fuck out and put that bullshit on hold. He ain't gonna trust nobody else to handle it, so we cool for a minute. While I'm laid up, I get time to think." Ice took a deep breath. "You ready?"

"What you want me to do with yo' jewelry?'

"I don't give a fuck, nigga. Keep it, sell it. Just snatch it. Now, do the damn thang."

Supreme fired.

Four hours later

Ice talked so fast it was as though he was trying to explain everything to Ivan in a single breath, and judging from the look of pure sympathy on the Russian's face, Ice was sure his story had been well told. He certainly had rehearsed it often enough.

Ivan, who had flown down to Charlotte immediately upon hearing of the robbery, had not seemed suspicious in the least, and when Ice apologized for slowing their work at hand to a crawl, Ivan had waved away the notion, insisting instead that what was of utmost important to him was Ice's full recovery.

"What about the cops?"

"Worthless as usual. Plus, I don't want them in my biz'ness."

"Of course. I can understand that."

"Anyway, I got my own people on it. My jewelry was specially made for me. It's registered so if it's sold, I'll know 'bout it. The fools who did this are living on borrowed time. They just don't know it yet."

"Just get well, that's my only concern. Everything else can wait. The New York office did a good job of putting all the orders on hold and everyone is willing to wait, though not for long. My staff in New York can sell sand to an Arab, but all our customers are eager to purchase one of the so-called queens from black America." Ivan grinned from ear to ear. "And it's our job to make sure they get one."

"And we will," Ice said with an exaggerated bravado. "I feel it's our patriotic duty to make sure that every motherfucka, who wants a queen from black America, gets one."

Then the sedative did its job and Ice fell fast asleep.

"Wake up, nigga. What the fuck up?"

It was three hours later and Ice was rudely awakened by Supreme.

"What you want, dawg," Ice mumbled, "to come by to check out your homework?" Ice smiled. "You did good, dawg. Ivan cool."

"Man, fuck that Russian thug. I came by to see what was up with you, but that ain't the first time I dropped by in. Me and Eve was up in heah first thang, but you was fucked up, had tubes and shit running all out your nose and arms. I thought yo' ass was a Martian."

Ice grinned weakly. "Like I said, you did good work."

"I mean, ain't nothing fucked up inside your head, is it?"

"Naw, I hollered at my doctor 'bout that and he guaranteed that there was no brain damage or nuthin' like that."

Supreme sighed in relief. "Thank God. I would've been feeling guilty as hell if they woulda had to put a steel plate in your head."

"It's all good. Ain't no damage." Ice rolled over to face the wall, his voice sounded muffled. "Tell Eve I said thanks for coming to visit me. I'm tired, dawg. I'll see you when I get back on my feet again. Later."

   Later that same afternoon.
   Eve had been momentarily worried that the after-school staff meeting would get her stuck in the chaos of Charlotte's rush hour traffic, but the discussion ended early, allowing her ample time to navigate the highway as though she owned it. She had no problem speeding as she drove directly home, zipping merrily along West W.T. Harris Boulevard as though the wide, tree-lined street belonged exclusively to her.
   Pulling up to the front of her immaculate two-story home in a Mallard Creek subdivision, her eyebrows arched in mild curiosity when she spied a fancy sports coupe parked in her driveway. She had a visitor, and her plans changed on the spot. Whereas, all she had wanted to do had been to kick off her shoes, and to chill out with a bottle of Moet, she knew her guest would expect a whole lot more. She paused for a moment in the driveway, her body already beginning to tingle with excitement.
   "Welcome home, beautiful one." The smartly-dressed man pointed to a chair opposite him. "Come, permit me to luxuriate in your presence."
   Eve leaned down to kiss the man on the lips. "Hello, Ivan. Long time, no see."
   "Shall I take that to mean you have missed me or should we just go to bed so I can show you just how much I have missed you?"
   Eve smiled wickedly. "I think I'd like to fuck."
   "And so we shall, but only in the way you prefer."
   "Like two mad dogs?"
   "Precisely. I love it when we have sex like wild animals."
   Relieved to be doing something other than having to tell Ivan what was truly going on in Charlotte, Eve threw her entire being into the sexual act. She twisted and turned, grinding and humping her body until her muscles ached, but she took comfort in knowing that once she was finished with him, Ivan would be exhausted both physically and mentally. Good pussy had

the tendency to rob a man of his energy, rendering him almost childlike. Still, at some point, she knew some hard questions would be put to her. She also knew she would be too afraid to lie. At any rate, she calculated that due to the callous way she was putting her coochie on Ivan, she had bought herself a few hours during which Ivan would sleep before awakening to learn of matters that invariably could---would---lead to bloodshed. Even now, hours before the fact, Eve knew that Ivan would smile and say that both Ice and Supreme must die. Then he would leave.

While Ivan snoozed, Eve plunged into the shower and then into a not-so-small glass of red wine, hoping to calm herself down although neither the hot water nor the cold drink were of much use. She was a nervous wreck.

Of course, she would tell the truth, but the most important thing she had to remember was that she personally had done nothing wrong. Therefore, Ivan would not harm her. Rather, he would give her a big bonus and a promotion. Perhaps she would be put in charge of the Charlotte operation. The odds of that were heavily in her favor, so maybe she herself should recommend it to Ivan. She would be perfect for the post although she didn't care to inherit the new direction in which things were headed. She had no problem advising young, teenage, black girls how to use their physical assets to their advantage. Stripping was one thing. Smuggling and kidnapping had never occurred to her, never once having shown up in her job description.

Occasionally, she had every thought and intention of assisting Supreme in the fall of GirlSmart, but the times she warned herself not to interfere outnumbered those moments ten to one. Eve was torn, but she felt that if she told Ivan the truth now, she would be less likely to blindly follow Supreme later.

"Oh my God!" Eve babbled in anguish. What was she to do? As soon as she came to understand that trying to find a happy ending to this dilemma would be next to impossible, she burst into her bedroom and shook Ivan awake. "We need to talk. Now!"

Chapter 20

"It's them, Chief. GirlSmart is the front."

"And you're sure about this?"

"100%," Walker blurted into the phone. "I'm in, but I've got a long row to hoe. These guys are aggressive and they mean business. I've learned enough to identify most of the major players here in Charlotte which appears to be the hub of this new, emerging trade in underage black girls. There's a Russian. I don't know his name yet, but he runs everything."

"A Russian?" Chief Dennis snorted. "I'm not surprised, but I'm just curious to know how Charlotte was spotted as an opportunity."

"I can't say for sure how Charlotte got to be in the position it's in, but what is certain is the Russian underworld has teamed up with the Queen City underworld to become a conduit for smuggling black girls out of the country."

The Chief grunted. "Like I said, the Russians are at the epicenter of this nasty business and they play hard-ball, so be careful. This is no game."

"Well, thanks for telling me all this after the fact, Chief."

"I just thought you should know the position you're in." Dennis took a deep breath, keeping his voice steady. "The idea is to get the job done without letting the job turn into some kind of black power crusade. You get my drift?"

"Loud and clear, Chief. I'll stay in touch. Goodbye."

The next morning it took Walker thirty minutes longer to dress than normal. She had promised Ice that she would wear an outfit to the hospital that was going to make his eyes pop out of his head. Trouble was that she was finding it difficult to find the right 'welcome home' gear. Ice had called earlier to inform her of his impending release from Carolinas Medical, and for her to come to pick him up. That didn't shock her.

By 10:15 she was having some success with the short, red dress and a matching silk blouse when it all came together. What she saw in the mirror encouraged her, and as she splashed her already kissable mouth with some flirty, red lipstick, she cheerfully pronounced herself 'the flava of the year'. She was all that. This was what she called her '*proof of life*' outfit because any man who saw her in it who had any life in him would get a hard dick instantly. Damn, she was hot!

Breakfast was a quick cup of coffee, black enough, she hoped to keep the lack of sleep from taking its toll on her. Since Ice was still in no shape to attempt to take her to bed, she had figured on having a lot of time to explore his house. She wondered what she'd find. Hopefully, much.

During the last few seconds of her liquid breakfast, she inspected her weapon then stuffed it, along with an extra clip, into her overnight bag. Then she was off.

By the time she had reached Scott Avenue by executing an illegal right turn off of East Boulevard, she had successfully managed to stop her heart from doing somersaults under her blouse. This was it, she thought, unless her luck ran out.

Adopting her Hoochie-Mama, I-could-care-less persona did indeed help her to feel calmer, but the pretense was difficult to maintain because on the floor where Ice was housed, she saw people running in and out of his room like there was an emergency. She pushed her way through the crowd.

"*What's happening?! What's happening?!* I'm Mr. Green's fiancée." Recognizing one of Ice's doctors, she rudely tugged at his sleeve until she got his attention. "Is everything alright with Mr. Green? Why are all these people here?"

"I'm afraid that something very terrible has happened." The doctor spoke in a dull monotone. "I'm afraid your friend, Mr. Green, is.....dead."

"That's ridiculous," Walker shouted. "I just spoke to him

earlier today."

The doctor suddenly sounded awkward. "At this moment, nothing is certain other than the fact that your friend is deceased. An investigation is pending which prevents me from saying anything more. I will say this though. The hospital regrets this tragic misfortune. Please accept our condolences."

Deciding to bully her way into the room, she was physically stopped by a burly cop who forcefully put his beefy hands in the center of her chest to impend her forward momentum. Walker let loose a string of obscenities and then threw an Oscar-worthy temper tantrum, but the cop wouldn't budge.

"I suggest you go to the waiting room."

Not a bad idea, Walker thought. There she could sort out this new, unexpected turn of events while getting a chance to see who else would pop up. She didn't think it would be long before Supreme and Brianna arrived. In the meanwhile, she would need an attitude adjustment since he had just gone from being the happy hooker to the grieving girlfriend.

She guessed that she wouldn't be able to snoop around Ice's home after all. That guess was just as good as her other one: The Russian had committed the murder.

Noon.

Supreme's phone rang. He answered it.

"Yo, Eve, what's up? Can you call back? I'm trying to handle a personal problem."

"Nigga," Eve hissed, "I don't give a damn about what problem you and that child got. Ice is dead----."

"Dead!?"

"You heard me right. Ice is gone. Call Carolinas Medical to verify what I'm saying if you want to, but I want your ass over to my house without any unnecessary delay."

"Bitch, I don't know what done got into you, but you better take some of that bass out of yo' motherfucking voice when you talking to me."

"Fuck you, Supreme. I'm in charge now."

"Hold up, Eve."

"Hold up, my ass. Just get over here."

Thirty minutes later when Supreme arrived at Eve's home, what was certainly more surprising than Eve's 'I'm-In-Charge' shit was that Ivan was there when he walked in.

"Hello, my new best pal in the universe," Ivan roared with good cheer. "Too bad about Ice, but what happened to him is now old news. As you Americans are so fond of saying, shit happens. And by the way, Supreme, this bitch, as you called her, is in charge of the entire operation in Charlotte, but since she is such a kind-hearted soul, she has appointed you to get the young girls at GirlSmart ready to travel at the earliest possible moment."

"But didn't Ice let you know that it couldn't be done?"

"Ice is asleep, so his views no longer count."

"Then why don't you ask this double-crossing bitch here for her opinion. She'll tell you the same thing."

"Find a way, motherfucka," Eve spat. She sat on the sofa next to Ivan, stroking his shoulder tenderly.

"I agree. Find a way. I need those girls, Supreme." Ivan leaned forward, menace in his cold eyes. "You could have very well met the same fate as Ice. Are you going to deny that you did not divulge info to a certain someone that you shouldn't have?" Supreme flashed his eyes angrily at Eve. "Oh, come on, my pal, you can't be truly upset with my friend here. She was simply doing her job and you weren't. You should have been severely reprimanded for your indiscretion, but yet you live, and I'm a firm believer in what is said about one good turn deserving another."

"In other words, nigga" Eve interjected, "he just scratched your back. Now, it's your turn to scratch his."

"Good job, Eve. I love your metaphors. How about you, Supreme? Did that beautiful metaphor work for you? If so, then I'd say that you've got some back-scratching to do." Ivan smiled slyly. "I itch for those young bitches."

"I'm sho' you do, but---"

"Shut up, Supreme, so I can tell you exactly how this is going to happen."

Supreme glared at Eve. "If you know so damn much, why the fuck don't you do it yourself?"

127

"Because it was her brilliance that put this wonderful plan together. I like it. She likes it. And you'd better like it....or else. Now listen to this delicious woman speak."

Supreme shrugged in submission. "Let's hear it."

Ivan smiled. "Cooperation makes me feel all warm and fuzzy inside." Eve kissed the Russian on his cheek. "Ah, now I'm really melting."

What Eve suggested shocked Supreme. "What we will do will be to organize a bus trip to Memphis for all the students at GirlSmart and while they're in Tennessee, we'll arrange for the whole bus to be kidnapped by terrorists, or at least we'll make it look like terrorists." Eve appeared pleased with herself. "Right now, we're working on the specifics to get all the kinks out, but so far the ability to do it is encouraging."

Supreme had to admit that it was a shrewd move and given the fact that Tennessee bordered seven other states, searching for the missing girls could turn into a logistics nightmare for the authorities.

"The alleged terrorists will release a demand for ransom which we imagine will cause the authorities to focus on that angle, but during the negotiations, the girls will be moved underground for subsequent removal from the country."

"Great plan, huh?" Ivan clapped. "Genius. And to think I was concentrating on the lower end of her body when it is her brain that is so very good."

"Not so fast," Eve laughed. "My coochie is outstanding also, isn't it, Supreme?"

Ivan winked at Supreme. "We're two lucky fools and maybe one day we'll have a few beers and compare notes, but not today. You need to go to claim Ice's body since you were listed as the next-of-kin. I will pay for the funeral." Ivan chuckled. "It's the least I could do."

Leaving Eve's home, Supreme saw how things were going to shape up and play out according to Eve's plan which was both genius and devious, but that failed to lift his spirits. Obviously, it was important that he come out of this alive, but he still was sympathetic to the plight of young sistas. He saw no viable way to resolve his dilemma, but he knew the longer he delayed, the more time Ivan and Eve's kidnap plot would mature until everyone at GirlSmart, including Brianna, would become victims of it, and he wasn't interested in dealing Brianna to the Russians.

By the time he had arrived at the hospital, a pair of police were waiting for him. It had been determined that foul play was involved in Ice's death and they had hoped he would agree to a few questions. Supreme was not in the mood, but did politely accept a business card, pretending he would call once he had finalized arrangements for the body. Finding this encouraging enough, the officers left.

Feeling sorry for himself, Supreme dropped his head in his hands and closed his eyes. When he looked up, a stunningly beautiful woman stood next to him.

"Are you Supreme?"

"Yeah, who you?"

"I'm Glo, a friend of Ice's. I was the one he called to come pick him up from the hospital today."

"Y-you talked to Ice this morning?"

Walker nodded her head solemnly. "I may have been the last one to talk to him before he was.....killed."

"I can't place you."

"I guess you could say I was Ice's flava of the month."

That Supreme could understand. "Oh."

Walker pressed a phone number into Supreme's hand. "I know you're going through a lot right now, but I would like for you to call me, okay?" Walker smiled warmly. "This is not a booty call, I'm afraid, but it could save your life." When Supreme's eyes widened, she smiled once more. "Relax, I'm a friend. I can't say any more than that right now, but we need to put our heads together. You know some things and I know some things. We need to see what it all adds up to. Look, Supreme, you'll have until after you bury Ice to call me. After that, I disappear. Call me, sweetie."

Walker sashayed off.

Two nights later after Supreme had been summoned by Eve to report to her house, he experienced the sensation of a virgin about to be deflowered by a gargoyle. Apparently, he would have to tread lightly around her or there would be problems.

As he drove south of the city towards his destination, he assured himself that the meeting would not be pleasant, and that he would leave as soon as he received his instructions although he realized that what he got could just as easily be an ultimatum. Either way, he would play it cool, hoping to find a way to counter at a later date. Right now was not the time for anything dramatic unless he got really heated at Eve and her bullshit.

Eve met Supreme at the front door and they exchanged obscenities over him being late.

"I don't like having to wait," Eve snapped, "and you, of all people, should know that." Eve pulled Supreme into the spacious living room by his arm. "How soon we forget."

"Tell me 'bout it." Supreme looked around for Ivan. "Just last week, you was sucking my dick and now you ready to cut my head off."

Eve remained silent, allowing Supreme to fume for a few seconds. "Did you get everything straight for tomorrow?" Eve spoke casually as if Ice's funeral was a dreaded media event. "It should be nice since Ivan sent a mighty generous check. With that kind of money, you could've went the whole New Orleans route, complete with brass bands and whatever else they do down there to make their funerals such fun." Eve poured two drinks. "There is the word fun in the word funeral, you know?"

"Why don't you just quit it, Eve. Ice was my friend."

"Mine too, dammit."

"Yeah, but he made the mistake of trusting yo' ass, and look at where that got him."

"Don't even try that shit, nigga," Eve hissed. "You're the motherfucka he should've never trusted. You the one that ran his mouth, and you knew you were taking a big risk when you told me shit that Ice had told you."

Supreme sucked in a sharp intake of air.

"That's right," Eve cracked, "suck it up like a goddamn real soldier." She stood in front of Supreme. "Do you want this fucking drink or not?"

"You drink it. I wanna make it back to view my boy's

body, so if you would be kind enough to tell me what this is all about, I'll be on my way."

"But I have other plans for tonight."

"*To-motherfucking-night?!*"

"That's right, nigga, tonight."

"Listen, Eve, I just tole you I got shit to do tonight."

"But you won't find this difficult at all."

"Why don't you let me be the judge of that. What is it?"

The silk dress slipped easily off Eve's shoulders. "I want you to stay her and fuck me all night long."

Supreme's breath caught in his throat just at the mere sight of Eve's voluptuous naked flesh. "Shit." He muttered under his breath.

"I don't think Ice would mind. Plus, I'll go with you to the funeral tomorrow." Eve pulled Supreme into her arms. "Let's fuck and make up. I still want us to be lovers."

"After what you done?"

"Why not, Supreme. That's life."

Eve led the way to the bedroom.

Chapter 21

At the funeral, Supreme's emotions swirled. Already he missed Ice, the finality of their friendship finally got to him and he almost broke down in tears. In his own way, Ice had felt he was coming to Supreme's rescue by inviting him into The Organization, but the mere fact that he did not play the game well enough or toe the company's rigid policy close enough was the very thing that had doomed Ice. In essence, he had killed Ice or at least had kick-started the process.

With his eyes fixed on Ice's face as he lay stiff in the bronze casket, Supreme relived the events of their lives together. Man, there were a pocketful of memories; some good, some bad, but at this last moment, they all counted.

When Eve attempted to move Supreme away from the bier, he still delayed the line of mourners. He deserved the extra moments. No one else had known Ice like he had, none of them went as far back. Ice was a nigga with whom he had fucked bitches, had run from the police with, and had ate at the same table with, but now would soon lie buried beneath the dirt.

Supreme broke down and cried, and when Eve looked around for the ushers, even they knew better than to move him until he had completely finished saying goodbye to his beloved partner, the Ice Man.

Meanwhile Walker played the role of a grieving girlfriend. Although her head was bent and her eyes lowered solemnly, she took careful note of everything around her as she shuffled in line, waiting to pay her last respects to a man she felt had escaped justice. If she had had her way, she would have preferred to have faced Ice in a court of law rather than staring him down in a coffin. She cursed softly to herself as she found her mind fast-forwarding to a courtroom where all of the GirlSmart defendants would be on trial. That day would still come because she would see to it, but it just wouldn't be the same minus Isaac Green.

Walker disturbed her private fantasy long enough to wonder what Ice's burial would represent to Supreme's plans. Would it make him want to take revenge on the Russians or would it make him more afraid of them? She grimaced. She would never know unless he made contact with her. So far, he hadn't and today her offer would expire, never to be repeated. After today, he would have to go down with the ship, and by the time she finished with them, that wasn't going to be a pretty sight.

When it came to be her turn to view the body for the last time, Walker had to beat back the impulse to spit in the dead man's face. Silently cursing his name, the detective turned up her nose and walked outside into the sunshine.

On the way the cemetery, she phoned the Chief.

"They're getting ready to dump the bastard in the hole."

Dennis noticed the venom in Walker's tone. "Trying times, I would imagine?"

"But it will all be worth it when I nail their asses."

"I'm sure it will be, detective. Was it a big funeral?"

"Sorta."

"Go have a drink later. Funerals can stress you out."

"The Russians killed him, you know?" When there was no answer, Walker called the Chief's name. "You still there?"

"Yeah, Walker, I'm still here."

"Did you hear what I said?"

"Yeah, Walker, I heard, but let's not jump to any conclusions."

Ready to argue, the detective thought better of the idea. "Well, Chief, I'd better hang up. We're moving pretty fast and should be at the burial ground in minutes."

"Keep me posted, detective."

"Sure thing, Chief. No problem. Later."

Hanging up, only a single thought egged her on. Maybe

Supreme would make contact. It would be a shame, she told herself, if her ploy didn't work because she wasn't going to bend the rules any further than she already had. She thought about that for a bit longer and concluded that not only would she bend the rules this time, she would break them. How could anything less be expected of her? These people---Ice's people---were the scum of the criminal underworld, the worst of the worst, and she intended to stop them in their tracks, so that meant she'd go as far as she had to in the attempt to end the victimization of young, black females. And that was that.

It was almost two o'clock when the funeral procession arrived at Oaklawn Memorial Park, and her thoughts drifted back to Supreme. He had better do something soon because the clock was ticking, and once his time was up, she would commence to treating him like the scum he was.

Time was sometimes cruel.

That night

The last metro bus was to leave Center City in about five minutes, and Supreme had told her to be on #7 which ran the Beatties Ford Road route. She was to disembark in front of The Excelsior Club. He would be waiting inside.

Walker could not recall the last time she had used public transportation in any city where she had lived or worked, but it was her hunch that with all the precautions Supreme was apparently taking that he had her pegged as a cop. That had to be it because no other possibility would make sense, but Walker wasn't disturbed. It meant Supreme was willing to come in out of the storm, and that she wouldn't have to play games which would allow her to get right down to business. Still, she knew she would have to dispel his suspicions if she expected him to provide her with the hard, cold evidence to make a solid case against his associates.

Walking into the legendary black club which was only a few feet away from a busy highway, Walker spotted Supreme seated at a table, laughing and talking to a well-dressed woman. Walker surprised him by sitting down without invitation. "Shoo, sista," she hissed, "this one is spoken for."

134

"Who do you think you're talking too?" the woman angrily snapped.

"I'm talking to you and my friendly suggestion is for you to move on. There's plenty of men here and this one is not worth fighting for. The only reason I'm here is to get his address so I'll know where to send the child support papers."

The woman stared at Supreme, her mouth open. "You lying motherfucka."

"I'm busted," Supreme shrugged. "No hard feelings. I was just trying my luck."

The woman made a hasty exit.

"You got a lot of nerve." Supreme was clearly annoyed. "Getting all up in my personal biz'ness like that."

Walker picked up Supreme's drink and sipped from it. "Whatever this is, I don't want one. Order me a pina colada."

Supreme looked across the table at Walker, then had a drink brought to her. "I hope you find that to yo' liking."

Walker sipped, a glint of pleasure in her eyes. "Now, this is more like it."

"Good, now maybe you'll explain what all this is about. I just buried my best friend today and I ain't in the mood for no fun and games."

Walker flinched uncomfortably.

"That cuts a lot of your options, doesn't it, Glo? If you don't like my house rules, then I'll gladly watch you walk the hell out of heah and go back to wherever it is that you came from. You say you have some info that might help me stay alive, so, hell yeah, I want to hear it. I loved Ice, but I ain't too excited 'bout joining him any time soon. You see, Glo, at the moment, money is plentiful and pussy is good. I want to stick around for a while, so if someone pops up out of the blue with a plan to help me reach that goal, then I'm gonna play fair, you know what I'm saying, but a nigga like me gotta know who he playing wit', you dig?"

This was going better than Walker could have imagined it would , but now her stress level was up. She looked around the club furtively because all of a sudden she felt like she was under a white-hot spotlight. Supreme wanted to know if she was the law.

She already had the chilling premonition that he had figured it out, but had no reason to believe he would demand proof.

"You're not a friend of Ice," Supreme continued, "or I would know how good or tight yo' pussy is." Supreme shrugged. "That's just the way it was with me and my dawg. I know all the details of what went on sexually with any woman Ice pulled his dick out on, and he never said shit 'bout no Glo. I wonder why that is?"

"Probably because he never fucked me. After that pistol-whipping and the bullet in his leg, he wasn't in too much shape for it." When Supreme cut his eyes at Walker long enough to let her know that she had struck a nerve, she smiled. "It's like I said, I know some things." Walker figured it was time to take control. "Add what I just told you to the psychological profile you've already made of me in your mind and what do you come up with?"

"You know good and damn well what I come up wit', but I ain't tripping 'bout that right now 'cause I might not be on point." Supreme chuckled humorlessly. Anyway, I'm heah to tell you that I done had an amazing string of bad luck recently when it comes to trusting y'all females. Some of y'all ain't nuthin' but snakes in the grass and that ain't no bullshit."

"I admit this is serious business—"

"Too damn serious for me to get stung by another Jezebel."

Walker reasoned that Supreme was being purposely tactless in the hopes of provoking her to anger so she'd say something stupid or reveal something she didn't want to. Instead of being furious over the name-calling, she would maintain her inner resolve. There would be only one chance to do this right and this was it. Therefore she would let him vent his frustration on her, so she let him rant. She'd been trained to know genuine anger from mere bluster, and how to interpret what was truly being said no matter how loudly or profanely spoken.

As a professional, she understood that certain words used in certain ways were as reliable as a good fingerprint. In fact, that's what she called them: verbal fingerprints, because they let her know when a person was crying for help or when they really wanted to be left alone, so she listened carefully as Supreme unpacked his psychic baggage.

At length, she nodded agreeably. "I'm not coming from where Eve was coming from. I know what she did."

"You know a mighty motherfucking lot. What else the hell you know?"

"Wouldn't you like another one of your nasty-tasting drinks?" Walker had assumed that an argument would yield her little that would be of any value to her, so she turned the conversation to something more recreational. "I would have broken Ice's back in bed."

Though the sexual banter of the next few minutes was extreme, it did help to diffuse Supreme's earlier tension which was exactly what Walker wanted to do, if only long enough for the second round of drinks to arrive. Alcohol, if used properly, routinely worked excellently in breaking down defenses, and Walker hoped the stuff worked its magic on Supreme. Otherwise, it was going to be a long night.

"Listen, Glo, even though I know that's not your real government name, it'll soon be last call for alcohol up in this joint, and you still ain't tole me nuthin'."

"So, what's up?'

"I wanna see it?'

"See it?!" Walker gasped. "See what?!"

"Stop fronting, sista, you know what I'm talking 'bout. I gots to see it."

Walker pretended shock. "So what you're telling me is that after all this time, you think I'm a damned man, and I have to flash my private parts to you as proof of my gender. What about if I pulled out one of my titties?"

"So, you got jokes? I'm glad you got a sense of humor, but until I see your badge----"

"Badge?!"

"You the motherfucking man, ain't you? The motherfucking police. Show me your damn badge. You do that and we got a game going. Otherwise tell Ivan I said hello."

Walker leaned closer. "What if I told you I don't have it on me?"

"Where is it?"

"Put up. Safe. It's not something I put into my purse like a tube of lip gloss."

Supreme flipped out his phone. "I'm fixing to call you a cab so you can get missing, but later on today, I needs to see yo' badge and some other confirmation that your phat ass the police for real." Supreme extended his hand. "Deal?"

"Deal."

"In that case, Supreme said, "I'll be seeing you later on."

The following morning

For their own safety and protection, arrangements were made for Supreme and Walker to meet in Gastonia, a city that was only a short drive outside of Charlotte's city limits. They agreed to rendezvous at 10:00 a.m. in one of the hotels that dotted the highway coming into Gaston County.

Walker arrived first and as a professional courtesy gave Supreme a warm reception. She wanted to instantly put him at ease, and Supreme seemed relieved, eagerly accepting the invitation to relax.

Walker's Hoochie-Mama persona of last night was completely gone, replaced by a severe departmental look that oozed authority and self-confidence. The look was definitely the kick-ass-now-take-names-later style.

To make sure Supreme got everything he wanted by way of proof, Walker pushed her badge across the table along with a laptop computer. "Here's what you asked for, my shield. Now, all you'll have to do is to type in my badge number and you'll be able to pull up my law-enforcement history. I don't want there to be any doubts."

While Supreme studied her profile, Walker remained silent except to occasionally make a clarifying comment. She wanted him to come to his own conclusions about her. She wanted him to know how good she was, so that he would come away with the impression that outside of Wonder Woman, she was the next best thing. She also knew how important it would be for them to have a good working relationship, and she knew that the bedrock of that relationship would have to be based on trust.

It was almost twenty minutes later when Supreme shut down the laptop. Walker, who sat several feet away, browsing through a newspaper, glanced up from the article she had been reading.

"Satisfied?"

"Yeah," Supreme nodded, "you straight."

Having cleared the first hurdle, Walker sighed in relief before speaking. "I have been advised to talk openly about what it is that I can do for you in return for what you can do for us. Is that something you would like to discuss now?"

"I ain't really done committed no crimes," Supreme replied flippantly, "so I ain't worried 'bout looking at no Judge."

"Are you sure about that? If the Justice Department wanted to, which I'm sure they will, they could indict you for conspiracy which doesn't separate your actions from anyone else's on the indictment. This means that even though you didn't participate directly, you are just as culpable as any of the principals who committed a federal offense on behalf of your group, so if it is discovered that a single girl has been smuggled, then there just might be a Judge staring in your face." Walker pressed on, not waiting for a reaction. "Furthermore, if it turns out that GirlSmart is the front we believe it is, then the charge of contributing to the delinquency of a minor looms big on the horizon."

"Okay, okay, you made your motherfucking point."

"Have I really? In any event, I think your major worry would be more about staying alive than staying out of jail. It has been my experience that Russian gangsters are a pretty tough bunch." Barely a second later, she commented flatly. "Who is Brianna and what is she to you?"

Supreme let his guards drop. "I don't want nuthin' to happen to Brianna, and I want both of us put in the Witness Protection Program, and sent to live somewhere else, maybe even in another country. Can you promise that kind of a guarantee?"

"I'll do the best I can."

"Not fucking good enough," Supreme snapped.

Walker lied. "If that's what you want, then you've got it. I give you my word on that. Deal?"

Supreme shook his head. "Not until I get something in writing. No offense, but motherfuckas down at the police station good for tricking niggas, sell a brotha a dream in a heartbeat, and then drop his black ass off in a back-alley with the wolves. I ain't trying to go out like that. Nosiree, not Supreme." Reveling in the fact that he held the better cards, and that the deck, for once, seemed stacked in his favor, Supreme boldly reached over and touched Walker's thigh. "That's it for today, sista. I'll holla at you again when you get them papers hooked up." He leaned closer, looking the detective in her eyes. "I like you a lot better now that you out of that ho outfit. That ain't you. This gear, I really dig." Supreme grinned devilishly. "What you say 'bout that?"

"Nothing except that if Brianna was enough woman to fill it out, I would give it to her. Now, remove your hand from my leg and don't ever, ever think of touching me again."

Supreme snatched his hand away. "My bad, but damn, you soft as cotton."

Chapter 22

Noon. Two days later

Eve was late for lunch, but when she did finally show up at The Olive Garden on Freedom Drive, she kissed Supreme as if she had sincerely missed him, but didn't apologize for not being on time. "Things are falling into place," she said pleasantly. "I have more details."

"Don't you think we moving too fast? We got less than a week. Ivan got a motherfucka on the clock and he cracking the whip like we slaves. I say we slow it down."

Eve ignored the remark about Ivan. "Are you familiar with a group called TWB?"

Supreme nodded.

"Well, that's who we've got." Eve spoke as though Terrorists Without Borders were a R&B singing group. "They're good at dirty deeds."

Apparently so. TWB had been responsible for a spectacular rash of kidnappings, murders, and similar activities over the last decade which had placed them on every terrorist watch list in the civilized world.

"What assurances do we have that TWB won't just turn this into another one of their jobs, and bomb the bus to grab attention?"

"Money." Eve's voice was controlled. "They've also been promised some toys."

"Toys?"

"Rocket launchers, automatic weapons, and other black market military stuff. I don't know the half of what Ivan offered them, but evidently it's quite a package." A smug look of anticipated success flashed across Eve's face. "TWB will make it right. They'll snatch those bitches up with no problem." Eve laughed happily, then noted the displeasure on Supreme's face. "Oh, I'm sorry. You're probably concerned over your beloved Miss Brianna."

"She's not going."

"The hell she's not." Eve's eyes turned cold. "Don't play no silly games, Supreme. Now is not the time. I want Brianna on that fucking bus. Do you understand me?"

"What's the big deal? Brianna ain't nuthin' but one girl. If the motherfuckas counting, I'll find a replacement."

"No," Eve snapped angrily. "I want Brianna's ass on that goddamn bus. If she doesn't go, then none of the other bitches will want to go. Brianna is a kind of superstar to them, and they all would line up to kiss her ass if she asked them to."

Supreme looked defeated. "You're jealous of Brianna."

"That's the silliest thing I've ever heard you say, nigga. Me, jealous of Brianna?"

"The girl adores you, Eve. Don't you know that? She worships the ground you walk on. I just can't believe that you would do something like this to her, somebody who looks up to you as a mother figure."

"I'm sorry, sweetheart. I can't save Brianna. Just look at the bright side, you'll still have me. I'm twice as old, twice as fine, and my coochie is probably twice as good. I'd say you just doubled your pleasure."

"You want me to yourself, don't you?"

"I'm going to have you for myself. That's been decided already, so get used to it."

During the rest of the conversation and throughout the ensuing meal, Supreme tried not to appear angry or flustered. He knew TWB would make good on their word to kidnap the girls, but it frightened him to know what would happen afterwards. Eve had given him no information on where Brianna and her friends would be held after their abduction. It wasn't even clear if she knew or cared, but Supreme needed to have this info if Walker and the feds were to have any chance at all of a rescue.

Eve put down her fork. "What's the matter now? You keep on staring out that window instead of talking to me. You look like you want to fly away." Eve reached over and stroked Supreme's hand. "If you do fly away," she smiled, "you have to take me with you. Tell you what. Once this shit is wrapped up, why don't we fly to France. Oh, Supreme, you'll love Paris. It's so romantic. Want me to make plans?"

"We'll talk about it later. Anyway, I ain't thinking 'bout flying nowhere."

"Then what are you thinking about?"

"It's gonna rain."

Eve laughed. "You concerned about the weather?"

"Can't help it. When I see the clouds rolling in like they doing, I go into my rain mode. It ain't nuthin' but some leftover shit from my hustling days. Ain't important."

"Tell me about it, Supreme. Everything about you is important to me, so go on, tell me about the rain. Please. I'd love to hear it."

"You serious?" Supreme was surprised by Eve's sincerity. "Like I said, it ain't nuthin'."

"How can it be nothing, sweetheart, when it concerns you. Tell me."

"You see, when a nigga on the streets hustling, the rain the best friend he ever had, especially to a stick-up artist like I used to be. What you gotta understand is that when it rains, that means there's less people out to see what the fuck you doing. The police ain't wanting to get all wet, so they got they asses parked somewhere or they hanging out bullshitting. Plus a motherfucka can bring out the heavy artillery 'cause when it be pouring down rain, people don't think twice 'bout a nigga with a long coat on even though it ain't cold. And then after you done put in your work, you can run without looking suspicious. Crime-watch motherfuckas will just think you running to get out of the rain." Supreme leaned back, a faraway glint in his eyes. "You better believe that every stick-up boy in town got his eyes on them clouds, waiting on the rain to fall so they can get busy."

"Wow." Eve had awe in her voice. "I never knew that." She licked her lips seductively. "Now, I know why good girls love bad boys so much." Caressing Supreme's hand again, she whispered huskily. "Oh, Supreme, you've got me so turned on, my panties are all wet. Let's go find a hotel close by, so I can show you what I like to do when it rains."

The following morning.
"And just what kind of strategy do you call that?!"
"It's called what happened, happened." Supreme was amused at Walker's reaction. He could almost swear she was jealous. "Plus, it wasn't no harm done."

Walker strolled over, standing in front of Supreme. "You're pathetic, but I guess you know that. I send you out to gather information, and you can't keep your fucking pants zipped up. At this rate, it's going to be hard for us to do our job until you learn how to get on the ball instead of getting into bed."

"I didn't come heah for no lecture 'bout the birds and the bees."

"Well, you getting one," Walker snapped. "Do you realize what a disaster it would have been if you would have been wearing a wire? The mission would have been blown."

"In that case," Supreme cracked, "I would've just got my dick sucked."

"Think business, not pleasure. That might help."

"Since you telling me when I can and when I can't get me some pussy, what would really help would be if you took up the slack."

"Don't even go there with me."

"Why, you scared I would break your back."

Walker exhaled. "Brianna is going to die if you keep on wanting to play house with every woman you see. I'm not eager to see young sistas die. Yeah, we, black woman, can be difficult to live with sometimes, but we all deserve our chance to walk on the sunny side of the street. Brianna and the others may not get that chance unless you bring us a tip we can use to turn this thing in our favor. To be quite honest, I'm scared for those girls."

Supreme listened attentively, suddenly having every reason to renew his efforts to persuade Eve to find out more of Ivan's plans so he could convey it to the cops. For a brief fraction of a second, he thought of suggesting that he introduce Walker to Eve because he was convinced that the detective could persuade Eve to switch sides, but that notion could prove dangerous. Eve was too mercurial which meant he would have to get the info himself. Still, he couldn't afford to rouse Eve's suspicions or else the bitch might squeal to Ivan. What else became obvious to him was that he would have to continue his fucking/sucking strategy with Eve since that was the only way he could get close enough to her to sweeten her up. Supreme glanced at Walker. "Ain't nuthin' like a sista."

"Then here's your chance to save some."

Supreme pounded his chest like a warrior. "Imma handle mines."

"Great."

Standing tall, Supreme squared his shoulders. "Don't do nuthin' 'til you hear from me 'cause I'm fixing to bring home the bacon."

Walker smiled. "The sunny side of the street, remember?"

"Don't worry," Supreme bragged, "Brianna and them gonna walk on the sunny side of the street or Imma be walking in hell. Bet that."

7:00pm. Same day

The meeting at the Ramada Inn between Walker and the two FBI agents got underway on time. The black detective stood beside a highly polished desk, starting her report from an angle that most supported her hopes for a crack in the case. She didn't say much about Supreme's misconduct with Eve, and she said nothing at all regarding TWB until she had exhausted all her other information. Then she figured it was time.

"I wish I could go on without having to make mention of this, but the group TWB is involved with the impending snatch and grab of the GirlSmart bus. This is not their baby. They're hired goons, being used as a diversion. The ploy will be to trick everyone into believing the kidnapping is political, an act carried out against America in the name of terrorism which these days is nothing new. However, while we're concentrating on the bogus negotiations, that will give the real people, Ivan and company, the needed time to smuggle the girls out of the country."

Walker told them everything. Neither man interrupted her even though her pauses were marvelous opportunities to either interject something or to accuse her of wrecking whatever plans they did have. They did neither. They simply listened.

"I know the presence of TWB puts a new twist in our operational plans, but the fact remains that we will have to readjust our strategy because of them. I do not believe they are invincible. For us, it may be better because in addition to knowing the way they function, we also can gain perspective from their many encounters with law enforcement agencies throughout the world. What we should be able to glean from these sources should provide us with valuable insights which will help us to prepare to the utmost of our capabilities." Walker paused. "I think not knowing who we're dealing with is a much bigger risk than knowing."

As a conclusion, Walker nervously asserted how she intended to put more scrutiny on Eve. The agents responded that they would take responsibility for tapping her phones and putting her under twenty-four hour surveillance. Walker also got permission to outfit Supreme with a wire whenever she deemed it appropriate.

"I'm sure you can understand my position." Walker took a seat on the corner of the bed. "Now, I'd like to hear your thoughts on how well our timetable is developing."

The tall, thin agent named Babcock responded, first scratching his beard thoughtfully. "Of course, TWB ups the potential for violence, thereby exposing the children to greater danger. That means we are going to have to direct a lot of our resources towards countermeasures, but it is also crucial that some energy be devoted to preventive measures."

"What do you suggest?" Walker asked.

The other agent, Crewes, picked up on cue. "If we would have been dealing with a true kidnap scenario, then there would be expectations on both sides. The kidnappers would be expected to treat their hostages well, at least until the negotiations fell through, but with TWB we have no such guarantees, so we have no sure way of knowing how the girls will fare. I don't consider rape a possibility because their prestige in the international world of terrorists would become a factor, and they wouldn't want to do anything to jeopardize their credibility, and for lack of a better word, their integrity. However, they may not feel obligated to feed them properly." Crewes spoke directly to Walker. "Detective, do a medical check of every student at GirlSmart and if she is on any type of prescribed meds, be it for asthma, ADHD, whatever, your boy Supreme must make sure that she does not board that bus without it."

Walker found that smart. "Good thinking. Anything else?"

"Since food may become a problem," Crewes added, "we'll need Supreme to throw some sort of bon voyage party. We will provide him with canisters of a substance to mix in the fruit punch." When Walker's eyebrows raised in question, Crewes resolved her anxiety. "No need to worry. The drug is a safe but effective way to slow down the girls' metabolism so they can go for longer times without experiencing hunger. I'll be sure to have the contents of the canisters ideally suited for intake by teenaged girls."

"And while you're at it," Babcock said, "have the lab techs to add a mild sedative drug that will force them to remain, if not calm, level-headed."

"When would be the best time for them to drink their----?"

"Cocktail." Crewes found a word for Walker. "It would be best not to let them drink it until a few minutes before they board the bus."

"Yeah," Babcock added, "we'll calculate the required travel time between here and the Tennessee state line. We'll want the sedative to kick in about then. Don't worry, Detective Walker, our lab rats will figure it all out and everything will be calibrated to act on time."

Walker felt relief. "I'm impressed."

"You should be," Babcock grinned, "we're good at this."

The very next morning, Walker flew out of Charlotte to

discuss strategy with Chief Dennis who had complained that things were moving too fast, but she had basically written the grievance off, viewing it as only another instance of the age-old animosity between state law enforcement agencies and the FBI. The bond between the two groups had always been prickly, so she didn't give the Chief's argument a second thought.

On the flight back to North Carolina, Walker pretended that their plans were perfect, but decided not to lie to herself so she went on to admit that she was getting more and more spooked, the closer it got to the day the GirlSmart bus would take off for Tennessee. Sometimes it felt as if they had climbed too far out on a limb, that their whole counterplan was nothing more than a blind alley that would lead nowhere except to the deaths of the girls. Despite Babcock and Crewes' assurances, too much of their plan depended on luck, something she felt they were short of. The only thing they probably had less of was time.

It disturbed her that nothing they had come up with had put them in total control of the situation, and it wasn't like they hadn't tried. It was just that nothing would work.

She tried to be tough, but it was hard. It wasn't easy to concentrate when she couldn't determine if Brianna and her friends would be alive this time next week.

As the plane touched down in Charlotte, she hurriedly made her way out of the terminal and to the C section of the parking deck where she had left her Camry. She stared at the huge statute of Queen Charlotte and then got into her car and drove towards West Boulevard. She wanted to see what the hood looked like, to see if she could feel neutral about a black community that turned out big-butt young girls like Krispy Kreme turned out doughnuts.

Fearlessly, she steered her way through the streets of the Little Rock Apartments, and Boulevard Homes, a pair of housing projects not far from the airport, located on the same strip of road. Although she felt ill at ease in her assumed role as clinical psychologist, she turned her mind to her task, coldly analyzing how these bleak surroundings pre-packaged young, black girls like they were some sort of sexual refreshment designed to give black males a jolt of pleasure. It wasn't right, but it was true.

The despair of the neighborhoods was so strong that Walker could feel the threat just by driving down the streets. There were no places to stretch out or to grow, so the risk of becoming desensitized was all too real. Over-crowdedness made you feel you had to fight to survive. And here, you did.

This was the world that black girls across the country experienced on a daily basis, but it was a nightmare that Walker wanted to get away from. Having seen enough, she veered right and exited back onto West Boulevard. At the corner of Remount Road, she swung into the vacant parking lot at The Grapevine. She needed something for a headache. On her way out of the store, her phone rang. It was FBI agent Crewes, who excitedly explained to her that they now had a viable answer to the puzzle of how to manage the GirlSmart episode.

When she pressed for more details, Crewes became deliberately vague saying that it was the ultimate resolution, and that she would be posted with further instructions on where they could meet once it was sufficiently dark. He told her to go home and try to sleep. It was going to be a long night.

The rest of the drive home took her no time. After leaving West Boulevard, she had put the pedal to the metal, pulling up into the driveway of her rental property in record time only to discover that resting, let alone sleeping, would be out of the question, especially when she knew that Crewes could call at any minute.

She carelessly shucked off her outer garments until she was in just her undies. Then she made her way to the den, wondering about the FBI's ultimate resolution. She had a chorus of questions, but knew she would just have to wait, so she nervously played with the remote control, channel-surfing.

Forty-five minutes later, her phone rang.

"Tonight. 8:30. The Days Inn on North Tryon."

At The Days Inn, Walker asked tough questions. The chore of buying into the feds' ultimate resolution scenario was turning out to be a lot harder than she thought it would be. She had detected enough flaws to have the whole operation blow-up in their faces, but she knew it would be a waste of time trying to convince them that it wouldn't work. The bastards had already dug in and would be unwilling to disengage.

Despite her skepticism, Walker was still willing to pitch in with them if she could get some guarantees. "I'm still suspicious of some of your details," she admitted. "I need to hear more."

So Crewes told her again about how the counterstrike was to go down. Speaking with commanding authority, he hoped to gain Walker's confidence this time. He was clear that he had hoped to win her support with the initial report, but when it became obvious he hadn't, he had to struggle hard to keep his frustration with her from showing. "Presumably, our prime objective is to secure the lives of everyone on the bus, and every agent involved with this operation has been briefed with that point in mind, so there is no possibility that we'll storm the bus. As I said earlier, we will have one of our own men on board the bus as the driver. The bus will be wired for sound so we will be able to hear precisely what is going on at all times. In addition, we'll have the bus on GPS so we'll be able to track it by the satellite pictures we'll be receiving, so there is no way we won't know what is happening."

"What you don't know is where the bus will be taken."

"No, we can't be certain just where the bus will be commandeered, but since we'll stick to I-40 the whole trip, we'll try to limit any action to that perimeter. Perhaps, the attackers may even wait for the bus to reach Memphis although I find that improbable, so we've guessed that it will be at a rest stop along the route."

Walker pursed he lips. "Well, I'm still worried, and what worries me most is the intentional use of gas."

"The gas use has been approved by the proper authorities, and only enough will be used to render all the occupants on the bus unconscious. The driver of the vehicle will be fitted with a special apparatus for his nose that will prevent the gas from knocking him out so there will be no cause to worry that he'll pass out and lose control of the bus. However, the rebels from TWB and the girls will be instantly put to sleep."

"But wasn't that also the idea in Russia. It probably seemed like a great tactic to gas the theater, but the outcome was horrendous. The gas killed many of the hostages."

"We've studied that incident well and I assure you that this won't be another Moscow."

"I'm glad to hear that," Walker retorted glumly. "I just hope your people in the lab know what the hell they're doing. After all, those are young girls and the amount of gas it might take to put an adult to sleep may be enough to kill them."

"We're not a fucking bunch of pansies, detective," Babcock snapped. "I'd rather assumed you'd be responsible enough to accept the feasibility of our plan. I would have thought that given the nature of this operation that it was one you'd want to win."

"You know good and damn well that I want to win." Walker was angry. "But I also want to spare lives, especially those of the girls."

"Then this is the operation for you."

Walker still didn't see eye to eye with the feds, but she reluctantly caved in. "And then what?"

"Once we have gained control of the bus and zoomed everyone to another location, the rebels will be removed to a federal prison in Memphis where we'll hold them overnight before whisking them away to another secure location outside of Tennessee." Crewes' voice was filled with enthusiasm. "In our talks with TWB, we'll let them know that it was someone close to Ivan who tipped us off. From there, we'll negotiate. All we want from TWB is evidence that demonstrates that Ivan sponsored the kidnapping of a busload of American school-girls. In return for that info, we'll free the rebels."

Walker gasped loudly.

"It's an imperfect world, Detective Walker, and sometimes the best you can do is to trade one evil for another. Right now, we want Ivan Gugarin. TWB has no loyalty to a child pornographer, so the exchange should be a no brainer. We're even hoping that once TWB finds out the true purpose of the kidnapping, they'll feel insulted that Ivan used them is such a way. Hell, these guys are in the terrorism business, not the sex trade. TWB could lose face if it ever got out that they were involved in child smuggling and kiddie porn."

"And given that scenario," Babcock interjected, "a quiet deal can be quickly struck. Everything will be hushed up, nobody's business."

"That's the best case scenario," Crewes added, "but it's highly unlikely. People along the kidnap route are bound to notice what is happening and we just can't pretend they didn't see what they saw. Plus, it is very likely that TWB will go for something spectacular so they can grab the headlines, but even if they do put on a good show for the evening news, we'll have the bus back before they can issue any press release. This way, we can put our own little spin on the episode."

"And TWB won't even be mentioned?" Walker asked

"After we contact them and tell them that we're getting ready to tell the world they're child smugglers, they'll beg us not to mention them in connection with what really went down."

"So, basically, it will be our word against Ivan's?"

"Pretty much" Crewes answered, "but when we get finished with our smear campaign, detective, TWB is going to be fully convinced that Ivan double-crossed them." The FBI agent smiled. "What do you think now?"

Walker smiled back. "I like it. I like it a lot."

Chapter 23

The entire staff at GirlSmart as well as a small group of
people unrelated to the school showed up for the 10:00 am going
away party. Eve had gone to great lengths to make sure it was
festive despite the early hour, and she had truly succeeded in
turning what was slated to be a casual affair into a special occasion.

Supreme watched Eve from a distance, eyeing her as she
went from girl to girl, hugging, smiling and kissing each of them
warmly. This was, for all practical purposes, her kiss of death.
The bitch was a monster, Supreme reminded himself, and he
visibly flinched when he witnessed Eve emerge from a corner
with Brianna in tow for a photo opportunity. Supreme wanted to
snatch Brianna up, and to get her as far away from Eve as possible.
Instead, he waved bravely.

A little later, McKay gave a brief speech about how
GirlSmart would one day become the stuff of legend and about
how this group of girls, in particular, would be immortalized since
they would be the pioneers of the school; the first graduating class.
The talk made Supreme develop cold chills.

The chartered bus arrived about ten minutes later, and a
tremendous cheer rose from the throats of the gathered assembly.
The young girls were so excited that one could have believed that
the 'Sweet Chariot' sung about so reverently on Sunday mornings
in black churches, had finally sung low, and had come to take this
group on a wonderful joy ride. Supreme, for his part, was getting
sicker and sicker by the minute.

Following a few moments of merry-making, Eve decided

that it was time to bid the girls farewell as she saw how they were looking forward to boarding the bus. It was 10:45 and it had indeed been a gala event, and after deciding that anything further would be anticlimactic, Eve ordered everyone outside to the parked bus.

Supreme tried everything he could to generate some enthusiasm over the scheduled departure, but all he could feel were butterflies in his stomach. He glanced at Brianna and winked his eye. She returned the gesture. Both were saddened they were unable to hug and kiss each other goodbye, but they couldn't. They had to keep their illegal relationship a secret. Or Supreme would be arrested.

He quickly turned to walk away. First, he no longer had any desire to be near Eve or McKay or any of the others in the GirlSmart organization. More than anything else, he wanted to be alone to sear this last image of his beloved Brianna in his mind's eye so he could remember it forever----in case something went wrong today.

"Hey, stranger."

Supreme didn't have to turn around. "What's up, Eve?"

"You, nigga, that's what's up. You in the mood for some good pussy this morning?"

Supreme spun around. "This is it, huh? The dirty deed has been done and all you got on your evil mind is fucking. We both need to go somewhere and fall down on our knees to pray."

Not expecting that, Eve took a step backwards. "Whoa, my brotha, all I've done this morning is offered you some good coochie. Don't bite my head off." Quickly gaining her composure, she acted offended. "Besides, what can I do? I think I have already told you a thousand times if I've told you once that everything happens for a reason."

""Eve, you amaze me."

Eve shifted her body until her neck was right under Supreme's nose. "Sniff, nigga," she commanded. "I'm wearing that perfume your ass claimed to love so much."

Despite himself, Supreme inhaled the intoxicating fragrance, instantly sensing his resistance to the woman weakening. He sniffed her again, knowing he was leaving himself little chance of not becoming aroused. "What kind of people are we, Eve?"

"The kind who do what they have to do." Eve's demeanor changed. "I'm sorry about Brianna, Supreme, so I don't want you running around thinking I got rid of Brianna just so I could have you all to myself because it's not like that. I had told you a long time ago that I had no problem with sharing you with the tenderoni and I meant that. You could have had us both. Again, I'm sorry." Eve's demeanor changed once more. "But Big Mama is not lying about how bad she needs some dick this morning." Eve boldly stroked Supreme through his jeans, staring at the budge. "And it has just become public knowledge that you want to skeet, so why don't you let me finish what I've started." Eve opened Supreme's car door for him. "If that swelling in your pants goes down on your way to my house, don't worry about it." She smacked her lips lewdly. "I know what to do. I'm so nasty, ain't I?"

After Supreme finished doing Eve, he sped across town to a hotel where Walker had promised to secure a room where they could follow the route of the GirlSmart bus as it traveled up I-40.

True to her word, Walker had reserved a corner room in a hotel just off I-85 and when she let him in, he rushed to the monitor to see where the bus was.

"It's still early," Walker commented casually. "Nothing is going to happen any time soon. I assume you ate at the party. That is where you were, wasn't it?"

"Damn," Supreme groaned, "I thought you was the police, not a P.O. Anyway, I'm grown, go where the hell I feel like going."

"Forget it," Walker blurted heatedly, "but I'd like to offer a tiny suggestion. Don't ever leave a woman's house smelling like her."

"What?"

"The woman you've just been with, I smell her perfume on you. The scent is in your clothes. If I was your woman and you came home smelling like another bitch, I'd slap the shit out of you."

When Supreme turned to face Walker, he could see that

her eyes were alive with interest, but just at that moment the car carrying Babcock and Crewes pulled up. "Later for you, sweetheart."

"You wish." Walker went to the door to let the FBI agents in.

"Miss anything?" They joined Supreme at the monitor.

"Naw, ain't nuthin' happening yet. They ain't got to Tennessee yet."

"Where are they now?" Crewes asked.

"I-40 is all I can tell you," Supreme responded. "I been waiting to see a road sign, but ain't one yet. Wherever they at, it's all good as long as it's on a map. Sho' don't want that bus getting lost or nuthin'."

After thirty minutes Supreme left, but found it difficult to not wonder what was going on. He phoned the room. Walker, as expected, picked up.

"Where they at now?"

"If you were that interested, you'd be here." Walker hung up.

"Bitch!" Supreme screamed into the dead line. He headed back to the hotel.

Unexpectedly, the room now bristled with undeniable tension and Supreme noticed how the three occupants were uncharacteristically edgy as they hovered around the monitor like vultures waiting on something to die. They all knew that it was about to go down so Supreme rushed over, joining his crackling energy to the almost combustible energy in that one spot. It was as if they were all kindred spirits united in a devious plot to dominate the universe.

Time seemed to stand still. No one noticed it. Talking was unimaginable, especially during one five mile stretch of highway where I-40 began to loop itself around the city of Memphis like an asphalt noose.

"They almost inside the city limits," Supreme uttered hoarsely, breaking the deep silence, "and ain't nobody done shit yet." He didn't know whether to be relieved or more concerned. "What's the deal?"

"I don't know," Babcock answered. "I would have thought that TWB would have had made a move long before now. Hell, that stretch about an hour and a half ago was a picture postcard for a highway job. I dunno," he whispered mostly to himself. "What's the rest of the itinerary, Crewes?"

Referring to a mock-up," Crewes frowned. "According to this, the driver has been instructed to take Danny Thomas Boulevard off of I-40 and to proceed downtown."

"I dunno," Babcock mumbled again, "but who knows what---."

"Look!" Crewes shouted, "there it is, coming up." Crewes' voice was choked. "It's going to go down on Danny Thomas."

Immediately the room turned deathly silent as everyone watched a massive roadblock being erected slightly inside the exit leading onto Danny Thomas.

"This is it!" Crewes repeatedly tersely. "Those guy are not cops. It's getting ready to go down, my friends, so hold onto your hats." He nudged Walker. "Activate sound. I want us to be able to hear what happens once they take the bus. This is fucking it!" His voice was tense with adrenaline. "Let's go to work, boys," he exhorted the FBI agents on the mission although he knew they wouldn't be able to hear him. "Let's kick some ass."

When Walker hit the button for sound, the hotel room came immediately to life with the incredible gaiety of schoolgirl chatter. Until now, they had agreed not to watch the interior of the bus even though from time to time Supreme had begged to see what Brianna was doing. Each time, out of consideration for the primary objective of tracking the movement of the bus, he had been overruled. Now, he gasped audibly although he didn't say much.

The bus rumbled up to the roadblock.

"What's wrong?" one of the girls yelled at the driver. "We gonna get a ticket or something? You wasn't speeding…were you?"

"No, I wasn't speeding. Everyone just relax," the driver ordered, "and let me handle everything, okay?"

"Okay," Danisha said, "but tell them to hurry up. We got other shit to do than to be stuck out here on the side of the highway."

The bus was flagged over to the shoulder of the road, and the four people in the hotel room watched, their breath caught in their throats, as the men dressed in law enforcement gear approached the bus, beckoning the driver to open the door. After a second, it hissed open. The men boarded.

"Where is this bus bound?"

"Memphis."

"I don't think so."

The occupants of the hotel room saw it coming even though the bus driver never did.

"No!" Babcock screamed as the second man, lower on the boarding steps and hidden behind the lead man, drew a weapon from beneath his jacket. "No!" the FBI agent screamed again as the man fired the gun, striking the driver between the eyes.

Out of nowhere, armed TWB members emerged. They quickly swarmed the bus amidst the terrified shrieks and cries of the startled GirlSmart students.

"Brianna!" Supreme shouted helplessly as he saw the masked rebels rounding the girls up, but he went mute as it dawned on him what type of masks the men were wearing.

"They-they're wearing fucking gas masks!" Babcock exclaimed in shocked disbelief. "The bastards knew!"

There wasn't any time for discussion as Supreme and the others stared transfixed as a second bus pulled up. Brianna and her friends were quickly herded off the GirlSmart bus, and into the waiting vehicle with a methodical precision that caused Walker to gasp at the speed and manic orderliness of it all. The entire operation had taken less than two minutes. The second bus moved.

Crewes leaned forward, rubbing his eyes as though he couldn't believe what he had just seen. He started to speak, but before he could utter the first words, one of the rebels tossed a hand grenade under the GirlSmart bus. It exploded with a spectacular burst of noise and flames. All four people in the hotel room in Charlotte jumped. The monitor went blank.

"It fell through?" Babcock wailed. "It fell through!"

"What fell through?" Supreme demanded to know.

"Our plans, that's what. They knew. How they know, I'll be damned if I know, but they knew."

"So, what does that mean?"

Babcock faced Supreme. "It means, dammit, that we're lost control and that we may never see those girls again…not alive anyway."

Supreme screamed. "Brianna!"

Chapter 24

The very next morning Walker flew out of Charlotte to huddle with Chief Dennis. She was in no mood to stick around, and to get dumped on by the federal agents whom she felt would try to use her as a scapegoat. Even though she had no proof, she was thoroughly convinced it was one of Babcock's and Crewes' own people who had squealed to Ivan, divulging every aspect of their well-organized counter-strike. The only other option would be to suppose that Supreme was responsible for the leak, but she didn't think so, and since she hadn't breathed a word of the plans to anyone other than the Chief, that left no one else to blame but the FBI.

Walker was terribly upset over the fiasco because after all the time and painstaking energy that had gone into developing the plan, it had still come undone. And at the worst possible moment, with the worst possible results. In an operation of this nature, everyone's primary job was to keep their mouths shut. Evidently, someone had forgotten that basic rule, and Walker hated to think about what that mistake might cause Brianna and her friends.

Two hours later as she sat with the Chief, Walker admitted that she would prefer not to know what happened to the GirlSmart students because she feared it would be horribly grisly, and such news could derail her ambitions to continue her career in law enforcement.

"You can't just give up, Walker," Dennis offered in a paternal tone. "For one thing, you're too damned good and secondly, you're acting way in advance of the final outcome. For all anyone knows, the girls are safe."

"That is probably correct for the moment. The girls are probably physically safe, but they, more than likely, are traumatized, terrified out of their minds. I can't begin to imagine what their families must be going through. Jesus Christ, Chief, this is the low point of my life. I-I feel so helpless."

"That's a normal enough reaction."

"So, I'm just not supposed to worry about it?"

"Not until they conduct their own internal investigation."

"And guess what that will do, Chief? Not a damn thing. If it's like you said, you think they're going to admit to something going on. They'll only look somewhere else....like at me."

The Chief shook his head. "They come at you, I've got your back and I promise that I'll hit the jackasses with all the fucking resources at my disposal. I might be local," Dennis snorted, "but the feds don't want to get into a pissing contest with me."

"Thanks, Chief, I knew I could count on you. It's people like you who keep me inspired, and if you want to know a secret, I would have quit a long time ago had it not been for your excellent example." After a brief pause. "Do you think the feds will find the girls?"

"I hope so. That was quite a show TWB put on for the public's benefit, but what we have to remember is that now that the fire and explosions extravaganza is over, it's out of TWB's jurisdiction. They've probably already handed the children over to Ivan." Dennis reared back in his chair. "The feds can provoke me if they want to and that's what they'll be doing if they come after you. I know how to fight fire with fire, so don't worry, I'm in your corner."

Within minutes, Walker was headed out of Chief Dennis' office feeling like she had an ace in the hole if the feds fucked with her, but by the time she had gotten back to Charlotte, the local media was in a frenzy. Accusations and rumor flew back and forth dramatically between public officials and spokespeople for the FBI, but there had not been a mumbling word about TWB. There had also been no signs of the 'getaway bus' as it had came to be called by the national press. It was as if the vehicle had magically vanished from the face of the earth which so far had proven to be a tough speculation to refute, but veteran law enforcement personnel felt the kidnappers had utilized a specially-constructed tunnel. They just didn't know where it was, so the search remained centered around the Memphis area, particularly the vicinity bordering I-40 and I-240.

Walker followed what was happening, or better yet what was not happening, with keen interest, but most important for her at the moment was her meeting with the feds. She had rehearsed and memorized her lines, but was thrown for a loop when she discovered Babcock and Crewes' unanimous in their belief that she had not corrupted the investigation. Internal Affairs was also equally adamant that none of the feds had gone blabbing to Ivan, so 100% suspicion fell on Supreme.

"Would you be willing to wear a wire to see if you could get Supreme to admit to saying something?" Babcock asked.

Walker found that implausible. "Do you really find it necessary to waste energy on that when the overall objective is still to locate those girls?"

"They wouldn't need to be located, dammit, if someone hadn't opened their big mouths and that person, whoever it is, is the one responsible for what happens to those girls, so hell yeah, the Bureau feels it is necessary. Besides, we're making it a special assignment for you."

Walker laughed bitterly. "Who dreamed that up? Special Assignments. It's a saving face mission for you guys, so don't bullshit me."

"You in or not?"

"I'll talk to Supreme, yes, but I'm not wiring up."

Babcock sipped his coffee. "I thought you were our friend?"

"Call our working relationship what you will, but I don't feel I owe you guys anything."

Crewes' voice sounded tired. "Right now, all we want is for this to end in the right way, and the only way to do that is with the arrest and conviction of all the players, from those who buy and sell girls to those who recruit them, all the way down to those who have those little, black schoolgirls as well as the son-of-a-bitch who caused this needless aftermath."

Walker hesitated, the need for closure uppermost in her mind despite her not wanting to have any further dealings with the feds. "Look, guys, I'll do a number on Supreme, but I can't wear a wire. I don't think it would be wise."

"Why not?" Crewes sounded worried. "It's not like we're asking you to take off your clothes and jump in bed with the guy." When Crewes saw Walker flinch, he steadied his tone. "There's not anything personal going on between you and----?"

"Hell no!" Walker snapped. "I'm a professional. I don't screw my colleagues or my fucking informants."

"Just asking," the FBI agent said defensively. "No offense."

"Well, mind your own business."

"We can find out for ourselves," Crewes yelled.

"Then that's your damn Special Assignment," Walker yelled back. "Do it."

She then made her exit.

Chapter 25

A week later.

The feds think we're fucking."

Supreme kissed Walker's nose. "We are."

"I mean before now."

"Well, we just gave 'em something to talk about."

Walker snuggled up closer to Supreme, rubbing his chest. "Anyway, where is it written that I've got to play by anyone's rules except my own. I'm a big girl and I declare today the day I start doing my own thing." She ran her hand up and down the inside of Supreme's thigh. "I'm off to a good start, wouldn't you say?"

"I'm just glad to be a part of the new you."

"And you know what? I like it down here on the ground, and I don't think I want to be resurrected. All these years, I was walking on air with my head stuck in a cloud, never having a private life. I never had anyone to go home to." Walker shuddered. "It's a wonder I'm not neurotic."

"So what you gonna do?"

"Quit. Retire. This last operation did it for me. I'm finished with trying to make the world a better place. I've lost all my ideals the same time you lost Brianna, but at least you've got me as a replacement. I felt I owed you me." Walker glanced at Supreme hopefully. "Does that make any sense to you?"

"It don't have to make sense to me as long as it makes sense to you. I just don't want you feeling guilty if you find out that being with me is not what you want."

"I want it, Supreme. I want it bad. I haven't been with a man like this in years."

"But what if Brianna comes back?"

"No problem. I'm not going to give you any trouble or beg you to let me stay. I'll move on and take my memories with me. All I ask is that you let me give you all of me for as long as it lasts. Is that asking too much?"

"No", Supreme reasoned, "and you got that. Bring it on," he grinned. "Put all of you on me, especially if it's gonna be like what we just got through doing."

"But there's so much more to me, Supreme, that you need to get to know. I'm more than just good in bed. I want to do things with, for, and to you outside the bedroom that will make you feel complete. Don't underestimate me, my friend."

"I won't."

"I know it's going to be a day to day process because we don't know if or when this case will be broken, but right now, it's going nowhere. I'm afraid Ivan has already won because in my heart I don't feel like we're ever going to see those girls again."

"You really feel that?'

"Yes, Supreme, I feel it and it's a feeling borne from experience. As a detective, I know instinctively when I'm winning or losing. I feel like this is a lost case. I'm sorry, baby. I know you loved Brianna….even though it was wrong."

There was a note of sadness in Supreme's voice as he changed the subject. "I sho' would like to know who flipped the script and fucked everything up."

"I assure you, baby, that it wasn't me. No matter what it may seem like with me laying here beside you, I wouldn't have done away with Brianna to make this happen."

Supreme put his arms around Walker. "I'm not accusing you. Plus, I knew you were a dedicated cop from the jump. I picked up right away how much you loved your badge and your work, but this shit is crazy. You didn't do it. I didn't do it. The feds say they didn't do it. All I know is that somebody is lying 'cause somebody told everything. Trust me, Eve taught me to keep my mouth shut."

"As far as that goes, I didn't have a man or a lover to whisper into his ear, so there was no one for me to pillow-talk with. I don't know a soul in Charlotte so I didn't have any friends.

The only person who knew what was up with the investigation that I spoke with was my supervisor back home. I felt I could trust Chief Dennis."

Supreme raised up in bed. "Who!?"

"My boss. Chief Dennis."

Supreme started thinking. "You know dude like that?"

"He was my mentor. Why?"

"Just something that Ivan tole me one time. I remember him bragging 'bout how he had all the police in Eastern Europe in his pocket. He said he hadn't gotten around to corrupting the police in this country yet, but that he was getting around to it." Supreme looked at Walker. "He might've got to yo' peeps."

Walker sat up in bed. "No, not the Chief. I'm sure of that."

"But you gotta admit it's possible. Your peeps could be the traitor. No one would ever think about him 'cause he wasn't supposed to know shit in the first place, you dig? I'm feeling this. It's a perfect fit." Supreme became hesitant. "But is there any way we can prove it?"

"Or disprove it. Yes, there is. If, as you suspect, Chief Dennis passed along info to Ivan, there would have had to have been some contact which would mean at least one phone call." Walker draped her arm around Supreme's shoulder. "Do you have anything with Ivan's number on it."

"Yeah. I got it when I got Ice's stuff. The number is in Ice's personal organizer, a little electronic jimmy."

"Okay, good enough. I got a contact back at home who works for the phone company. I can have her pull up the Chief's phone call sheet for the last billing period. We'll see what we come up with, but I think this is a wild goose chase."

"Famous last words," Supreme commented dryly. "I trusted Eve."

"In that case, let me get to work. Hand me my phone."

Once Walker had made her call, she dressed and went downstairs to the hotel's lobby to retrieve the fax. It wasn't long before she had returned to the room, waving the phone records.

"Let's start digging," Supreme said eagerly.

Sitting down at the desk, Walker spread out the documents.

"Even though I don't think this will achieve anything, I want you to have peace of mind. Here, look this sheet over and see if any familiar numbers pop up." Walker extended a listing to Supreme, but no sooner had he scanned the list than he let the paper slip from his hand with an audible gasp. "Wh-what is it, baby?"

Supreme's eyes went dead. "Ivan's number is on there."

"No," Walker shrieked. "It-it can't be." She picked up the paper. "Here, look again. Your eyes must be playing tricks on you."

Supreme shook his head. "I saw what I saw and I know what I saw. Ivan's number is on there."

"Well, let me see. Show it too me."

Gripping the paper firmly, Supreme's eyes roamed down the list. He pointed. "There it is. Right there."

"And you're sure?"

Supreme grabbed Walker by the hand. "Let's go to my crib. I'll show you the number on Ice's private digital organizer. Maybe then you'll believe me."

Walker involuntarily shivered as a chill ran up her spine. She didn't relish the irrevocable knowledge that the Chief had betrayed her and that she, in return, had indirectly betrayed others. But it was a part of her job to know, and why not, the wheels were already in motion. Her temples pounded at the choice she would have to make next if it proved correct that she had been used by a man she had respected like no other.

On the drive across town, she cut off the car's radio. She needed to think and the thumping bass of the Prince song only added to the pressure inside her head. After this, there might not be anything left in her life to salvage. She pounded the dash in utter frustration. She cursed. The trip didn't take long.

At Supreme's house, he instantly sensed that something was wrong. He stopped Walker just inside the doorway. "Hold up. Somebody done been in heah." He looked around slowly, his eyes taking in everything as they swept the living room for signs of anything missing or disturbed. "Ain't nuthin' been fucked wit'," he said confidently. "At least not in heah."

"You're sure someone---"

"Just like you got yo' skills, I got some of my own.

Anybody in prison can walk into his cell and automatically know when somebody done been up in his spot. It don't matter if it was a guard or another convict and it don't make no difference how careful the motherfucka was, a nigga still can tell when his space done been invaded."

Walker pulled out her weapon.

"Now, you on point" Supreme said respectfully. Now, let's go through the rest of the crib.

They chose the bedroom first because that was where Supreme kept both the organizer and his gun, but he experienced a numbness in his head when he discovered both were missing. He sat on the edge of the bed to think, but Walker discouraged him.

"We've got to get out of here, baby."

"Why, the motherfuckas got what they wanted and gone."

"But don't mean they ain't coming back."

"For what?"

"For you, Supreme. If this is like you say and it is the Chief, then chances are he has told Ivan that you were our informant."

"It is your fucking boss and if you give me a second, I'll remember…." Supreme stopped talking and jumped up. "I know it would come back to me." He dashed to his closet and pulled out a box of brand new sneakers. Peeling back the flap of the box, he called Walker over. "I was scared the battery might go out on Ice's electronic gadget and I didn't know if that would erase the numbers or not, so I wrote Ivan's number down for safekeeping. Another jailhouse trick. Sometimes a nigga's mind will go blank on him and he can't even remember the combination to his lock, so you write it down and hide it in your books or your shoebox for safekeeping." Supreme held the number up. "Look at them digits and then look at the digits on that phone list and tell me what's what."

The numbers matched!

"Let's get out of her." Without elaborating further, Walker tugged Supreme towards the door.

"Wait," Supreme retorted, "we gonna need some paper."

"Hurry up. They've probably got someone watching the

house and they've probably let it be known that you're here, so our time is running out."

Supreme quickly emerged from the closet with a backpack stuffed with cash. "C'mon, let's get missing."

On their way back to Supreme's Beemer, Walker spotted two men cutting a diagonal path across the street, coming quickly towards them. "Supreme!" she screamed, "get in the car quick!"

The man on the left drew his gun first, firing twice as he continued to walk in their direction. The other, more cautious, stopped, assumed the standard shooter's stance and aimed his weapon. Walker shot him first, then in the next drawn-out second, hit his partner. Both were head shots. Both were effective. And fatal.

"Drive," she said calmly as she got into the car, "but don't speed."

"Where to?"

"This is your city. Drive us somewhere safe." At a red light, Walker asked Supreme if he had any dependable friends in any of the housing projects on West Boulevard.

"I got a good friend, Randy, in Little Rock."

"Then we need to go there, but not in your car. We must go in a cab. Does the city bus---"

"Number 10 runs right through the street Randy lives on."

"Where do we catch the bus?"

"Down below the Square, across from where the Charlotte Hornets play when they at home"

"Then take us there and say goodbye to your BMW."

Chapter 26

Ivan was in shock. He kept on telling himself that this was a bad dream, a nightmare from which he would soon awake to find that Supreme and
Walker were both dead.

"They have no choice but to lay low," Uri growled. "They're scared shitless---"

"If scared shitless makes that bitch shoot like that," Ivan snapped, "then you had better pursue some other way to manage this problem. You continue scaring them shitless and you're going to have your men getting bullets in their heads left and right."

"I think---"

"Think! Think! Think!" Ivan hotly declared. "That's the problem. Everyone is fucking thinking and while all this thinking is going on, no one is doing shit. Do! Do! Do! Leave the thinking to the scholars, Uri." Ivan gripped his brother's shoulders between his huge hands. "Scholars think, killers do, Uri. Understand? I recommend more doing and less thinking." Ivan let his hands drop lifelessly to his sides. "You say, for a fact, that the two are holed up in Charlotte. Is that correct, my brother and comrade?"

"Yes."

"Then may I offer a solution?"

"Yes, Ivan, you may."

"Tear the fucking city up."

Friday evening.

"Whew!" Randy remarked earnestly. "Shit serious as cancer."

"And that ain't even half the story," Supreme said. "That's how big this is."

"And it's only gonna get uglier, so that mean y'all gotta get outta Charlotte with the quickness. Them motherfuckas gonna tear this city up."

The next few hours were desperate ones for Supreme and Walker who both understood they didn't have much time to straighten their affairs, but if there was one thing they both knew, it was that they had to depart North Carolina and neither had the slightest idea of how to do it.

Randy had offered them the use of his apartment for as long as it was needed, and it was he who had put them in a better position to get away by buying them another car and securing for each, false identification. For the time being, that was the best he could do for them. He knew that even this little bit of assistance could get him in hot water if the people looking for them found out he had provided it. If that became the case, he expected the Russians would make his life miserable. The only loyalty they could honor was the type owed and paid to them.

When Randy came back from another one of his errands, this time for clothes, Supreme gave him two envelopes. One stuffed with money which Randy eagerly accepted. The other was a brief account of what had happened to Brianna and her friends. Supreme wanted it mailed to Ryanne Persinger at The Charlotte Post no sooner had they left town.

"Where y'all going?"

Supreme shrugged. "Don't know yet. Ain't nowhere safe, but we're trying to put together a location even if it's only temporary. At least that will give us a moment to sort shit out."

"I know where the fuck I'd go."

"Where?" Walker asked. "Where would you go if you were on the run?"

"Memphis."

"Memphis, Randy? Damn, dawg" Supreme wailed, "didn't you just finish hearing me tell 'bout the shit that went down in

Memphis?"

"I heard all that, soldier, and that's why I would go there. It's the last place they would think you'd go after what went down. Another thang I can tell you is that in all the world, ain't no place hotter than Memphis. Whew, with all them police and feds and shit up there, man, the block is hot, but at the same time, if you get my drift, ain't no spot safer. Fit it all together," Randy grinned. "Do you really think the bad guys really return to the scene of the crime. Hell naw, dawg, and you know it. Motherfucka get in the wind and don't look the fuck back."

Supreme looked over at Walker. "How that sound to you?"

"Crazy, but in a way that made sense. I think it's something we need to consider and considering we don't have a lot of other options, it's the best idea we're going to get. I really don't think Ivan's people will want to go anywhere near Memphis right now."

"Can I ask y'all something," Randy inquired. "How y'all gonna get there? Can't fly, can't ride the bus, or take the train 'cause yo' boy gonna have all them spots covered."

"I guess we gonna have to drive."

"Yeah, that's what I thought, but y'all gonna be asking for trouble if y'all try to roll out together. Them people ain't no dummies so they gonna be on the look-out for a couple, a man and a woman, riding together, trying to get missing."

"Man," Supreme said dismissively, "I gotta give Ivan his props and yeah, you right about him having people at the airport and shit, but it ain't no way I can credit him with being smart enough to have motherfuckas sitting at every exit leaving town. I could see it if Charlotte was a lil' rinky-dink city with just one way in and one way out, but it ain't. There's too many ways to get out of this bitch."

"Plus, I don't think we should split up," Walker added. "At least, I don't want to."

"Okay," Randy shrugged, "it's y'all thang. I'm just throwing shit out here for y'all to beware of."

Supreme studied Walker. "You don't gotta go, babe. The FBI will look out for you since you the law like them. Anyway, we ain't even seen the big picture yet. Ivan might not even know who you are."

"Why shouldn't he know?"

"Maybe the Chief didn't give you up. If you and him cool like that, maybe he didn't kick your name. He might not have revealed his source. He might have protected you. As long as Ivan was getting his info, he probably didn't give a shit 'bout who was supplying the Chief wit' it."

Walker rejected the idea. "If the Chief turned rotten, he turned rotten to the core. I feel much safer and wiser thinking that he did rather than he didn't."

"Ain't but one way to find out," Randy asserted, "and that's to approach his ass and find out."

Walker and Supreme looked at each other.

"That's right, peeps," Randy continued, "call his double-crossing ass up, not on my phone, though," he laughed, "and holla at his punk ass. On the strength of y'all relationship, the motherfucka, if he any kind of man, should tell you what he did. The cracker owe you the chance to protect yourself even if he the bitch who set you up."

To get her answer, Walker would have to wait until Randy returned from purchasing a cheap cell phone, one which would be used expressly for the one call to Dennis and then dumped to the bottom of the Catawba River.

When Randy got back to his Leake Street apartment, he was grinning from ear to ear. "I got y'all the hook-up." He pulled a phone out of a plastic shoe bag. "Check this baby out. Now, hold on before you start asking a bunch of questions and let me hip you to what's up with this gizmo."

"I know it ain't what we sent you for."

"Sho' you right, my nigga. This heah damn sho' ain't no cell phone. It's a spy phone."

"A what?"

"A phone equipped with some high-tech shit. Belong to a Spanish friend of mine. Jose, he into some space-age spyware shit, so I got him to let me borrow this motherfucka for a minute. Calls can't be traced neither." Randy looked at Walker. "I was worried that dude would front on you, say he didn't flip on you when the fuck he did. Well, Jose's phone will let you know if he straight up or if he lying. This bitch got a voice stress analyzer on it."

Walker nodded appreciatively. "I'm familiar with this program. Yeah, it will give me an advantage. Smart thinking, Randy."

"Good looking out, dawg," Supreme was grateful. "Now the Chief won't have no room to wiggle his ass out of this. If it's him, we'll know."

"But you gotta work the cracker," Randy interjected, "and here's how you do it."

Supreme glanced at Walker, shaking his head. "Get ready. I should have warned you. This brotha got a scheme for everything."

"And that's because I ain't met the situation yet that I couldn't finesse my way out of. Now, check this out and tell me it ain't the shit."

"Give it up, dawg," Supreme urged. "Put down game."

"Since you ain't gotta worry 'bout if ol' boy lying or not, you move to phase two, provided he is a double-crossing dog. My money is on the fact he gonna lie. If he do, cool 'cause you gonna know anyhow. Tell him you need to meet his ass somewhere, just you and him. What he probably will try to do is to set you up, but you beat his conniving ass to the punch and snatch his bitch ass up, take him somewhere and hold him hostage."

"And then what?"

"You use him to set Ivan up. Tell him that if he don't do it, ya'll gonna off his no good ass. If he play the double-cross for money or whatever it was the Russian gave him, he'll play the triple-cross to save his life. Once you snatch Ivan, then you in a position to call shots, you dig?"

"That's a whole of snatching."

"True dat, but if you work it just right, it'll work." Randy shrugged. "Either you stand and fight or you run for the rest of your lives. One thang that ain't no joke is that no matter how big and bad Ivan is, he scared like anybody else when the gun in his face. Life is a whole lot different when the shoe on the other foot." Randy took a breath. "If it sounds like a waste of time, then I'll figure out a way to sneak y'all into Memphis. Y'all put y'all heads together and see which way y'all gonna roll. In the meantime, I'm gonna go put a lil' somethin' somethin' on the ol' stove."

And then it was time.

Walker knew exactly what to do. First, she dialed a private directory which allowed her to make an electronic inquiry via a secret switchboard to

put her in direct contact with Chief Dennis on his hotline.

She punched in a code. He would know it was her.

"Detective." Dennis answered on the second ring. He sounded surprised, but maybe he wasn't. "I've been hearing some things."

"So have I."

"Are you still in Charlotte?"

"No," Walker lied, "but I can't tell you where I am. I need to see you."

"When?"

"Immediately."

"What's up?"

"You've never bothered to question me before when I've needed to see you. Why now?"

"Some very unfavorable reports have come across my desk, Walker."

"Such as?"

"Such as the fact that you breached the operation by having an affair with the very same individual you were assigned to handle."

"That's bullshit, Chief. You know I would never do any such thing."

"They say you went over to Ivan."

"Well, may I ask you a question, Chief?"

"I may not answer, but go ahead. Ask."

Walker paused. "Have you had any personal contact with Ivan?"

As the Chief spoke, Walker was almost tempted to shout at him and to let him know that despite how clever he assumed he was, she knew he was lying. In a way, it saddened her, then sickened her. The man she would have given her life for had betrayed her. It had taken her only a few seconds after that to begin to hate Chief Dennis and to want to kill him. Still she maintained her civility throughout the duration of the conversation.

"I still need to see you."

"Can you get to my office?"

"No way. Not there. Somewhere else where I'll feel safe."

"Where's that, I wonder." Chief Dennis scoffed. "You really set a fire under your bottom this time, Detective."

"Give me a second to think." Walker motioned to Supreme as if to say where. Supreme made a silent movement with his mouth. Walker nodded. "Come to Charlotte."

Chapter 27

The next night, In Charlotte

At 8:30 pm, Chief Dennis fidgeted, squirming uncomfortably in the front seat of the rental car. He had to piss badly. He looked around furtively for a safe piss haven and spied the garbage can behind the McDonalds'. Perfect.

"Fuck it," he softly cursed when he realized he had left his gun inside the car, lying on the seat. He wouldn't need it since he wouldn't be gone but a quick second or two.

Chief Dennis ambled towards the dumpster, unzipping his pants as he went.

Across the street, Detective Walker unzipped her gun holster, moving quickly through the dark.

Supreme made his move.

The white man tried to run. He screamed. The knife had ripped through the fabric of his jacket, shredding it like paper, finding soft flesh. The long, sharp blade plowed deep into his right shoulder, bouncing off bone, sawing through meat. The terrified man screamed again.

Spinning around, Chief Dennis side-stepped, manipulating his neck muscles to fling his head away from his body. The knife whistled past, but soon, much too soon, it came back round, aiming at his chest. In a flash, as quick as lightning, Chief Dennis' brain summed up the nature of the threat and in one frighteningly swift movement, calculated the response that would save his life. His body twisted to the side. The knife whistled past.

Panting wildly, the bulging eye-balls of the Chief followed the parry of the knife as it slithered off course, striking past his body, tampering with emptiness. He gripped the black man's arm, but Supreme snatched free from his hold. Instantly, the knife was back on course. This time it came higher, ear-level high, the hard glint of steel illuminating the squalid blackness with sparkling ferocity.

Chief Dennis stood transfixed as the blade leveled, watching as it bent itself into a crazy, looping arc. This dizzy pattern confused him, cheating him of any effective counter-move. He shrieked, knowing that payment for this miscalculation would be exacted in blood. The knife seared through his stomach, piercing his intestines, painting the blade red.

After a blood-curdling scream, Chief Dennis's arm snaked out, doubling up at the elbow, smashing down mightily upon Supreme's head. His left foot kicked out. The crunch of splintering bone was heard. He kicked once more. The knife fell free, dropping to the ground as both men emitted savage, animal grunts. They charged. Chief Dennis ignored his assailant's grappling arms and lowering his head, crashed it into Supreme's middle, relieving him of oxygen. They plummeted to the earth, rolling over and over in the grass. Chief Dennis was on top. He punched wildly at the face below him, tearing open a gash beneath Supreme's left eye. The man on the bottom clawed back, toppling Chief Dennis from his heaving chest. Again, they rolled. Over and over and over. Once again, Chief Dennis landed on top. He punched methodically.

The tired, desperate heart-beat of both men went thump in the night. Joining. Separating. Dissipating.

Supreme was weakening. Chief Dennis was encouraged. His barrage of punches intensified, time after time, finding their mark. He sensed triumph. He reached down, wrenching his left hand vise-like in Supreme's collar, pulling, elevating the black face. He drew back his fist, drenched in power. The black face drew closer; nearing. The white fist, packed with power, waited.

From deep inside the bowels of the now terrified Supreme, emanated a horrible wracking cough, a septic rumbling that spilled across the girth of his body and spewed out of his mouth in a steady, fetid stream. The vomit splashed Chief Dennis' face, smearing it with a smorgasbord of vile, putrid filth. Chief Dennis flinched. That reaction, though involuntary, was enough. Supreme dislodged him from his chest.

Both scrambled solidly to their feet.

The eyes of both men located the knife.

They let out a final, savage yell.

Both dived for the blade.

Only one of them was successful in getting it.

Chief Dennis grinned in joy. Victory was his.

Just as he made ready to finish his prey, a shot rang out and Chief Dennis collapsed.

Suddenly, Supreme felt blessed.

Chapter 28

Bright and early the next morning

"DETECTICE CHIEF FOUND DEAD!" screamed the newspaper headline after the body of Chief Dennis was discovered by a group of children on their way to school.

At around 5:30 the same evening, a burly Russian with the physique of a hockey player wandered carelessly through the aisles of the soup kitchen and had a seat on the back bench. He didn't look hungry and he didn't approach the service line where the free food was being passed out. Tanika Nelson thought this odd.

As chance would have it, just before she walked into the back of the kitchen to end her shift, she noticed a second man enter the building, then a third.

Tanika panicked, and darted inside a food cooler to collect herself. These evidently were men from the two cars she had spotted earlier. Who the hell were they? It was clear they were not bums or vagrants, but what was their objective? By God, this was a church charity.

Inside the cooler, the outside noises had quieted down until she could no longer hear the clang and clatter of the silverware scrapping across the tin plates. Still, she was starting to hyperventilate.

Struggling but determined to calm her nerves, she let the cool chill wash over her, but the moment she felt relaxed, the aluminum door was yanked open. Instinctively, she jumped to the side, but the two men were on top of her in a flash. Though she was unable to move, she shouted for help, trying to get someone's---anyone's---attention, but snarling like a mad dog, one of the men popped her in the mouth with the back of his hand.

"Shut up!"

"Who are you?" Tanika gasped, tasting the blood in her mouth. "What you want?"

The men pushed Tanika through the cooler's door. "Let's go."

Dismayed that the commotion had gone unnoticed, Tanika screamed again. "Help!"

One of the men grabbed Tanika's wrist and applied pressure until she was whimpering in pain. Then they quickly shuffled her through the back exit where two vehicles idled, sitting in the dark.

Left alone in the backseat of the lead car, Tanika's panic increased. Three men piled into the car, one in front, two in the back, and one, with amazing speed, bound and gagged her. Abruptly, the cars sped off.

When the cars made a sharp, veering right turn, Tanika's fears mounted as the car bolted past the city limits and out into the darkening county. Passing through a deserted intersection, the county grew even darker.

Several miles farther, one of the men signaled with a flashlight, and in the distance from a northeasterly direction, a beam of light streaked back through the darkness. Using the intermittent flashes to get his bearings, the driver swerved off the road onto the padded shoulder of a dirt path.

About a mile away, Tanika was snatched down into the back seat and made to huddle in the well of the floor, but she could still feel the car circle, the tires frantically crunching on the loose gravel.

The vehicle stopped.

Ten seconds passed, then another two. Finally Tanika heard footsteps followed by voices. Next she was out of the car and on her back being forcefully dragged across a path of fine, dry sand. The trees on either side of the path seemed to vee into a crossroads not too far from a steamy bay of still water.

On the front porch of a very tiny cabin, one of her captors opened the door with a key. Everyone barged in. Finding nothing particularly strange about the room, Tanika observed the men.

They frightened her. And for good reason. None of these guys were stick-up kids or car-jackers, the usual suspects she had been taught to be on the look-out for. This was something her boyfriend hadn't warned her about, and Tanika had never felt so unlucky in her whole life.

And it didn't seem as if things were going to get any better. If anything, Tanika felt that her chances for release had just grown a lot slimmer when one of the men released his shoulder holster and remover the 9mm.

"My name is Uri," the man declared in a commanding voice, "and at this moment your life is in my hands. Do you want to live?"

Tanika nodded.

Uri continued. "Good. I hope I don't have to hurt you." He then showed Tanika a photo. "Do you recognize this man?"

Tanika shook her head

Uri quickly stepped into the breach between the chair and the wall, slapping the terrified woman across her face. "Are you sure?"

The pain blurred Tanika's vision and the impact of the blow snapped her neck backwards, but she was bound to the chair and could do little more than flinch when she saw Uri raise his hand a second time. This blow hurt worse than the first one had.

"And you've never seen him in the company of your boyfriend?"

Tanika tried not to gag as she swallowed a mouthful of blood. Her boyfriend!? So this is what this was all about she thought to herself as she tried to clear her head.

She would talk.

So it had come to this.

The kidnapping of Tanika Nelson was the first visible sign of Ivan's emerging conviction that if he put the squeeze on the family members of the big-time ballers in Charlotte, that someone would tell him something about the whereabouts of Supreme and Detective Walker. He would consider the next phase when and if it became necessary. Right now, there was a second batch of people to kidnap.

The current mission was to kidnap one of the family members of each of the biggest dope dealers from each neighborhood in the city, and then to hold them until he got the info he wanted. He knew that despite the hood's well-known attitude about keeping silent, he knew that once he started to execute the hostages that someone would break.

If, by chance, he didn't get what he wanted, what would then unfold would be an all out assault upon black Charlotte. Ivan weighed this aspect of Plan B which called for the entire Beatties Ford Road area to be encircled by Uri's men while another core group invaded North Charlotte. An even larger group would push to the south and ride into Wilmore and West Boulevard.

In a way, though, Ivan somehow believed that Plan B would not be called for. He trusted that when the reports of the kidnappings started to hit the Charlotte streets that all the local ballers, playas, and thugs would get the message that he was not to be fucked with. He also knew that it wouldn't take long for them to decipher what the kidnappings were all about and to understand exactly what he wanted from them.

And he was correct. Within minutes of the news hitting the hood, Ivan knew that every nigga with loot in the city would start believing that he or one of his loved ones could be next in line to get snatched, and once the fear quotient was up high enough, someone would step forward. Ivan automatically suspected that this urban version of "chickens coming home to roost" would take an immediate toll on the Charlotte underworld which wouldn't be able to make any money because the police and the news media would have the hood under a white-hot spotlight.

"Goddamn!" Ivan cursed, shaking his head in stunned disbelief. How had this situation gotten so far out of hand? No sooner than he tried to help black thugs get rich than they set out to destroy him. Well, he would destroy them first. Almost as soon as Ivan had poured himself a shot of Grey Goose, he cursed again, only this time he cursed Supreme. Downing the drink, he suddenly felt his energy returning, but he also got an ugly mental picture of his Charlotte empire crumbling. That prickled his skin. All he had wanted to do was to introduce the international world to the beauty of the black woman. That skin, that sass, that ass.

Despite feeling the soothing warmth of his favorite drink, it still took considerable effort on Ivan's part not to snatch out his phone and to call Uri for an update. This burning desire seized him countless times but he beat back the impulse time and time again. Whenever something happened, he would be the first to know of it.

Shortly before his third drink, his phone rang. Ivan quickly answered.

"Good news," Uri muttered, "we got action."

On the surface, Ivan gave the impression that he was cool and unfazed by what he had heard, but the truth was that his insides felt like they were boiling. He spoke calmly. "How soon will everything be finished?"

At best, Uri knew not to lie although his instincts told him to. "Soon."

Ivan grunted, saying nothing.

"Why don't you go back home. Me and my people will handle it from here."

"No way," Ivan laughed bitterly. "Supreme and his bitch just might still have a few tricks up their sleeves and I don't want to be a million miles away while they continue to play cat-and-mouse with your ass."

Uri ignored the stinging rebuke. "It will be finished soon." Without dwelling on the fact that he was on a time-table, Uri sighed. "Very soon. I have total confidence in my plans."

"That is like music to my ears." Ivan chuckled. "It's times like these when murder is sweeter than money."

Ten minutes later Ivan fell into a fitful sleep. He had murder on his mind and his mind on murder. That's how sure he was that Supreme was breathing the last of his free oxygen.

Chapter 29

By three o'clock, the roomful of thugs looked shaken to the core.

"I know it ain't much of a motherfucking choice, but there it is." Butch Nelson shrugged in resignation. "We either work with the feds or we work with the Russians." He shrugged once more. "By ourself, we can't do shit but get our peoples killed." For sheer audacity, nothing in his life compared to the near-mythical spectacle he and the others in the room faced, and it failed to surprise him to know that everyone was scared as hell. "So what up?" He had to know how they were going to cope with this current crisis.

"On the up and up, I ain't wanting to be fucking with no feds," Casino croaked. He stared directly at Crewes and Babcock who had called the meeting, held in a conference room in a hotel on Nations Ford Road. "No offense, but if the feds can't catch me doing what I be doing and I ain't shit but a nickel and dime dope boy, then how the fuck they gonna stop them Russian motherfuck-as who be on some hard-core murder shit?" Casino threw his hands up in defeat. "Man, I think we got a better chance of getting our peeps back if we deal with them Russians."

"I'm wit' that," Jap Junior rasped. "Feds sat right heah and said they blew the mission with that busload of bitches. What up? You think they done got smarter overnight? They fucked that up. They'll fuck this up, only thing is that this time it'll be our peeps who take the bullet."

Crewes felt like shit. "Okay, so we don't look too good in your eyes right now, but at least you know where you stand with us. How do you know the Russians will honor their word?"

"All they want is for us to find out where Supreme is and---

--"

Babcock shook his head. "The Russians don't want you to just find out where Supreme is. They want you to find Supreme! They want you to do their dirty work for them."

"Then that's my next job," Butch Nelson cracked, "if it gonna keep Tanika safe."

"Maybe our next job", Bo Edwards snapped, "should be to posse up and tear this motherfucking city up looking for our peeps. Fuck that nigga Supreme. They want his black ass dead, let them find him and kill him theyself. My beef ain't with that nigga. My war wit' them Russian motherfuckas who done violated all of us by snatching our loved ones."

"But that's it," Casino shot back. "we don't know where Supreme is and we don't know where our folks at either. Finding one is gonna to be just as hard as trying to find the other. At least if we looking for Supreme, our people will be safe as long as we let the Russians know we trying. They done said that."

Ten minutes later, Chilly, a dope-boy from West Boulevard, asked to be heard. "Yo, I can get this shit ended." He spoke with 100% confidence. "But it's gonna cost ya."

Butch Nelson now had a question of his own. He glared coldly at Chilly. "Why you gonna carry us like that? Why we gotta kick when you helping yo'self just like you helping us. They got yo' peeps to or else you wouldn't be up in heah wit' the rest of us."

"True dat and sho' you right," Chilly said slowly. "They do gots my old lady, but da thang is, you see, is that I don't give a fuck 'bout her trifling ass. If they cap her ass, they doing me a favor. I done been tired of the gold-digging heifer a long time ago, so if you thinking I'm gonna lose sleep over not getting her ass back, then you dead wrong. Fuck that ho, but it's like I done already said, for a fee I can make everything gravy, bring this bullshit to an end."

"Yo-you know where Supreme is?" Crewes barked.

"Ain't talking to you, Mr. FBI. This shit 'tween me and my boys."

Casino stood up. "Well, I ain't the damn feds and I'm asking you. You know where that nigga, Supreme, at?"

"No disrespect, playa, but I think y'all better go check yo' stash and load me up wit' paper. I can handle my end of the deal."

The next morning when the call came in, Chilly dressed quickly and since he wasn't concerned about making a good impression on the Russian never considered brushing his hair. However he did brush his teeth, screwing up his face when he rinsed his mouth, gargling loudly with a capful of Listerine. Taking amused pleasure at the dark stubble on his chin and his bloodshot eyes, Chilly stared impassively at his reflection in the mirror. He'd looked better.

The crisp early morning Queen City air felt good on his face as he walked briskly to his car. He drove four blocks before turning left at the light. He parked. He half-listened to the zany antics of No-Limit Larry and The Morning Madhouse Crew on WPEG until a dark-colored sedan pulled up beside him.

Chilly got into the car and was driven to the new YMCA on West Boulevard. There another man climbed into the backseat.

"You have information?"

"Absolutely."

The Russian grinned broadly.

Halfway down the block, the car picked up speed.

"You know the deal. We will exchange the hostages only for relevant info. What gives? Do you know where Supreme is?"

"No."

Uri grunted. "No?!"

Chilly casually lit a cigarette. "I don't know where Supreme is, but I know somebody who does."

Uri patted Chilly on the shoulder gently. "For a brief moment, I thought I was going to have to kill all the hostages, you to." Uri leaned back. "Who is this person?"

"Dude named Randy, live over in Little Rock. I know for a fact that the guy named Supreme and a broad stayed with him for a few days."

"And you're sure about this?"

"Yeah, I'm sho." Randy is a fiend and one night when I went to his house to serve his ass, both of your peeps was there. I didn't know neither of them, but Randy called Supreme by name."

Uri pulled a photo from his jacket, handing it off to Chilly.

"Yeah, that's dude. That the motherfucka that was living with crackhead-assed Randy."

His face set in a cold mask, Uri whipped out a cell phone. He took a deep breath and relayed the info he had just received. Then in complete silence, he listened attentively as he got instructions. When the call was over, Uri's eyes were alive with fire, and Chilly was ready to swear on a stack of Bibles that the Russian emitted a menacing heat from his body. Chilly had felt it before. It was the flame of death.

"How do I find this person named Randy?"

Chilly provided the required address and directions. "Anything else?"

"Yeah, buy a wreath and dust off your black suit."

Fifteen minutes later, Russian gangsters burst in Randy's apartment.

Forty-five minutes after that

Numbed that they had been discovered, Supreme craned his neck towards the barely flickering red and white EXIT sign, then pushed Walker towards it. "We ain't got much time 'cause they already in the hotel lobby. Let's go."

The steps seemed like a maze, winding down into an underground parking lot, and when Supreme hurtled through the heavy door, tugging Walker through behind him, he was shocked at how cold the air felt. He shivered involuntarily.

Supreme squinted in the gloomy darkness, moving towards the car he had parked there just in case they had to make an emergency exit. He snatched open the door. "Hurry up! Get in!"

Speechlessly, Walker peered as Supreme fumbled to insert the key into the ignition. It was as though she was watching a movie in slow motion. She could see his fingers working, but it was as if Supreme was wearing a pair of boxing gloves. Time passed slowly until Walker was jolted back to reality as the Exit door slammed against the concrete wall with a loud metallic thud.

"Oh my God!" Walker screeched. "Here they come!"

Supreme quickly pushed Walker down into the floor of the car as he tried to start the car, but the engine refused to turn over.

"Surprise, nigga!"

"Don't shoot," Supreme yelled, "I'm unarmed."

The man with the gun stepped from the shadows. "Stop whining like a lil' bitch and face this shit like a man."

"Randy?" Supreme stared, caught off-guard. "Randy, is that you!?"

"Yeah, nigga, it's me. Surprise, motherfucka, surprise. Now, get out of the motherfucking ride." Pausing, he asked. "Where that bitch at?"

"She ran off and left me." Supreme smiled nervously. "Randy the Dandy. Man, what up? Me and you dawgs, go back a ways. Why you rolling with them other people?"

"Shut the fuck up and open the motherfucking car door so I can look inside."

Supreme winced. "Let's talk, Randy. Don't kill me, man. Please."

As soon as the words were out of Supreme's mouth, he rested his hand firmly on Walker's head, pushing her farther down into the floorboard. Then he swiftly and smoothly removed the gun from his ill-fitting jacket, shoving it into Walker's hands.

"Step out of the ride, nigga. Now!"

"Ain't no need to get heated. I ain't offering no resistance….. Let's talk, Randy."

"Get the fuck out the car. I ain't telling yo' ass twice."

"Okay, dawg, just tell me what to do."

"Put both your hands out the window where I can see them and then open the door from the outside with your right hand. Do it slowly, nigga, or you hit."

"Look, Randy, please----"

"Open the goddamn door and be the fuck quiet."

"Fuck you then, nigga. I ain't scared to die."

"Bitch-ass could've fooled me. Now open the door."

Supreme flicked the door open with his right hand and as the door swung open, he could sense Walker swinging into action. Involuntarily, he grew stiffly rigid as he felt the heat of the gunfire as the bullets whizzed past his ear. Wrinkling his nose as the first bullet knocked a hole in Randy's forehead, and after what could not be described as a pause, the second and third bullets rapidly lodged into Randy's surprised face.

"Is he dead?"

"Hell yeah," Supreme shouted over the ringing in his ears. "Now, scoot over and let me drive."

It was almost half past the hour when Supreme and Walker raced into the department store. They halted just inside the front entranceway. Supreme leaned forward, his arm cradled around Walker's waist. "Damn," he cursed, "not much of a crowd, but come on." He hustled Walker through the thin throng of shoppers, examining all the exits because he knew that soon the Russians, the feds, and God knows who else would soon swarm the building to seal them off.

"What are we going to do?" Walker inquired.

"Just act normal and don't look scared."

"But we've got to get out of here."

"And we will. Trust me." Supreme turned to the right and quickly approached the escalator. "Going up," he said. At the top of the landing, he paused only long enough to glare bemusedly at the three Russians who had just burst onto the lower entrance perimeter, scrambling around in apparent confusion. "Let's go."

Walker's heart beat like a drum as she clutched Supreme's arm tighter. "We're trapped," she groaned in defeat. "We don't have anywhere to go."

"Stop scaring yourself and stop looking around. Everything is under control."

When they reached the edge of the Appliance Center, Supreme moved to the rear of the department and advanced cautiously to a back office. He knocked softly. For several seconds, he waited, then rapped on the door again. Still no answer. He opened the door. "Wait here," he whispered, "and watch out."

Inside the musty office, Supreme ran to a glass-faced cabinet and deftly pushed the handle until it skidded in a circle to the other side. In response, the cabinet door swung open, revealing a pull-out drawer. Twisting the knob in a half circle, he slid the shelf out and greedily reached for the two sets of keys. "Thank God," he audibly prayed.

Barreling out of the office, Supreme hastily escorted Walker down a corridor that ran parallel to the office. There was total silence as he fitted the key into the lock. The key seemed to nestle inside the guts of the lock, but after a second the bolt moved grittily and then finally clicked open. Supreme and Walker immediately took shelter behind the door. Supreme locked the door back.

Walker spun around to find herself in some kind of warehouse where to the far right were rows of damaged appliances with an assortments of dents, dings, and twisted metal hanging from them. To the left, closest to them, were countless rows of brand, spanking new refrigerators, washers and dryers.

Supreme touched Walker on the shoulder. "We safe."

"H-how did you know about this place?"

"Used to work heah a while back." Supreme laughed. "Turns out to be the best damn gig I ever had."

"What happens now? We can't stay here forever."

Supreme squatted down beside a metal foot locker and pulled out two pair of work uniforms. "This one should fit you." He handed the jumpsuit to Walker. "Put that on." Crossing the room, he removed a cap from the rack and placed it atop Walker's head. "It's time to go."

"Where?"

"Anywhere you want to. Ice keeps a small private plane at the airport just in case of an emergency."

'Can you fly it?"

"Naw, but I'm calling Ice's friend who can. He'll be waiting for us."

Supreme led the way through the cramped warehouse and out of the ass-end of a tubular passageway that spat them out next to a decrepit, crumbling elevator shaft. To the left was a newer model. Both found it difficult to speak as they barged into the boxy enclosure, but they both exhaled deeply as Supreme punched the button and the elevator lurched, shook, and then moved downwards.

On the loading dock, Supreme guided Walker to one of the parked department store trucks. He kissed her on the lips. "We won, babe. It's over."

192

By two o'clock, they were in flight and as the plane reached cruising speed, a feeling of relief and celebration swept over both Supreme and Walker. They were headed for Cuba.

"You're a good woman, Miss Walker," Supreme said playfully. "The best I ever known."

"Marry me, then."

Supreme smiled. "Don't tempt me." He dropped his eyes. "I'm sorry if I got you in trouble, probably wrecked yo' life."

"You know what they say. When one door closes, another one opens." Content to let the issue rest for the time being, Walker opened a compartment door, slid a map out and plopped it in her lap. When she unfolded it, an envelope was tucked inside. "What's this?"

"Open it and see," Supreme instructed. "Must be something Ice-----"

"It's from Ice, but it's addressed to you."

"To me?" Supreme was puzzled. "Read it, see what it says."

Walker began to read. *"Nigga, if something were to happen to me, here is how to get to all my loot. I want you to have every nickel. You my dawg."*

Supreme couldn't contain himself. He felt so good he gave Walker a long kiss as a feeling of serene calm enveloped the small plane. The pair sat together in a deep quiet, hugging, gazing into each other's eyes lovingly.

Then, without warning, the pilot bailed out of the plane.

A mountain loomed ahead.

The plane exploded into flames!

EPISODE 3

short.

Supreme stopped feeling sorry for himself. After all, wasn't it said that life was simply a point between birth and death where a motherfucka was given a little bit of time to fuck as many bitches as possible, to smoke all the weed he could, and to stack paper like crazy. Well, he had done all three like a champ, so if God wanted him, he sure as hell wasn't going to be too hard to find.

Then he blacked out.

Days later
The nurse pushed the wheelchair out onto the south-side of the patio so the patient could get some sun.

"It's a great day today, isn't it, Mr. Lucky-to-be alive."

Supreme grunted. "What day is it, anyway?"

"Wednesday, the 23nd."

"Wednesday!" Deep down, Supreme knew that he was not 100% mentally sharp, but he couldn't recall losing a day or two. "What happened to the other days?"

"You were in surgery all day Tuesday."

"You mean it took that long for them to put me back into one piece?"

"You're lucky that you escaped with only a few broken bones, some scrapes and bruises, nothing major." The nurse smiled. "You're the second person I have ever met who survived a plane crash."

"Second," Supreme cracked, "who was the other person?"

The nurse looked at Supreme quizzically. "You really don't know?"

Supreme sat up straight in the wheelchair. "Know what?"

"Who the other person was? You mean they didn't tell you."

"Tell me what?" Supreme snapped."

"That the lady, Miss Walker, who was in the plane with you survived as well."

"Oh my God!" Supreme yelled. "My baby is alive! Thank you, God, Thank you." Tears streamed down his face. "I-I thought she was dead. Take me to see her."

Without delay, the nurse strapped Supreme into his

wheelchair, and after touching his hand gently, said, "And off we go."

At first, there was the enormous feeling of relief at the fact that Walker was still alive. Then, there was, for Supreme a terrible moment of anxiety. What if Walker was really fucked up? Would she blame him for her medical woes? Would she accuse him of ruining her life, of maiming her? Suddenly, this anxiety exploded into widespread panic. Of course, she would hold him responsible just like he blamed Ice.

Growing nervously excited again, Supreme had another brilliant idea. He grinned happily. Today was the first day of his forever. Then he detected a tiny flaw in his plan. What if his proposal was rejected? What if Walker said hell no?

As he was pushed down the hallway, he courted a whole new class of 'designer ideas', but none had enough flava to detour him from his original plan.   Today, he would ask Walker to marry him.

What a brilliant idea, he thought.

As he was carted onto the elevator, he kissed his old life farewell, but just before he got off on the eighth floor, he carefully went over his hopes and dreams as well as the chances of coming up with something that would make Walker want to spend the rest of her life with him. He would take his chances. Warming up to his quest, he assured himself that he had a winner.

By the time he had been wheeled out of the elevator, he had declined to do any further thinking. Now was the moment of truth where he would let his heart take over.

Although he had always felt that getting down on one knee and proposing was lame, he somehow now felt he had been misled. For some reason, he now saw the beauty of it even though he understood that he wouldn't be able to pull it off in a wheelchair.

Supreme spoke to the nurse. "Do you think you could make arrangements to have my food brought to Miss Walker's room so we can eat lunch together?"

"I don't see why not," the nurse smiled. "How can anyone deny the two luckiest people in the world. Anything else, Mister Lucky?"

Suddenly, Supreme did feel lucky. The nurse's enthusiasm was so contagious that he also felt like he could run through the rest of his life coming out on top. Maybe this was God's way of pacifying him for all the hardship He had put him through. Supreme felt joyful. Good luck was such a wonderful pacifier.

Entering the room, Supreme gazed lovingly at the bed.

"She's sleeping," the nurse whispered, "but I'll push you closer so you can get a better look at her, okay?' Once she had wheeled Supreme to the head of the bed, she hurriedly left the room. "I'll go see about your lunch request."

"Take your time," Supreme muttered, "you ain't got to be in no hurry to get back." This was, in essence, the only time since he had been in the hospital that he didn't want to be bothered with any nurses or doctors. He now had his baby to watch his back, to hold him down, to be his Boo until the end of time.

Looking nervously around him, he couldn't find any reason to keep himself in suspense any longer. He was interested in discovering just what Walker looked like now. Had her face been damaged in any way? At the moment, nothing seemed a better thing for him to do than to lift up the bedcovers and have himself a peek.

He took a big breath and eased the covers up s-l-o-w-l-y.

Supreme couldn't believe his eyes. Were they playing tricks on him? What the fuck was happening?

Once the greater sense of what was happening dawned on him, Supreme tried to push himself away from the bed, but the nurse had applied the brakes which prevented him from going either backward or forward.

"You...you are not Walker!"

The knife in the woman's hand looked shiny, new. "I know."

But before the imposter could get out of the bed, a middle-aged white man burst through the hospital room door, and pumped three bullets into the woman's body. She fell back onto the bed, staining the crisp, white sheets.

Other men rushed into the room quickly. They grabbed Supreme.

"You're safe," the man told Supreme. " Then he gave orders

to the others in the room. "Get him out of here. Now!"

The men were pros. Without missing a beat, they hustled him back out of the hospital room, to the elevator, and back down to the lower level where he was escorted out of the hospital to a waiting van. And not a damn soul tried to interfere.

"Who the fuck are you guys and what the hell just happened back there?"

"You're still alive and well," the thin, white man, Bostic, offered, "that's all I'm concerned about."

"Who cares?" Supreme looked at the man. "Look, I know the drill and I respect what you guys did for me back there, but if you will kindly let me out somewhere, I promise there won't be any hard feelings. I can make it on my own."

The man smirked. "We have orders to personally escort you to Washington in one piece."

"But why," Supreme wanted to know. "I ain't got no beef with nobody that nobody in DC should give a damn about. I believe in letting by-gones be by-gones."

In the back of the van, the men checked their weapons.

"Good job, ladies," Bostic joked in a congratulatory tone. "Now let's get to the chopper."

Supreme visibly flinched. "The last time I was up in the air, there were some technical problems like the damn pilot bailing out on me."

Bostic laughed. "Never get on a plane where the pilot is the only fucker with a parachute. Anyway, just sit back and relax, the skies will be a lot more friendly this time." After a another brief moment, Bostic felt it was time to make an acknowledgment. "Your friend, the real Sally Walker, is dead. She did not survive the crash." Oddly, the white man felt apologetic. "I'm sorry."

"What now?"

"All I know is that I'm to bring you to Washington to testify before Congress."

"Testify," Supreme barked, "about what?"

"Sex trafficking"," Bostic cracked, "what else?"

By the time Supreme said something else, he was haunted by the busy, nerve-wracking push and pull of how desperate everything now was. He knew that if he didn't testify before Congress that he would never get the help he needed to keep Ivan off his ass, and somehow he didn't actively court the desire to have the rest of his life dictated by violence and bloodshed.

Seeming to read Supreme's thought, Bostic whispered. "Ivan Gugarin is only a mortal man."

"But so am I," Supreme shot back. "Let's not forget that."Supreme paused. "You have to kill him quickly or else my life……" Supreme's breathless voice became muffled, then ended abruptly.

Bostic squared his shoulders bravely. "Don't worry, Ivan is already scheduled for some hot-lead therapy. It's not going to end well for his Russian ass. I guarantee you that."

A cloud of dark energy enveloped the van. It hovered over every nook and cranny of the vehicle, making bold contact with all the men. Following this was a period of absolute, heart-pounding silence. Then Supreme uttered the most famous words he could think of. "Kill that motherfucka!"

"Like I said," Bostic boasted, "it's a done deal, but if I may offer a word of advice. When this shit is over, I advise you to leave the street life alone." He glared at Supreme. "Now, would be a good time to learn how to flip burgers."

Getting near the top of the curved intersection, Supreme let his window down and instantly the glow of sunshine and fresh air invaded the interior of the van with a dazzling glitter. Supreme breathed greedily, aware of how sweet the oxygen seem to feel as it flickered across his parched tongue and filtered down into his constricted lungs.

The scene that happened within the next second reminded Supreme of a fast-moving clip from one of those made-for-TV action movies. There was no predicting just how fast the truck was going, but just as soon as Supreme saw it, he knew it was going to crash into them.

Gripping the steering wheel tightly, Bostic watched the approaching truck lurch forward like a great, wounded beast, clawing across the center lane, heading straight for them. At the same time Bostic realized the man would not be able to gain control of the truck, he also recognized that he wouldn't have enough time to take any extraordinary evasive measures so there was nothing he could do to avoid contact.

When Supreme grew tired of watching the truck barrel towards them, he turned away, hoping to discover a way to brace himself for the impact, but he found nothing to save him from the crash which crumpled the van like a pack of empty Newports.

This crash he wouldn't survive.

Chapter 31

Even worse than being locked up 24 hours a day in a dark basement, everything had accelerated for Brianna. Now, all the vague shit about not knowing what was going to happen to her and her friends were gone. They all were being sold.

Too her, this concept was as real as anything else she had ever believed in. Besides this, nothing else was clear except the fact that she would not be rescued. Still, she felt tormented by the fact that she had been the one who had enticed Rena and the others into this nightmare. She was also yoked to the almost unbearable burden of trying to be the one to get them out of this nightmare.

It was hell on earth. No matter what it looked like on the outside, the basement was a dark, damp, dungeon. Each of the five girls had a separate cot where they slept chained to a steel stake, planted in the floor. Makeshift alarms, which would emit a high-pitched screech, if any of the girls were to get loose, were rigged to the posts.

Set into a man-made niche in the far corner was a plastic commode that was hid from view with a sheet of black plastic. The kitchen, where the food for the girls was prepared, was on the next level above the basement. The girls ate at a card table with forks and spoons bought from a neighborhood Family Dollar Store.

The only door that led to somewhere else in the house had no knob. The bare walls had no windows, and there was no running water in the basement. The girls were so disoriented they never knew if it was day or night. They also had no clue as to the weather outside of their dungeon, and time stood still.

Whenever the girls were freed from their bed posts for some leisure time, they were handcuffed with plastic restraints, and when they were allowed to shower, they were tied to a metal chain that was fastened to a pole in the floor.

Brianna watched as Rena stirred in her restless sleep, hoping that her crying would not awaken the girl because sleep, when it did come, was the only freedom they had.

Left to her own devices, Brianna would kill herself, but how could she? There was nothing in the basement that could be used as a weapon, and she sure as hell couldn't starve herself to death. Sabrina had tried that, and they had force-fed her through IV tubes. Plus, she couldn't truly guarantee that she would have the guts to starve herself because how could she, in all actuality, encourage herself to perform an act that was so contrary to life as she knew it. Fully conscious of this fact only gave her more incentive to consider the seemingly impossible task of bringing the girls out of this ordeal alive.

Brianna's heart skipped a beat when Rena awoke in a cold sweat. Throwing the covers from her bruised body, Rena muttered about how much she hurt. Brianna knew the complaint was legitimate because the kidnappers had been ruthless in their disciplining of Rena who had refused to suck one of the men's dick.

Hurrying over to Rena's cot, Brianna did what she could to comfort her friend, but when she got there sadly realized that she could do nothing more than to gently massage the scars on Rena's back and legs which protruded from her body like train tracks.

Even though it could possibly mean jumping out of the frying pan into the fire, Brianna understood that if they were going to survive long enough to be sold, they would have to open up a new chapter in their lives. They were going to have to use their powerful sexual mystique to their advantage. So rather than attempting to hide their feminine assets, they would have to flaunt them. This was their only defense, the only weapon in their arsenal, and they had better use it or else they would face a certain early death. They were now in a crisis situation where they had to use the same thing---titties and ass--- that had enhanced their lives to now save their lives.

Brianna got an idea. She would stop worrying about when the men would rape her. Instead, she would offer them the pussy, hoping to weaken one enough so she could take advantage of any opening the weakness would give her. Suddenly, she was in no mood to die. She was prepared to fight back. After all, good pussy had been known to open more than a few doors.

The dry taste in her mouth got even drier. She would beat the kidnappers at their own game. She knew they wanted black pussy. Well, they would get it, but she and her friends would have to make it not simply a new experience. They would have to make it the best sexual experience of the men's lives. They had to make the first fuck any of the men had with a 'black Queen from America' a slightly larger version of a wet dream. Only, this would be the real thing.

If Brianna had her way, the sex had to be a thousand times better. She would tell the girls to pay special attention to all of the kidnappers' sexual needs, known and unknown, and when they introduced the men to the phenomenon of licking young, black pussy, it would have to be mind-blowing.

Brianna woke all the girls up.

"We are going to have to let our coochies get us out of this," she preached.

A week later

Even though they were not any closer to making an escape, the girls had managed to secure concessions that made their lives a whole lot better. For starters, they were not chained up all day, the food had gotten much better, and the basement had now been equipped with boot-leg cable. These 'come-ups' had given them a renewed sense of security, and they had acquired a sexual reputation that had a great influence on their kidnappers, but they all knew that in order to stop the brutal beatings, they had to continue to use coochie to pay their protection fees.

The girls felt drained, but relieved. It may not have been the best of plans, but it was an opening, a smaller part of something that could ultimately lead to something bigger.

When Brianna examined the little things she had managed to get done, she was convinced that better things were just ahead, their freedom being one of them. She was wise enough to know that it was coochie that was keeping them in the game, and she was quick to put pressure on the one thing she absolutely believed in: PUSSY POWER!

The fact that the rest of the girls sometimes didn't appreciate what she doing or didn't take pleasure from slanging pussy, it sure was a lot better than being dead.

"We don't have much time," Rena reported that evening at supper. "I found out from Igor that they plan to move us this Sunday." She looked at Brianna with fear in her eyes. "What we gonna do now, Miss Know-It-All?"

Brianna brushed off the remark. "We just gonna have to come up with something, or else somebody better come rescue our asses before Sunday."

Chapter 32

FBI agent Ronnie David felt spooked. He had just been granted immediate release from his regular duties because starting right now, he had no official assignment. He was a 'ghost'. Wasn't that a bitch?

He was a forty year, law enforcement vet, but at no time did it ever cross his mind that he would, one day, have to go back to chasing pimps. He hadn't done that shit since he had been a rookie back in Memphis. What he was then was not what he was now. Today, he considered himself a first-rate master agent, not a street fighter, although that is what he had been back in the day; a ghetto, super-cop who was out to tame the die-hard pimps who would rather 'mack' than eat.

Back then the Macks had come out of nowhere, pimping their way to the top of the hustling world. They were a bunch of pretty boys who talked slick, drove El Dorados, and who had mastered the dirty business of 'turning women out'. David's hand shook as his mind played tricks on him. It was the 70s again.

Back then no one in the law enforcement community had known a fucking thing about how vicious the pimp game was becoming until gorilla pimps like Iceberg Slim started to take the game in a new direction. Right after this, violence replaced finesses as the best way to flip a bitch.

Taking a sip of water, David shook off the mental cobwebs and snapped back into 2017. He knew what would come next, and he didn't have to wait long for the question.

"When did your obsession with pimps begin?" His supervisor scowled. "Pimping? That seems odd, especially when other, real crimes were being committed." The supervisor glared knowingly at David. "The one thing I do know to be true is that most cops develop a passion for crimes they feel really deserves their wrath, so I figure you had a good reason for chasing pimps."

It was the summer of 1972 and nineteen year old Ronnie David was in New York, having the time of his life. All of his cousins were going to the Loew's Theater on 125th Street to see 'The Mack', the movie that was all the rage at the time. He went along.

Later as he had sat in the park on St. Nicholas, he had heard an old pimp telling a young pimp that if he wanted to catch hoes that all he had to do would be to stand outside any movie theater in the country where The Mack was being shown. He told the young mack to forget about the movie. Instead, he was instructed to stand outside and to wait on the females to come out. Then the young pimp was told that all those bitches were his for the taking because why else would a female go to see a movie about selling coochie unless she wanted to slang ass herself?

Once he had returned back home, Ronnie David had wanted to watch The Mack with some of his local friends. They had opted to attend the second showing of the movie, and had made it to the theater just as people were filing out of the first showing. What he had found so absurd was that he had seen one of his sisters coming out of the movie.

Recalling the message of the old pimp in New York, he had rushed up to his sister and hadgrabbed her angrily, shaking her. He wanted to know why she had wanted to see that kind of movie, why she had wasted her money?

Six months later, she had been turned out and was hoeing.

And that was when his hatred for pimps began.

"Wow!" the supervisor exclaimed. "Now, I understand which gives me even more reason to believe that you are the right man for this mission. Young, black girls are being snatched and sold into sex slavery. Someone has got to put the brakes on this shit, or else we're going to have more faces of missing black girls on milk cartons than we do in the elementary school yearbook.

"Oh shit," David groaned. What if he was staring into the

newest edition of pimps gone wild. What if this was actually a new movement to cheat young, black girls out of the urban version of the American dream? At sixty-four years old, he sure as hell didn't need the action. "Please, be wrong about this."

The supervisor shrugged. He knew that he would have to bring the info to David's attention sooner or later, and now seemed as good a time as any. He rubbed his temples. "Have you ever heard of the legendary pimps from Atlanta; Sir Charles and Batman?"

David had not.

The station chief plopped an envelope on the desk. "In there is a video made by Sir Charles called 'Really Really Pimpin' In Da South.' The second video, 'Pimps Up, Hoes Down', explains the rules of the pimp game." The supervisor sighed. ""Take 'em home with you. Study up. And in case you're wondering what happened to Sir Charles and Batman. They went to federal prison for operating a juvenile prostitution ring."

This videos gave David a headache.

In the pimp brotherhood, there were "popcorn pimps", "finesse pimps", and "gorilla pimps". But no matter what your status was, the pimp was required to invent a world where the ho was completely dependent upon him, and if the pimp was capable of 'spreading his game like butter', then he could get rich.

Despite the fact that the game was laid down to benefit the pimp, the bitches did have one, single, solitary right. She could 'break bread' elsewhere. Under no circumstances could a ho leave the game, but she could choose to leave one pimp to be with another. David remembered that a ho who broke bread constantly by jumping from one pimp to another was called a 'Choosey Susie'.

David shook his head. The punishment for a bitch who went against the rules of the game was severe. She get her ass whupped with the 'pimp stick' (two clothes hangers braided together) or she could get 'trunked' which meant she would be locked into the trunk of a car for a certain period of time.

Shit was serious.

After viewing the tapes, David went over all the documents

left by a now deceased detective, Sally Walker, who had been the first to link individuals such as Ice and Supreme to the wave of terror that was now sweeping through black neighborhoods.

Back in the day, he, like everyone else had no real clue as what it would be like to lose a whole generation of black girls to the 'fast track'. At the time, no one could have imagined the damage that was being done by the seeds that were being planted in the 70s.

David understood that nowadays, no one mentioned that it was during the golden age of black radio that cheap commercials helped lure sistas to their present state of immorality. As part of their daily grind, black radio disc jockeys, with their smooth talk and fancy lines, constantly invited black women out to nightclubs to participate in Hot Legs, Big Butt, and Wet T-shirt contests. Once the idea caught fire that they could cash in on their butts, titties , and legs, sistas started displaying themselves in public in pursuit of a dollar. The other pieces of the puzzle started falling into place once black women, who were the benefactors of such great physical assets, decided to not only show their asses in clubs, but to shake their asses in clubs.

The grind was real.

Chapter 33

By the end of the second week of the new year, January 11th, FBI agent David had been reassigned to Charlotte, and had got his first assignment, and by the end of the month still hadn't made any progress. He had visited all the gas stations and convenience stores inside the large perimeter around the Glenwood Avenue neighborhood where the young girl had been abducted. No one had seen shit.

The entire morning had been eaten up by his need to connect the dots, and he had counted on the convenience stores and gas stations in and around Hoskins and Hovis Roads to be a good jump-off point for his investigation for two good reasons: a kidnapper's great unintentional fear of running out of gas, and a twelve year old girl's intentional craving for sweets. Both never thought they could have enough of either.

So far the person who had snatched Ebony Jenkins had steered clear of all the places he had targeted.

Dammit.

No problem. He would just had to expand his search area. If he could just get something or someone on camera. He was enticed by that idea, but he had no clue if the kidnapper smoked, chewed gum, drank coffee, or did any of the other countless things that might bring him to a convenience store or gas station.

He was worried because his probing mind was well-suited for such a job, but this mental game kept tossing up the same need---gas.

After a burger and fries lunch at the Stockyard Restaurant on Rozzelles Ferry Road, he hit another Kangaroo Express next to a highway exit off I-85. The security camera gave him nothing. He decided on a long shot and ventured way out into the county, heading towards Newton.

At his next stop, a man with a prosthetic left leg hobbled out even before David was out of his car. "Fill 'er up?"

David stared at the LIncoln's fuel hand, and felt angry that he didn't need gas. He smiled lamely at the crippled man, shaking his head. "Probably can use a quart or two of oil, though." He tried to think of something else the car might need, wondering how the man made a living way out here.

While the man checked under the hood, David fixed his eyes on the harsh landscape across the road. Basically, what he saw was a hollowed-out scoop of hell. It was like a postcard for the garbage-pail kids.

When the man brought out the oil, David paid with a twenty dollar. "Keep the change," he said. "By the way, you wouldn't happen to have any working, security cameras----"

"Sure, I do."

David flashed his badge. "I'd sure as hell like to see the videos from a few days ago."

The poor quality of this footage was more pronounced than in any of the others he had viewed so far. It was almost completely a mix of white lines and fuzzy static. David yawned, but just as his boredom reached its peak, he was jolted upright and frozen stiff. The hazy image of Ebony Jenkins zoomed onto the screen.

David stopped the frame, and jiggled the controls, hoping to make the image clearer, but nothing helped. It didn't matter because he was positive that the little girl standing at the back of a Jaguar was the girl who had recently been snatched.

"Move, Ebony, dammit, girl," David cursed at the screen, "get out of the fucking way. Move out of the damned way." He sounded hysterical, and he groaned bitterly because there was someone just outside the frame that he couldn't see.

In the very next frame, he still couldn't see the person, but he did see a part of the body. It was a hand and David was certain that it was a woman's hand.

The parting shot was of the expensive car as it lurched

forward in an elongated blur as the sun's ray bounced off the chrome headlights. Grabbing one final look, he tried to see what else he could see through the dark-tinted window. Though he couldn't truly see shit, what he could make out from the driver's feminine silhouette was that she was tall.

Just as he started to turn the video off, he saw one more thing of interest. He watched as the driver opened the window and flicked out a cigarette butt.

"The bitch smokes," he muttered.

When David had learned, later that evening, that the Jaguar was registered to a Helen Jacobs, he didn't count on the woman to be a school teacher or a health care provider. He already had her pegged as a female pimp, but he was dead wrong. Helen Jacobs was a rich, white bitch who lived out in the suburbs. It turned out her Jag had been stolen.

He felt sick to his stomach, like he had just been kicked in the gut by a white-mouthed mule. He knees wobbled because he felt that he should run as far away from this case as he could. Already, he was clutching at straws.

When he had initially thought of calling his daughter back home in Nashville to make sure his granddaughter was being watched after carefully, he dismissed the idea. He didn't wish to offend his daughter. Of course, she was taking precautions to make sure that the 'body snatchers' didn't get her little girl. Needing someone to talk to, he called a friend instead.

"I know this may sound silly , but what is it about black women and this obsession with their bodies?" David paused. "Whatever happened to the old saying about beauty coming from within?" He sighed. "As a psychologist, I figured you might know. And while you're at it, why do black women, as much shit as they talk, have such low self-esteem?"

"Slavery."

"Slavery? I thought that was over a few centuries ago." David grunted. "Come on, Michelle, you're going to have to do better than that."

"Can you imagine how hard it was for black women to find their femininity? Slavery sure as hell didn't give us any. We were worked in the fields just as hard as the men, so when we were freed from bondage, we didn't know a damned thing about how to be feminine. What did we know about hair, nails, or makeup? That meant we had to discover our own femininity, had to define ourselves. Of all the women on the planet, black women are the only ones that had to learn how to be feminine. All we had was a blank slate on which to draw ourselves, but we didn't have anything to go on but our physical assets so we used that as our foundation. Therefore, titties and ass became the building blocks of black womanhood."

"I'm sorry."

"And your black ass should be."

"Why, what I do?"

"Black men let black women down big time." Michelle shook her head. "We expected so much more from you bastards. Do you know why? We were there, Ronnie. The black woman was there, a personal eyewitness to everything you had done for the white man. We saw how you made crops grow like magic from a earth that wasn't supposed to produce crops. We saw how you erected grand homes out of sticks and stones for the massa." There was bitterness in her voice. "We were there, Ronnie. We witnessed all the marvelous shit you guys did as slaves, so quite naturally, we assumed that you fuckers were going to do the same for us once we were free. We expected you lazy, no-good motherfuckers to go out and to conquer the world for us, but you guys were bigger bitches as free men than you had been as slaves."

Unable to conceal her disappointment, Michelle hung up.

David wasn't about to call back.

Chapter 34

From across the room, fifteen year old, Benji Latham, realized he was being watched. It was Mike-Mike, his Mama's young, thuggish boyfriend. Benji's body grew warm as the man looked him up and down slowly, and then sought him out with his eyes. Mike-Mike's eyes gave a warm welcome as Benji moved out of sight.

As soon as the party was over Mike-Mike approached Benji. "I thought that shit was never going to end." He laughed. "Your Moms has good intentions, but she gonna spoil yo' baby brother and make him soft. Can't have that shit in the hood 'cause we in the jungle, and the motherfucka who ain't got no heart ain't gonna clock no paper, you dig?"

Benji looked uncertain.

Mike-Mike stepped closer to Benji. "I know I ain't yo' Pops, but right now, I'm yo' Mama's peeps, so that gives me the right to come at you like this heah. Plus, you probably gonna find out sooner and later, and I feel like it's my duty to keep you from finding out the hard way, that is if you open." Mike-Mike shrugged his shoulders. "If you ain't, you ain't."

"Go head, then, Mike-Mike, kick it."

Mike-Mike pulled out a roll of money. "Come closer, get a good look. All them motherfuckas hundreds and fifties. Real paper."

Benji peeked at the money greedily.

"Shit pretty, ain't it?"

Benji nodded stiffly.

Mike-Mike licked his lips. "A motherfucka should

215

never be afraid to tell another motherfucka exatly what's on his motherfucking mind." When Mike-Mike handed Benji a fifty dollar bill, he caressed the young boy's hand. "You a fine motherfucka, Benji."

They were standing face to face in the hallway when Karen walked up. "Oh, there my two niggas. I was beginning to think ya'll had gotten missing on a bitch." Karen pointed her finger at her son. "Benji, you better listen to Mike, nigga know some shit, don't you, baby?"

"Yep, and I'm fixing to school this nigga real good and proper so his come up will be as smooth as butter." Mike-Mike thumped Benji in his chest. "Put together a crew and let me teach you how to get some of this free money."

Not much later

For sure, the new crew of young niggas should have known that life as thugs wouldn't be easy, and Benji had to fight against the impulse to slap one or two around just for the hell of it. He had the three young boys lined up in formation, and as he drew level with each one of them, he laid a stiff finger on each of their noses.

"Who don't understand that I'm the boss of this crew?"

Benji was pleased, almost joyful. He paused in front of Jamie, clenching and unclenching his fists. "What about you, J-Dawg? Yo' understanding don't need fixing or nuthin', do it?"

"You the boss, Boss."

Benji reached into his back pocket and angrily yanked out a crumpled sheet of notebook paper. He thrust it at Jamie. "Since you so smart, I want you to read this heah shit on this heah piece of paper."

For a second, it looked as if Jamie wasn't going to read the paper. He just stared at it.

"Out loud, dammit!" Benji yelled. "Read the motherfucka out loud."

Jamie read slowly, his voice cracking. "On this.....day..... before---."

Benji snatched the paper out of Jamie's trembling hand. "I'll read it myself. Bow down!" he thundered, "and listen."

The boys all knelt.

Benji stood tall. He read. "On this day, before all we love and hold dear, it is hereby proclaimed to the whole motherfucking world that we are a crew, and starting right goddamn now, we gonna be known as The Come Up Kids!"

When he had finished reading both sides of the paper, he made them stand and they burned the document, each boy striking a match to the paper. Then Benji led them in prayer. After the prayer, he rewarded each member of his crew with a knife.

Following Benji's example, the boys opened their store-bought knives and thrust the blades defiantly into the sky.

"WE ARE THE COME UP KIDS!" they cheered.

Three days later, Benji addressed his crew once more.

Though he was only fifteen, Benji spoke like a seasoned vet of the streets. "Which one of you bustas got a beef with stacking paper?" The basketball game was forgotten about. "Cars. Bitches. Reefer. Gotta pay for that shit and since we ain't no rap stars on the come up, we gotta claw our way out of the hood the best way we know how." He kicked the basketball over the fence. "Ain't none of us gonna get no damn call from the NBA, NFL neither." He looked his friends in the eyes. He quoted the bible. "When I was a child, I spoke as a child. I did childish things." He thumped his chest. "Well, I ain't no fucking child no mo' so I'm finished wit' all that peewee bullshit. It's all about getting paid, about getting the motherfucking ends."

"Money the shit," Baby Rip added. "We needs to get rich."

Benji pulled a wrinkled newspaper out of his back pocket. "Been keeping up with the prices of cars and shit. In a lil' while, if we do this thang for Mike-Mike and them, we will be able to get us a nice ride. Man, just think. Our own transportation."

"Who gonna drive it?"

"Since the motherfucka gonna belong to all of us, we'll all take turns driving the bitch." Suddenly, Benji balled the newspaper up and punted it over the fence like he had done the basketball earlier. "Fuck that. Got a new plan. What about if we all bought us some motor scooters."

217

Baby Rip liked that idea. "That's the kind of shit I'm talking 'bout."

Benji interrupted Baby Rip long enough to pass out a crisp twenty dollar bill to each of his three friends. "Do somethin' nice for yo'self," he said graciously. "Get used to this, my niggas, because spending motherfucking paper is something that we, 'The Come Up Kids', gonna be doing a lot of."

Baby Rip threw his hands in the air. "Raise the roof, motherfuckas."

After the celebrations had died down, Benji took center-stage again. "Y'all gonna love me for the surprise I got Mike Mike to give us."

"What is it?"

"Don't trip. Just meet me at the clubhouse when it gets dark."

What The Come Up Kids called a clubhouse was nothing more than an old abandoned house with no lights or running water, but tonight it wouldn't matter.

"This is Valentine's Day, Thanksgiving, The Fourth of July, and Christmas all wrapped up in one. Oh yeah, I forget to throw in there about when it snows and there ain't no damn school. Anyway, it's all them shits and more." Benji clapped his hands and immediately a naked, full-grown woman crawled in on her hands and knees.

Wow!

Once the woman had let everyone play with her pussy , Benji got the party really started when he stuck the first 'ceremonial dick' down the woman's throat. After this, Benji stepped aside, declining to participate further.

"This is for y'all," he commented grandly. "Treat yo' dick real good."

Right away the boys sexually swarmed the woman, greedily searching for somewhere to slide their dicks.

"Whoa, my niggas, slow the fuck up," Benji warned. "Ain't but so many holes available so you gonna have to take turns or you might poke the bitch's eyes out."

Two hours later when the orgy was over and the woman

gone, Benji clapped his hands to get everyone's attention. Now, we in debt to Mike-Mike and them, but it's all good. To pay our dues, all we gotta do is to trick that phat young bitch, Shanna, out of her Mama's house, and get her to come down to the store."

"Then what?" Baby Rip wanted to know.

"Then the body-snatchers gonna get her ass," Benji laughed. "J-Dawg, you gotta make the call. The bitch like you." Benji handed a phone to Jamie. "Man up, nigga. Make that call."

To prove just how down he was with the come up, J-Dawg punched in the phone number.

"Hello."

"Shanna, this heah yo' nigga, J-Dawg."

"Oh, hi, Jamie. Who phone you on?"

"Don't worry 'bout that. What you need to be thinking on is 'bout this good green I got. It's fire. You wanna get down?"

Shanna was excited. "When?"

"Right the fuck now. You can come out the house, can't you 'cause if you can't then that'll mean that I'll have to find somebody else to blaze up wit'."

"I ain't said nuthin' 'bout I wasn't coming. Where you at, anyway?"

"Meet me at the store in about fifteen minutes. I'm right across the street from there right now, so what up?"

"Don't go nowhere, boy. I'm on my way."

A week later

"You see," Benji ranted before the funeral, "this is what a bitch gets when she doesn't follow the script. Bitch know she wasn't s'posed to try to escape and run away. That's a classic case of a bitch trying to do too much."

Nearly all of The Come Up Kids suspected that Jamie, J-Dawg, Martin felt guilty about Shanna's death. After all, he was the one who had lured her out of her Mama's house where the body snatchers could get at her.

"We better get ready for the funeral," Baby Rip said softly. "We got to carry the casket so it won't look right if we late."

"Look alive," Benji commanded. "We still The Come Up

Kids. After we say goodbye to Shanna, we gonna say hello to some hell-raising. Let's look alive."

During the funeral, Jamie was uncomfortable. The contrast between life and death was too clearly illuminated at a funeral, and already he had decided he didn't like them. It was well-established that your first kiss, your first shot of pussy would always call up unbearably pleasant memories. There is also a dramatic impulse to feel good about your first day at school, your first day at summer camp. Your first funeral conjured up no such pleasant memories.

Jamie was ready to go home. To shut out the pain and misery of the funeral, he launched into a daydream where he was getting his dick sucked. He concentrated more intently on his imaginary lover, and in terms of sheer size, the daydream was stimulating, but when the choir started singing, it knocked his fantasy aside. Even the thought of good pussy was not strong enough or big enough to shut out the pain and anguish of a burial.

The preacher, Glover Redding, stood over the casket, giving the police a tongue-lashing, calling them shareholders in Shanna's murder.

Listening to the preacher, Jamie felt something deep within him began to thaw. He struggled to put the freeze back on, but it was too late.

Jamie wept.

Almost midnight

The blunt and the warm water had calmed Benji down some. He appeared relaxed as he absently slapped at the mountain of Calgon bath beads bubbles. He playfully snatched up a handful of the bubbles and blew them at Mike-Mike as he walked into the bathroom.

Mike-Mike blew a kiss in return.

Benji looked away. "I ain't wanting to kill nobody."

"You stop bringing me hard-headed hoes and it won't be no drama."

"Why don't you put a damn ad in the paper," Benji shot back.

"Lean back, young'un. No bullshit. Don't get it twisted.

Just because you doing me don't mean I won't bust a cap in yo' dumb ass. Them hoes out there worth five grand apiece, so get you some money, motherfucka."

"My bad." Benji whispered.

"You wanna eat somethin' before I drop you off." Mike-Mike stuck his tongue out. "Plus, the next time we get together, I want you to make it up to me for the shitty way you acted today. What you gotta say 'bout that?"

"Let's just wait and see, how 'bout that?"

That was so funny that Mike-Mike laughed, but the first thing he noticed when the laughter stopped was that his phone was ringing. He scowled at it evilly, but picked it up just the same.

The voice on the other end got his attention. "You gonna need to come by the drive-through tonight 'cause Imma have some pick-ups for you."

"That's great." Mike-Mike sounded cheerful. "Get money, my nigga. Get the fuck paid." He chuckled happily. "If a nigga broke, it 'cause he wanna be broke. Snatching bitches the best hustle to hit the hood since crack, and I ain't the kind of nigga to blow no opportunity like this heah. Imma stack my ends."

Apparently, a lot of other people thought the same way.

Chapter 35

Ever since learning of the so-called "Cash 4 Coochie" grind that was sweeping through urban America like an out-of-control wildfire, Sandra Benson had already cashed in once. It had provided her with enough money to buy herself a mountain of crack, but now the rocks were gone, and she was leaning on the bottle of cheap wine to get her sloppy drunk so she could be protected from the demons of her crack addiction.

"Shit!" She had the urge to bash her head into the wall. Her mouth was wide open and her breath came out of her mouth smelling like stale, day old onions and French fries. She had to get high.

She took a cold shower to de-sensitize herself, but after toweling herself dry, she was facing a decision. Up until now, she was not sure if she would snatch another bitch. Now, it simply a matter of when…..and who.

She put on her clothes, and in the space of five seconds had decided which of her nieces would be the next to come up missing. Suddenly, she became very competitive. This was a chance of a lifetime, and she was going to trap off as many bitches as she could. Mo' honey. Mo' money. The temptation to put some paper in her pocket was just too good to pass up. Already, she felt rich.

Sandra wanted to make a good choice, but the momentum was putting so much pressure on her, she could hardly think straight. Her blood-shot eyes rolled back in her head. Then she brightened. Her brother had four daughters, so surely one of those young bitches would do. Any one of them would make a perfect sacrifice.

She made the call that would get her paid.

"Aunt Sand. How are you doing?"

"I'm okay, girl, but.....well, let me ask you something. Have you seen that movie with Taraji P. Henson in it?"

"No," Angie replied, "but I want to. Everybody say that it's like that."

"Well, I got two tickets. I was thinking about inviting---."

"I wanna go, Aunt Sand. I ain't got nuthin' to do or nowhere to go. When we gonna go?"

"Tonight. I'll pick you up just as soon as it gets dark."

Angie smiled. "I'll be ready. Thanks, Auntie."

"No. Thank you." Sandra giggled. "Yo' company will enrich me."

Meanwhile. Across town.

"Yeah," the girl answered hesitantly. "Who is this?"

"A friend."

"Who?"

"Are you alone?"

"Yeah."

"Can you talk privately?"

"Yeah, I guess."

"Do you want me to lick your pussy?"

"What?!" the fourteen year old girl exclaimed.

"You heard right," the man purred softly. "Do you want me to suck your pussy?" He paused. "It's me, Val, your internet boyfriend, Kevin."

The line went dead.

"Remember how I always told you that one night I was coming. You do remember me telling you that, don't you?"

"I remember."

"Well, let me ask you something else. Do you still want your pussy licked?"

"Umm-hmm, I do."

"If you want me to pull down your panties and stick my tongue in your pussy, then all you have to do is to slip out of your backdoor. I'm right across the street in a red car. Come on, Val, be a big girl. Come, get your pussy sucked. Let me make you cum."

Val was excited. "And you gonna bring me back?"

"Of course. Are you coming?"

"Yes, I'm coming so I can cum."

Kevin was already counting the money he was going to get from the impending sale. This was his third girl this month.

Even later that same night.

She was a sexy, little thing. Happy Jack stood apart, looking the girl over, almost certain that her phat, juicy ass would split the seams of her jeans any moment. He had not expected quite a catch.

He knew that he had to stop staring and get his shit together. The rec center would be closing soon, but he wasn't too worried. He had enough charm to seduce any sixteen year old girl on the planet, and this magnificent one should not be any harder to pull than any of his other 'fishes' had been.

Weighing his options, Happy Jack swiftly rehearsed his opening line.

"So you like basketball?" he said .

The girl turned up her nose at the dark-skinned stranger. "I play basketball?"

"You do?"

"Evidently, you don't come here much 'cause if you did, you would know who I was."

"Excuse me, my bad. I appreciate you straightening me out."

"No problem," the girl snapped.

"Well, I tell you what I'm going to do to show you that there are no hard feelings." Happy Jack smiled. " I'm going to call one of my partners up and see if he can't help you snag a shoe deal. My dawg, you see, is a sports agent, got mad connections."

"Oh shit," the girl gushed. "You got it like that? You can put me down?"

"Sure. Why not. By the way, what's your name?"

"Jameka."

"Okay, Jameka, what about this. I don't want you to think

that I can't deliver so this is what I'm prepared to do." Happy Jack paused as if he was thinking. "Okay, let me know what you think about this." Happy Jack grinned slyly. "Why don't you let me buy you seven pairs of Air Jordans?"

"Seven?"

"One for every day of the week."

"Wow! Seven pairs!"

Happy Jack touched the girl's arm. He pointed. "Are those your friends over there?"

"Sorta."

"Do you want to go with them……or with me?"

"With you," Val answered quickly. She wanted those sneakers.

They did not speak again until he had herded the girl into the station wagon. Happy Jack rubbed the girl's leg. "You a fine, young thang."

Happy Jack, a man who delighted in mixing business with pleasure, decided to rape the girl before he sold her. Talk about killing two birds with one stone!

Chapter 36

Speedway Lake sat in the hub of an U-turn, down along a strip of used car lots where brightly-colored confetti flapped noisily in the breeze as you drove past to get to the water.

Under the watchful eyes of several local cops, FBI agent David helped to fish the backpack out of the lake. As soon as the backpack, filled with schoolbooks, was pulled out of the water, everyone seemed to speak at once. "Hey, David, does that belong to the kidnapped girl?"

"Naw, I don't think so." David's voice sounded so fake that he knew no one believed him. "I think this is different." He grimaced. As soon as he saw the name inscribed inside one of the books, he knew. It was another one. The book-bag belonged to the latest kidnap victim, a fourteen year old girl from the Eastside.

Less than one hour and a half later, the streets were no longer empty. The citizens of the city were wide awake, and starting to go about their business which meant that soon everyone would be aware that another black girl had been lost to this current madness; kidnapped from the bus-stop on her way to school.

The headlines in The Charlotte Observer were not nice, and throughout the morning, the intensity kept right on building, fueled by unending, relentless news coverage. Young Pamela Smith's senseless kidnap was broadcast in every detail as every reporter in town kept busy by stirring the flames of the city's discontent.

By mid-morning, the 'kiddie kidnaps' had boiled the city's

collective temperature too near hysteria. It was so fever-pitch high that by noon, angry black parents walked off their jobs, and stormed into local schools, demanding their children.

And the panic was just beginning.

When the Mayor issued a curfew, it was ignored. Thousands of black people, and some whites as well, refused to stay inside. They deliberately ignored the curfew, gathering in city parks, on street corners, and walking in large packs down the middle of town, daring the cops to arrest them.

It seemed that, for once, black people had had enough and weren't going to take it any damned more!

Chapter 37

Seventy-two hours later

After a while Karen stopped arguing.

"And that's why I feel certain that your son, Benji, is involved with the Cash 4 Coochie scandal along with your boyfriend, Mike Everett. With your help, I think your son will assist us."

Karen stared at David blankly. She felt half-dead, still unable to believe what she was hearing. Mike-Mike, a child molester! Before she could protest, she thought of Benji. And in quiet desperation glanced at the glossy photos of her boyfriend sucking her son's dick.

Was this a bad dream?

"I-I must be dreaming all this," Karen sputtered. "This can't be true, none of it. No way. Mike would never do that to Benji."

David gestured with his hands. "A picture is worth a thousand words." This was not the time for Mr. Nice Guy. "Bear with me as I go over a few things with you, alright?" He gently touched the back of Karen's hand. "You said earlier that you had allowed your friend, Sandra Benson, to borrow your red Honda on the night that one of the kidnappings occurred?"

"Yes, yes, yes," Karen shrieked.

"And that is the car right there?" David pointed to the photograph.

Karen nodded numbly.

Next, David forced Karen to look at the photos of the dead black girls. "These are the lucky ones because, for them, it's over. They can't be hurt any more. They're free. But what about the girls that are missing? They are going to be sold and used as sex toys, but after a while, when they get strung out on drugs, they won't give a damn."

Karen needed a blunt and a stiff shot of Hennessey.

David leaned closer. "Black girls are in danger."

Karen shook her head in dissent.

David nodded. "Sex trafficking is real, and it's happening now." He scowled. "And the money is good. There are very reliable sources that indicates that a single girl can earn a pimp up to quarter of a million dollars a year." He frowned. "The money must be pretty good on the other end as well because in North Carolina and elsewhere, a number of women have personally sold their daughters to sex traffickers."

Karen still wasn't convinced. "That shit be happening to white girls, not us."

"A whole lot of people right now in DC would disagree with you since a lot of black and Latina girls have been kidnapped there recently." David shrugged. "The Department of Justice reports that black and Latina girls, all of a sudden, make up 64% of girls forced into the sex trade."

Karen shook her head in disbelief. "This shit is crazy."

"Help me save those girls. Tell me where you son is so I can talk to him. He'll do the right thing. He's a good boy, Karen. He'll man up."

Karen spoke quietly. "Every night, him and his friends go down by the park to smoke weed. They'll be there tonight."

David sighed in relief. Now, at last, he was getting somewhere.

Eventually, David knew his breathing would calm down, but at the moment, his instincts told him that something just wasn't right. What was Benji and his friends up to, he wondered, almost aloud. He had been following them for thirty minutes, and they had passed the park a long time ago. He had no inkling of where they were now heading.

Next, they emerged from behind a closed parking lot and swarmed across the empty street, moving in a wrinkled line, talking shit to each other.

David's ear pricked up trying to hear what was being said, but he was too far away. He watched mutely as the boys dashed into the consuming dark of an open field, still talking shit.

A quarter mile farther on, they turned onto a dirt road. They slowed down. David reckoned that they must be close to their destination, but all he could see in the distance was a mess of blackness that hovered defiantly over the forked road. The boys followed the fork that led to a small building. A couple of yards beyond a naked oak tree, David recognized the building to be a church. His stomach knotted in apprehension. Surely, these boys had not come as worshippers. He felt that something was very, very wrong.

David allowed himself no time to play guessing games. His whole body was now aflame with the terrible dread of knowing that he was on the cutting edge of some brilliant new bullshit that was about to occur right before his eyes.

Watching the boys fan out like small soldiers, he, without giving it a second thought, whipped out his gun. He sensed that something horrible was about to happen. All the signs were there.

At the back of the rickety fence, the boys halted, taking position. David crawled closer. He peered through the emptiness, spotting Benji. He didn't want to lose sight of him.

Suddenly, a match flared, and David harbored hope. Perhaps, they had simply sneaked out here, in the middle of nowhere, to smoke marijuana. He spent a few seconds trying to convince himself that reefer was reason enough for all the secrecy and mystery, but just when he considered turning and crawling away, he heard a sound he clearly recognized. The clacking, metallic snap of a bullet clip being slapped into an automatic pistol.

David's heart pounded as he counted inside his head each time he heard the metallic clack. "Damn," he mumbled softly. They all were strapped.

Before he could decide what to do next, the door of the

church opened, and the worshippers began to file out. Everything slowed down as David felt himself raising up on one knee, almost halfway vertical.

The boys were going to open fire on the church-goers! David's first shot rang out, and it blasted the night to smithereens, but, as intended, the bullet landed harmlessly in the ground behind Benji and his friends.

"BENJI!" David screamed at the top of his lungs. 'EVERYBODY DROP YOUR GUNS!"

Seeing him, one of the boys dropped his weapon. Another ran. Then another followed. Benji turned around. He fired.

The next thing David knew he was no longer running in the same direction. Now, instead of moving forward, he was tumbling back, tripping over the red-hot darkness, falling down heavily. He was leaking blood.

Karen was worried sick. It was as if she had aged ten years within the last ten minutes. David had not called, and he had promised to call at eight. It was now nine.

Was something wrong? Had he changed his plans?

Where was Benji?

She sat patiently through the first half of American Idol, but the suspense inside her head was too much for her to keep still. She paced the floor. Somehow, David had managed to find out that Benji was supposed to sell Mike-Mike some girls, and for some reason he couldn't explain, he had a premonition that tonight would be that night.

Suddenly, Karen was afraid for her son. It was now 9:30. She couldn't take it any more so she grabbed her gun, and exited the house. She would confront Mike-Mike and Benji. This would be one sale they wouldn't make.

Mike-Mike was furious.

He shifted restlessly on the bar stool at the kitchen counter, peeking out of the window. Benji was late. *Young motherfucka!*

He stood up angrily, and he stared at his watch in horror. The latest he could wait on Benji was 11:30, so that meant he might be forced to leave without the girl Benji was scheduled to deliver .

Ten minutes later when there was a knock at the door, he froze in place, running a silent check over his plans. His biggest problem now would be to get to the rendezvous spot before the Russians left at midnight.

Mike-Mike opened the door, but when he saw Benji, he gasped. "What the fuck happened to you?" He angrily marched Benji to the bathroom where he examined him. "What tiger jumped on you?"

"Shut the fuck up, nigga," Benji said heatedly. "I don't want to hear that bullshit."

"*Bullshit?!*" Mike-Mike exploded. "You think it's bullshit when you walk yo' ass up in heah, empty-handed. That mean that 'cause of yo' no hustling ass, I'm gonna miss out on some paper. Tell me, where the bullshit at?"

"So, that's how it is?"

"That's how, what is?"

"I'm standing heah, bleeding like a bitch on the motherfucking rag, and you ain't asked shit 'bout my well-being."

"Wash up and stop bitching." Mike-Mike tossed Benji a face towel. "I'm gonna run you some bath water."

Moments later, Mike-Mike felt relieved as he slipped out of his robe, and eased into the tub of warm, soapy water.

"Let's chop it up for a minute," he said pleasantly. "What the hell jumped off out there tonight?" Mike-Mike soaped up the wash cloth. "I hope you don't mind me reminding you that I warned you not to try to snatch that church girl even though she did have a big ol' butt. Anyway, what happened?"

"I'm not sure."

Mike-Mike sighed. "Whatever happened, you can trust me." He washed one of Benji's arms, then the other. "It's not like you killed somebody."

Benji laughed bitterly. "If only you knew."

Karen was out of her car now. She dashed to the front door of Mike-Mike's house and felt foolish that she couldn't knock. She prayed that David was inside, and prayed that he had left the door unlocked. She twisted the knob.

Locked!

Instantly, her whole body shook with panic. It was as though her brain had become engulfed with fire, and there was no way to release the flame. She boiled.

She felt weak. The locked door probably meant that David was not inside the house. Why would he locked himself in? That made no sense to her. She stared at the door again. Tried it once more. *It was still locked!* The locked door may have suggested that David wasn't in there, but it sure as hell didn't mean that her son wasn't.

She turned her head away, and smashed the glass with the butt of her gun.

She stepped inside, annoyingly surprised at the soothing peace that smothered the house. All was quiet. At least, that was the impression she got downstairs, but for once in her life, she was not content with what she felt. She kicked off her shoes; her senses could be fooled, but she was determined not to be tricked. She deliberately hefted the gun in her hand, clicking the safety off.

Heading up the steps as quiet as a mouse, she made up her mind to shoot to kill if the need arose. Somehow, she felt the need would arise.

At the top of the stairs, she began to feel dark and aggressive. She looked around in the shadows, and half-expected to see David, but she didn't. Unfazed, she tip-toed towards Mike-Mike's bedroom. She stopped, trying to hear, but she heard nothing. She continued to move forward.

She shifted the gun restlessly from one hand to another before deciding to leave it in her right hand, her dominant hand, her writing hand; the hand she stirred her coffee with, the hand that had rocked Benji's cradle. Her shooting hand.

Moving down the hallway, she went cold with fright. Voices, only slightly heard, came from the bathroom. Straining, she could make out the voices more clearly, and she recognized them both. Her son's. Her boyfriend.

Karen's knees buckled.

A jumbled howl of protest went off inside her head. There

had to be a better way to break up a romance than by smashing a window, entering the house illegally, and then abducting her son at gunpoint. But she didn't give a damn. Tonight would be the last night her boyfriend sucked her son's dick, or sold another girl into bondage.

Karen thought it over. In theory, this was it, the end of the road for a romance that was supposed to last forever. "Dammit, Mike-Mike," she whispered softly. "Why, nigga, why?!"

With tears streaming down her face, and the gun dangling low, she took a deep breath to steel herself before bursting into the bathroom. Several things occurred at once, but what she saw erased away her weariness.

She fired the gun!

The dim light of the gun's flash cleared quickly, and when she peeked through the slit in her almost closed eyes, she screamed. "Oh my God!" Mistakenly, she had shot her son.

Benji slumped over in the tub, bleeding profusely. She dropped the gun and ran to the tub. Dragging her son out of the water, she pleaded with Mike-Mike. "Help me."

"Bitch," Mike-Mike croaked evilly, reaching for a gun under a towel "now, it's yo' time to die."

On a chilly Sunday morning, Benji died.

The day before, a bright, sunny Saturday, Ronnie David had been buried, his casket flanked by two columns of stiff-walking federal agents.

Karen had been devastated.

Mike-Mike's body had been claimed by out-of-state relatives, and flown up North to be cremated. The nigga had done too much damage for her to shed any tears in his behalf. For everyone in town, it was good riddance.

She was still baffled by everything that had happened because only now was she truly learning about the "Cash 4 Coochie" conspiracy that Mike-Mike had spear-headed, and that her son, Benji, had been a part of. Now they both were dead. And what about her friend, Sand? They had all been monsters.

Was she a monster as well?

Mike-Mike had been one, and from what Benji's arrested friends, The Come Up Kids, were saying from their jail cells, her son had been one equally.

Within ten seconds, she began to regret the fact that she hadn't had sense enough to see what was going on earlier because for little, black girls, across the country, there were indeed monsters under the bed.

Everything was crazy, and nothing made sense. Maybe, nothing ever would, and perhaps, that was the reason she just wanted to sleep. Forever.

Karen took the whole bottle of sleeping pills.

Chapter 38

President's Day. February

It was still fairly early in the morning when the dark-skinned man educated the other top FBI officials on the categorical breakdown of their mission to destroy Ivan and his organization.

He saw no use in kidding himself or the other men gathered in the room, and he scolded himself for not accepting the earlier invitation to cut his losses, and to scram, and, finally, to pass the task of saving black girls to another agency.

He silently cursed his foolishness because, to an astonishing degree, he had really believed that David's wild, crazy scheme would somehow work.

"Gentlemen," he rasped, "we are facing a national calamity, the likes of which we have never seen before." Adrenaline and anxiety, wrapped together, flooded the dark-skinned man's chest, pounding against his heart like the Hammer of Thor, but he didn't give a damn about these unintended side effects. All he knew what that he had to do what he had to do, and considering that now would be an ideal time to introduce the men to what was to come next in his attack against Ivan, he cleared his throat. "I'm calling in The Couple."

Sunday

When Sylvester Blackmon pulled into the parking lot of the restaurant, he saw that his wife's car was already there. This was their second dinner date this month. It was her time to pay.

"Sorry, I'm late," he apologized as he squeezed into his

chair opposite Sasha. "You're lovely," he added.

"What about my kiss, then?"

"Oh." Blackmon scrambled back to his feet and gracefully leaned down, pecking Sasha gently on her cheek. He loved the way she smelled. And looked. Her soft, flawless skin was a radiantly burnished copper, and her eyes were only slightly less brown. She was wearing her hair cut short, colored a silky, black gloss. Blackmon studied her. Without question, she was beautiful.

They gazed quietly at their menus, savoring the peaceful atmosphere of the restaurant. From time to time, one or the other of them would gaze over the top of their menu to stare at the other, and every time they caught the other doing this, they would giggle childishly like silly schoolchildren. But this was no game.

"How are things at the salt mines?"

The two of them took each other in as the question dangled between them. Sasha looked at her iced tea while Blackmon munched on a hush-puppy.

"I think I got the easier assignment."

Blackmon's expression didn't change. "You did." Suddenly, he noticed how uncomfortable he felt. "This could be the last time we ever see each other." His voice was flat.

"Yes, I know," Sasha replied sadly. She touched her napkin to his lips, wiping his mouth. "But this is what we do. We're closers."

Blackmon grinned, slightly relaxing. "You make it sound like we're ghost-busters."

"Sasha sighed. "Who else were they going to call? You represent the last chance to get those little girls back home safely to their mothers."

"And you represent the last chance to keep it from happening again."

"It's what we do." There was a hint of pride in Sasha's voice. "We either make it happen or we stop it from happening. Either way, we get the job done."

And for the last decade or so, the husband and wife team had done just that. Plucked right out of college, the pair had been recruited by the CIA, trained, and sent on various secret missions where the risks were high, and where the job needed to be done quietly and quickly. They were the best of the government's elite squad of 'people who got the job done'.

Blackmon shrugged as the waitress walked away with their order. He wondered if this was their last supper.

Monday.

Sasha's plan was simple. She would kill Ivan Gugarin. Still, she didn't have much time. She glanced at a calendar. It was already the 20th.

One week.

Seven whole days.

That's all she had.

Out of the next troubled days, she would have to piece together a way to take out one of the most heavily-guarded sex traffickers in the world, or get herself killed in the process.

On all of her other government-sanctioned missions, every move she had made had been plotted out with careful planning. On each of those hits, a situation that was very dangerous would be potentially reduced and lessened by superior, overwhelming info-gathering, but that was not the case this time. All her superiors had left her with were bare, naked notes; hardly sufficient to shape an effective assassination, but whether she liked it or not, in less than a week, something would have to be done. Her deadline was fast approaching.

She understood that men who took great pleasure in living sometimes took extra precautions, going against their natural instinct of following a routine. This prevented them from being predictable which made them more difficult to kill. Ivan, the Russian, was presumably one such individual.

However, now was certainly not the right time to get philosophical. She re-focused. She gazed at the key, running her fingers across the jagged, grooved edges absently. It was only 11:00am, not quite time for lunch.

After a brief moment, the realtor flipped the big book closed, and dashed across to a blank board where he entered the name and address of the property Sasha wanted to view. By force of habit, the realtor compelled Sasha to spell her name out slowly.

"S-T-R-U-T-H-E-R-S." Sasha pronounced each letter clearly, then repeated the process for the first name. "J-U-N-E."

Glancing at the name, the man appeared satisfied. "The twenty-five dollar key deposit will be reimbursed once you return the key. We close at five o'clock sharp. If for some reason, you don't return it by that time, you will have to pay a late charge."

Sasha exited the office quickly, walking swiftly past the red and white, peppermint striped Benson Realty sign, then turned the corner where her car was parked.

She drove away.

Shortly, the building she had chosen popped into view and Sasha checked her watch. There was no time for a walk-through. She would have just enough time to get set up since she had discovered that Ivan always had lunch at noon.

Parking the Maxima near a stone passageway to the immediate left of the building's front door, she snatched the long, tubular package out of the back seat and approached the property.

She stopped and tried to peek through one of the dirt-streaked, diamond-cut panes of glass. It was dark inside. She took a step backwards and angled the key, inserting it squarely into the lock. One turn and the door clicked open.

She stood at the staircase and put on the sleek, black gloves. They fit snugly. She purposely clenched and unclenched her fists, feeling the soft leather bunch up, crinkle, and then flatten out over her small hands, becoming more and more like a second layer of skin.

She climbed the stairs in the outrageous quiet and at the top, she tried the door. It was locked. She used the same key to open it and to her surprise, the room was larger than she had thought it would be.

A weak splash of light filtered through a window that faced out onto the avenue directly across from the restaurant where Ivan and his goons would be having lunch.

She gazed at her watch as she cracked off the plastic cap on the tubing, and slid the high-powered rifle out. At the window, she dropped down on one knee, and sighted the weapon along the front doorway of the restaurant. She enjoyed the view because there was an endless row of nothingness to block a good, clean shot. This was a shooter's paradise. The landscape outside was flat and topped with nothing shiny or reflective that would cause the lens of the scope to bend or to refract any light that could distort her aim.

So far. So good.

Everything on the left side of the building was an exact replica of everything on the right. Sasha grew still. A small column of pigeons had dive-bombed in on the outside ledge and set perched there, bobbing their elongated heads up and down. She dared not disturb them or else they would flutter off in fright, giving her position away to any alert bodyguard.

"Shoo," she hissed through the closed window.

The birds flew away.

Sasha tracked their orderly flight through the cold lens of the rifle's scope. She removed her eye from the scope and squinted. She was high on the third door of the abandoned building, but not too high. Still, she could see the speeding traffic plowing the Interstate to the north and south of her where a chesty blonde woman on a colorful billboard sat curled up elegantly on a sofa, drinking Remy Martin. She appeared to be winking her eyes.

It was now a few seconds before noon.

Sasha changed her position as she scanned the distance, watching; waiting. Slowly, she reeled her left leg back in, relaxing the muscles in her thigh. She stood. Apparently, Ivan wasn't coming today.

Monday. Mid-day.

Back at the hotel, Blackmon snipped through his throw-away driver's license with a pair of scissors, and flushed the strips of plastic down the toilet.

He studied the photo on his new driver's license and then glanced at the info that accompanied it. He digested the data it contained so that he would be familiar with the area where the address said he lived. That way if **anyone** quizzed him, he would be able to describe his neighborhood. However, this was a high-quality document and could stand the scrutiny of anyone wishing to inspect it, so he expected no questions to be asked.

Leaving the hotel, he now knew he faced the task of eluding anyone who might try to get in his way. He knew that Ivan had eyes everywhere, and that he had taken a lot of precautions to keep the whereabouts of the girls unknown, and that he would continue to put up defenses to stop anyone who did find a trail.

Another thing he had learned about Ivan was just how much of a visionary he was when it came to securing his precious cargo of black gold. He had pulled out all the stops on this caper, and Blackmon had to grudgingly admire the handiwork and ingenuity that had gone into not just the planning of the kidnapping, but also the execution of the deed. It had been an A plus piece of work.

What disturbed him, though, was the fact that so many people were involved in the scheme who had refused to talk. That meant a lot of money had been tossed around. Or maybe it simply meant that the Tennessee Department of Transportation was very stupid, but Blackmon refused to believe anyone was that silly, so it had to have been money. Lots of it. How else could a construction crew win a contract to fix a stretch of highway that was not in need of repair? Anyway, this bogus contract had permitted Ivan's crew to work around the clock on the highway, but instead of a repair job, what they did instead was to dig under the highway to erect a hydraulic lift just under the surface of the road.

When the bus with the girls aboard had been forced to stop, Ivan's escape vehicle had been parked on top of the lift. And to disguise what was truly happening, the bombing of the bus from Charlotte had been a ploy to divert everyone's attention as the get-away bus was being lowered into the ground. That was why the bombs were more smoke than flash. Blackmon applauded the smarts that had gone into pulling that off. Additionally, the crew had equipped the underground passage with everything required to keep the girls down there until the heat died down. Then, from all indications, they had been whisked off, a few at a time, back into the North Carolina mountains.

Blackmon knew what he was up against. There were indeed monsters under the bed.

Chapter 39

Tuesday. Morning

Sasha saw the revolving doors of the public library just
ahead and she pushed gently into one of the four angular, glassed-
in compartments. It spun around quietly and churned her out into
a softly-lit huge room lined with books. She briefly examined her
surroundings. Slightly to her right, she spotted the librarian coming
down a looped, triangular corridor. She gingerly shoved the horn-
rimmed glasses further up on her nose, and with a nervous swipe
of her hand, patted the wig in place.

From the maps and blueprints she had studied the night
before, the archives gallery sat in a northwest corner on the
second floor perpendicular to the computer room and the women's
bathroom. It also faced the shoulder of a barbershop where Ivan
got his hair cut. Today, Tuesday, was the day of his weekly visit.

That much she now knew thanks to a contact who funneled
her info via another contact in DC. What she didn't know was
whether or not the gallery had a fucking window. She approached
the information desk. She'd find out soon enough.

"Hello," Sasha said in a clipped British accent. "My name
is Victoria Blair. I called earlier in reference to some research I'm
doing and was interested in visiting your archives."

"Oh yes," the librarian answered politely, "I remember your

call, Miss Blair. The gallery is upstairs, second floor. I've already summoned someone to have the door unlocked in anticipation of your arrival." The librarian smiled brightly. "Enjoy your research."

"Thanks." Sasha looked around for the stairs.

Being helpful, the librarian pointed. "Take the elevator."

When Sasha met the woman's gaze, she noticed her slightly exotic features, her soulful eyes. She smiled. "Thanks, but I really should take the steps. I need the exercise."

"In that case," the librarian laughed, "the stairs are in the rear. Can't miss them."

Walking off, Sasha was vaguely aware of the woman watching her. She cradled the tube that hid her rifle, slinging it across her shoulder and took the first two steps clumsily. The sun poured through the open-topped atrium, depositing itself upon an awe-inspiring, still-life portrait of three apples and a stainless steel knife that hung high on the enclosed wall.

The climb was soundless, but by the time she had lost count of the steps she had climbed, her breathing was impaired. Anticipation had set in, but still climbing, she vacantly started the process of clearing her mind.

Once she was in the kill zone, she casually planned her escape. Instantly after she had assassinated her target, she would exit the gallery by way of the stairs. No elevators. A crowd on the ground floor would be helpful, but if none, she would still slip out of the side exit nearest the water cooler.

Once outside, she would pass under the bridge leading to the Interstate, shuck off her disguise in the bathroom at Wendy's, reverse her route, and catch the number six bus going downtown.

At the second floor landing when she peeked at her watch, she saw that she hadn't much time to reflect on anything else. It was time to set up.

She strode briskly down the carpeted hallway, past one room, then another. The third door led into the archives gallery. She stood motionless for half a second, looking over her shoulder to see if she was being observed. Feeling nothing, she pushed the unlocked door open.

She had barely stepped inside the gallery when she swerved,

stopped, cursed. The window was elevated. It was nothing more than a paned square of plexiglass. She would have to stand on a chair. Immediately, she yanked a high-backed wooden one from under a heavily-built research table, and just as she started to step onto the chair, the door opened. It was the librarian. Sasha was taken by surprise.

"I'm sorry, Miss Blair.....what are you doing?"

Sasha crossed the room and gripped the woman around her neck. She applied pressure. The woman gasped, grabbing Sasha's wrists, trying to break the iron grip. She twisted, foamed at the mouth, then died.

Sasha released the woman, and the body clattered to the floor. In a big hurry now, Sasha quickly removed the rifle and climbed onto the chair. Her breath caught in her throat as she observed the arrogant, athletic figure of Ivan Gugarin, moving slightly out of view to her left.

"Dammit!" It was still possible that she could hit her target, but the disappearing angle he was giving her might not insure a kill shot. Sasha stood erect in the chair. Desperation was to be avoided because the risk was not worth taking. But just the same......!

Without giving it a second thought, she stuffed the gun back inside the cardboard tubing. She dashed to the research table, leaping over the dead body of the librarian, and retrieved the key to the locked door.

Out in the mezzanine, beyond the classical film section, came the faint murmur of voices. Sasha, for a brief moment, fiddled with the notion of trying to locate the fire escape, but instead decided to return the same way she had come.

She suddenly felt amped up, the familiar heat of the chase that lived inside her head had her juiced up, but oddly enough, despite the jacked up energy, she felt that time had slowed down considerably. When she dashed out of the library's door, she found herself immersed in the cool, bright midday. Her training kicked in and without delay, her brain raced to systematically code and decode external temperature, wind pressure, sunshine, clouds, and any other weather data that could have any negative effects on her getting off a good, clean shot.

At the last minute, she flirted with the image of her getting a better shot from behind the bushes next to the big tree than from behind the parked delivery truck. In any case, time was running out. It had to be one or the damned other. Now!

She ran like a madwoman, her long legs free-wheeling across a dry patch of brown grass where she had to leap-frog a small puddle of shit-colored mud to reach the scraggly bushes.

Up the block, she could still witness the approach of Ivan, but he was almost at the entrance of the barbershop, There was hardly any time left. She was panting like a weary dog, her ruptured breath chugging out of her mouth in a heated rush.

She didn't have time to analyze her shot, but it was obvious that the bushes gave her a more perfect vantage point. But not much else. Her flank was exposed and her escape route was less clearly defined, but once she had made contact with her target, and had dodged the instant, subsequent pandemonium that would immediately erupt within the vicinity of the shooting, she could easily elude detection.

Seizing the weapon, she was annoyed by the manner in which the sun gleamed off the gun's shiny metal, but she could barely do anything about it. She knew that now the most important thing was not to be distracted because one shot would be all she got.

She quietly adjusted her sights. To her, Ivan was already dead as she focused on getting a clear head shot. Her concentration was zen-like as she grew Buddha-like still. She aimed. A fraction of a second passed. Then another. Ivan was filling up the rifle's crosshairs nicely; just right. Sasha's finger tightened on the trigger, curling back in a fierce semi-arc, moving the firing pin out of position.

Sasha was impressed with the shot she would get, but at the last nanosecond, a man walked deliberately out of the barbershop and stood directly in front of Ivan, squeezing him completely out of the crosshairs. Not even Ivan's head was visible.

"Move you moron," Sasha exclaimed too herself. "Move!"

Instead the man stood there---in the way---greeting Ivan and then opening the door several feet so that the target could enter the premises. Shortly thereafter, the sidewalk was empty.

Sasha shook her head in utter disbelief. It didn't take long for her fire to be put out, so she re-packed the rifle. "What was that all about?" she groaned, addressing heaven. "Or maybe it was you," she croaked, staring at the earth. "Please, both of you," she muttered, walking back in the direction of the University, "leave me alone."

Tuesday. 12:00

The big clock in the hallway gonged. Both hands stood still on the weary face of the ancient timepiece, pointing angrily towards heaven. Noon.

Hearing that sound, Brianna and all the girls jumped up obediently, forsaking their hard cots to stand silently for inspection.

Today, one of the girls was a little slow in "assuming the position". One of the men held a gun to Rena's head.

"Let me shoot this bitch in the head, Commander. Let me plaster the walls with her fucking brains."

The Commander shook his head.

"Just let me shoot one of these bitches. Just let me kill one of 'em." The man grinned fiendishly. "I'll let you pick which one, Commander. I don't give a damn. I just want to blast one of these whores into next week." He pointed the gun at Rena. "Don't move, bitch."

"You." The Commander indicated Brianna. "Come with me." He motioned to the others. "The rest of you bitches stand pretty."

Outside a black Mercedes parked in front of the building, and a man, Carlos Popovich, stiffly emerged from the car as if he had driven a very long distance.

"Inside," Carlos pointed at the building. "Black Gold?"

Stepping inside the front door, Carlos' heart seemed to skip a beat.

"Oh my God!" he yelped. He stared at the young, black girl who stood in the middle of the floor, naked. "I-I wasn't expecting this. I have never in my life seen a woman this magnificent."

"I only deal in high quality. You know that."

"How many more of these do you have?"

"Quite a few," the gypsy rasped gruffly. He pointed at Brianna. "What about that one? Does she meet your specifications?"

"You must understand that it would be foolish of me to buy a cow with only a single drop of milk. Plus, I must know precisely what I am dealing with. Therefore I want to examine each specimen." He glanced again at Brianna. "And yes, this particular one has quite a bit of appeal."

Brianna was terrified, but she stood there as she had been instructed by the men who had brought her there. If she moved, they had warned her, she would be shot.

"I can deliver," the gypsy bragged.

Carlos Popovich nodded happily. "Excellent." He marched awe-struck towards Brianna, running his hands all over her body, searching for imperfections. He stared at the gypsy. "Impressive."

"Then I would like to complete this deal as soon as possible."

"And so would I" Carlos rubbed his hands together greedily. "Everyone, it seems, is in love with black gold, and I'm most eager to sell them." The man grinned happily. "Give me your rock bottom price."

Tuesday. Evening.

A look of pain crossed Blackmon's face. This was a bigger mess than he had previously thought it was. Just days before the kidnapping, there had been intelligence reports that the Russians were gearing up for an enterprise to kidnap black girls. They were throwing money away left and right, setting up safe-houses throughout the country where the girls could be held until it was safe to transport them out of the country.

Suddenly, Blackmon found that he wasn't hungry any more. His 6'2", 215 pound body would have to wait until later to be nourished as he felt sick on his stomach. He did however drink some of his latte as his station chief continued to brief him on the current events surrounding the Russians. The older, dark-skinned man took a deep breath. He spoke with a northern accent.

"The reports started pouring in a few months ago when we

were told that Russian sex traffickers and domestic pimps were putting together this so-called "Black Gold" agenda, but no one listened."

"So when did things change?"

The dark-skinned man looked at his hands, then shook his head. "It just boggles my mind what some people with a little time on their hands can cook up. A few years ago, a convict looking for a favor made it known to the feds about what new crime was on the drawing board at the Big House." The dark-skinned man paused. "Actually, it's funny how this whole damn thing got started, but according to the intel…. you're not going to believe this. Anyway, the story goes like this. A Russian sex trafficker goes to the prison commissary and buys a pint of Butter Pecan ice cream for a small-time local pimp. It, the ice cream, was a surprise, from one scum-bag to another. Anyway, the Russian gets to the nigga's cell, and sees a poster of a beautiful, bigged-ass black woman on the cell wall. The Russian guy goes bananas over the girl's ass. Wow, he says. "If you could get me bitches like that, I can make us very, very rich." The dark-skinned man scratched his beard. "Can you believe that? A fucking pint of ice cream. We got a busload of missing girls all because of a damn pint of Butter Pecan ice cream."

Blackmon spoke haltingly. "I still can hear my grandmother telling my sisters about how their asses were going to get them in trouble one day." He smirked. "Nothing in the world is talked about more than the fabled ass of black women. Hell, it is easily the most famous physical asset in the universe."

"Well, guess what," the dark-skinned man said, "it's now your job to save that world-renown ass."

Blackmon leaned back in his chair. "Give me the real story, man. After more than fifteen years in this business, I know when someone is trying to hand me the short end of the stick. You may want me to believe that this is about Ivan, but I'm picking up the scent of some other bullshit."

"Okay, okay. What disturbs the Department most," the dark-skinned man explained, "is that the kidnapping of black girls is no passing fad, and if we don't shut this thing down before it can really raise its ugly head, it could provide a pretext for full-scale aggression against black communities everywhere." The man sighed. "Young, black girls won't be safe."

"How many have been abducted so far?"

"All we know about for certain is that busload, but we're in contact with all the states to see if any of the girls that have been reported as missing are merely missing, or if they were part of a Cash for Coochie program----."

"A what kind of program?" Blackmon asked. "Cash for Coochie?"

"Yeah, that's what it's called, but what it amounts to is a bounty on the heads of black females. All bullshit aside, young black girls are almost worth their weight in gold and trust me, there are hustlers out there who are looking for an opportunity to snatch and grab a few of them."

Blackmon groaned. "At first, it was the boys who had a bounty on their heads."

"Well, now it's the sistas turn." The dark-skinned man talked slowly. "I don't want to scare you, but just to let you know how big this is, it could lead to war."

"War?!"

"At the request of The White House, we have personally been in contact with some of the countries where the girls may be taken, and those countries have been told that if they allow any of these children into their country for the purposes of sex slavery, then they will suffer the military might of the USA."

Blackmon groaned again. "Who would have ever thought that World War III would be fought over coochie."

"Anyway, the president would rather that we handle this crisis discreetly."

"Under what conditions?"

"By any means necessary. That's how serious this is."

"That bad, huh?"

The dark-skinned man nodded. "And part of the problem is that many of the countries involved in the sex trade have pretty much told The White House to kiss their asses. They see this as a golden opportunity to wipe the President's face in shit." The man blew hot air. "This could be the straw that broke the camel's back for black people. For decades, Russian, Cuba, and others have waited on something to set black folks off, something that would send them rioting in the streets, something so terrible that we would destroy the country from within."

"And you think this could be it?"

"If you had a daughter and someone fucked with her, what would you do?"

Blackmon got the message. "So none of the other countries are willing to cooperate?"

"And miss watching America destroy itself. Hell, every country in the world will want a front-row seat." The dark-skinned man shrugged. "Right now, we know Ivan the Russian is calling the shots and we know that he is still here in this country, and from all accounts, so are those girls. The White House does not, and I repeat, does not want those girls to leave these shores. It's anyone's guess what will happen if they do, but I damned sure don't want to face that possibility."

"In that case," Blackmon bragged, "all I need from you guys is intel."

After spending about thirty minutes discussing the location of his jump-off point, serious questions arose.

"I don't trust that," Blackmon informed the dark-skinned man, pointing to the data regarding the possible location of the safe-house where some of the girls were being held captive.

"They're there."

"In the mountains?"

"Okay," the dark-skinned man shrugged, "let's have a look at a map of Asheville. The team that assembled this data was very thorough. From Memphis, they were able to crack the code of the girls' movement by unraveling the knot of vehicle traffic here." With Blackmon close to his elbow, the dark-skinned man reached for a piece of chalk. "It always helps to visualize your info. He drew a circle. "Boston." He circled another city. "Newark." Lastly, he pointed. "Asheville."

"Why can't I----?"

"Too risky, that's why."

There was always the possibility that he could be wrong but Blackmon truly felt he could rescue the girls, especially the ones in Asheville, but he had been put on hold. Apparently, the big-wigs had thought that it would be best to wait until all the girls were back together. A rescue attempt would be made then.

"But what if they never bring all the girls together again? They separated them for a reason," Blackmon argued.

"Breaking the girls up into small groups of four or five was sensible. It made moving them a lot easier, and it sure was convenient when it came to getting them settled in somewhere. Everyone believes that they will bring the girls back together when the time comes to move them out of the country."

Blackmon didn't buy that. "What a break that would be, but what if they don't?"

"Then we lose those girls forever."

"I can---"

"Didn't I just make myself clear on that, Blackmon? Too damn risky. What do you think would happen to the other girls once the Russians found out that we had rescued one group. What, you think you could get in and out, get the girls without it being known."

"I'm killing all of the captors. No one, except the girls, gets out alive."

"Great, Blackmon, great, but the only problem with that is that once you get finished with all this killing, who is going to be left to handle communications between the other camps. I'm damned sure that constant contact is going on between the safe-houses and Ivan. If one were to go down, he would know about it quicker than the President."

Blackmon said nothing although it would have been more satisfying for him to have yelled at the dark-skinned man, telling him to kiss his ass, and that he was going in after those girls. Yet he didn't. He had gotten his orders and he would obey them. He finally stopped sulking long enough to ask one more question. "Suppose this meeting between us never took place?"

"Which would mean----."

"That I didn't hear shit you just said about not going in to get those girls." Blackmon tilted his head slightly to the side and aimed his eyes at the dark-skinned man, awaiting a response.

"Stranger things have happened."

Chapter 40

Friday

In downtown Asheville, Blackmon guzzled a cup of premium java as he waited near the side entrance of a furniture store. It was not yet nine o'clock when the store would officially open for it daily business.

At the appointed time, a small, blue company van pulled up and parked directly in front of the loading dock, facing a smaller, more narrower side street. The man sitting on the passenger side got out first, lit up a Marlboro, took two drags and then passed it to the driver of the van who had now come around where Blackmon could clearly see them both. This man also took two, quick drags off the cigarette before tossing it to the ground and stomping it with his left boot. They then entered the store.

A few seconds passed, and it was now Blackmon's time to move. He approached the door of the store at an angle. Stepping cautiously inside the building, he saw that one man, the driver, was planted near the big glass window. His companion stood behind the counter, pretending to be studying a batch of invoices.

After a minute of browsing, Blackmon heard the unmistakable click of a door being locked, and the telltale metallic rasp of the blinds being drawn.

The phone rang. The man came from behind the counter. "It's for you," he said to Blackmon.

Blackmon brushed past the man with no comment, and

reached over the counter for the phone. By now, the other man was halfway down a flight of steps that seemed to descend into a lower level of the store.

When Blackmon hung up the phone, the man pushed past and came back around the other side of the counter to face him. "May I be of some assistance to you?"

"I am an interior decorator," Blackmon lied, "and a mutual acquaintance suggested that I ask you about a particular piece of furniture that I could use on my next job."

The man slid a glossy brochure across the counter-top. "See anything in there you like?"

Blackmon slipped an envelope stuffed with cash out of his jacket into the center of the brochure, then slammed it closed. Glaring intently into the man's eye, his voice was hard and steady. "What I had in mind was a bit more special."

The man took the brochure out of Blackmon's grasp slowly. "I see," he said. "Follow me."

Sure enough the stairs led to a storage basement where furniture waiting to be crated and shipped filled the entire floor. The other man was already there, waiting. He came over, pushing a small cabinet on a coaster. "Ta Da!" he said dramatically.

"We just finished it yesterday," the man who had accompanied Blackmon down the steps confessed. "Everything you requested is installed inside the body of the cabinet. Gut it and you'll see. Most of the electrical stuff is in the legs, but to get to the real goodies," the man instructed, "simply saw the face of the cabinet in two."

Blackmon nodded. "Take it out to my car, will you?"

"Yeah, why not."

"Thanks," Blackmon said politely. "I'll go bring my car around. It'll only take a second."

As soon as Blackmon got into the car, he pulled a high-powered pistol out of the dash. He hadn't dared to take it inside the store with him for fear of being frisked, but now he tucked it under his thigh, practically sitting on top of it.

Pulling the car around, he drove to the curb, and quickly jumped out. Using an extended clip, he swiftly pumped two bullets into each man's head.

Peering down the small, deserted side street, he saw no one so he loaded the cabinet into the trunk of his car and casually drove off.

A little later as the morning progressed, Blackmon gazed into the sky, visibly awed by the day that was coming on. At a different stretch along the same highway, he witnessed the sun perform a glorious splashing-on-of-colors, bathing the panoramic vista with a brilliant glow. So, this was Asheville.

Asheville sat atop the mountains in the western part of North Carolina, tucked away in a mile high valley on the French Broad River. The scenic Blue Ridge Parkway cut a path through the middle of town while the outlying area was pock-marked with deep blue, man-made lakes filled to capacity with all kinds of fish.

For the last twenty-five years, Asheville had been experiencing a boom time. Downtown had been spiced up and transformed into a trendy, upscale bohemian mecca. This was a city where literary giants such as Thomas Wolfe, O. Henry, and Carl Sandburg had once lived, but Blackmon didn't give a damn about that. What concerned him most was that Asheville was now the hiding place for some young, black girls which he fully intended to take home with him.

Blackmon checked himself. All he wanted was to rescue the little girls safely. He told himself that he could spare his heroics for another mission, that all he had to do would be to make this short and sweet. Nothing more. Nothing less.

On the move again, he listened to the radio, but found it hard to concentrate on the song because the mere thought of how he was going to rescue those girls made his bowels churn. He craved action. Still, he needed to sort things out before absolutely committing himself to any single course of action because once he made his move, there could be no turning back.

Sometimes, doing the right thing could get ugly.

Saturday
When Sasha saw the man looking in the direction of the warehouse, she was quick to understand that the man knew

someone else was there, lurking close by.

Strangely enough, she felt no panic until a second man came racing from between the buildings, a gun held tightly in his fist. The men stood there, talking with great urgency.

As one, both men looked up. First, the man on the left said something, then in response, the other one checked his gun. Together, they headed in her general direction.

Watching them, Sasha cursed violently. She would be trapped if they swept into the warehouse from the wide avenue in the back because there was no other way in----or out.

Taking one final glance at the pair as they swaggered carefully towards the gated mesh fence, she could almost feel the cold intensity of the goons.

Cursing again, she rushed back across the floor and quickly gathered up the rifle. They knew where she was. She looked around, knowing she had to act fast.

Even in retreat, a plan was forming. She jumped up on an empty barrel and lifted herself up into the ceiling, dragging herself over the beams swiftly.

In the darkness of the ceiling, she crawled into a corner, concealing herself in the sloping vee where the iron framework met the far right wall.

If need be, she saw that she could creep further over to a covered recess behind a cluster of rusty pipes. She studied the area, her body primed to move, but suddenly, the two men loomed into view. Silently, she hugged the rifle tight to her body, aiming it at the pair below her.

Sasha was on the move again. Securing a firm grip and pulling herself between the crossbeams, she kept on her belly through the iron and steel sprawl, the rifle clapped to her chest. In the inky, black, cobwebbed firmament, she slid across the rafters smoothly. She soared high above the men below, scurrying over the cold, impassive gridlock until she reached a glass partition rising over the rim of a block of granite.

Stopped at this dark portal, Sasha cursed. She sure as hell couldn't go back the way she had come.

Damn!

And to make matters worse, she calmly watched as one of the men easily hoisted himself up into the steel-jacket ceiling and burst into the iron-fisted blackness. He was coming after her.

She was trapped!

Calming herself down, she tried to open the glass partition, but couldn't. Taking a second or two to let her eyes adjust to the stupendous darkness, she ran a careful finger alongside the fringes of the glass where it cut deeply into the stonework. Using her sense of touch as a guide, she soon detected what she had been looking for: a trigger guard. It dipped down and was snugly fitted into a concave groove, and when she depressed it, an almost inaudible click was heard. This time when she pressed her palm against the thick plexiglass, it swung out easily, opening the way to another section where the steel crossbeams were burnt and had been disfigured by fire.

Sasha crossed over. The faded stink of charred smoke still clung heavily to the unwinking shadows, evoking mystery as she threaded the iron labyrinth. She moved fast.

Meanwhile, the Russian goon didn't find the darkness inviting. His vision was too limited and the front flap of his jacket kept getting stuck in the cracks as he slowly moved through the darkened gloom, riding the steel beam as though it was an iron horse.

As his eyes began to focus more sharply, he looked around because he knew that in one of these shadows, danger lurked. An intruder was here which made this such an attractive opportunity for death. All at once, air became almost nonexistent and the man grew sick on his stomach, but he didn't stop, To get to where he wanted to go, it was necessary for him to cross a corroded eight inch beam where the raised struts bit into his body like blood-thirsty iron leeches. Reaching the end of the snarling steel terminal, the man recognized that he was heading onto a double-tracked platform strapped to a massive stone arch. A storefront window was seemingly jammed down into the rock like a see-through tee-shirt. Seconds later, he pressed his face to the glass, staring into the vast darkness on the other side. A second or two after that, he pushed through the window into the blackness,

Like a slinky, black cat, Sasha curled up on the beam. She waited. She took it all in. She could clearly see the man and as he got closer, she kept absolutely still, continuing to breathe normally even though she was excited. The time to strike was near.

In the darkness, she tested the belt by running her hand up and down the length of the leather. It was strong enough.

The man slid closer.

To her left, the abrasive sound of clothing sliding across steel grew louder. She prepared herself. The man was only a few feet away.

As soon as she could feel the warmth of the man's breath on her face, she sprung out of the shadows like a caged tiger. She was as quick as a bullet. In that exact, same instant, the goon noticed something coming at him, but before he could do anything, his eyes began to water and he experienced a strangling sensation around his neck, and knew he was being choked.

Twisting his head violently from side to side, the man's hands flew up to his throat, his fingers trying desperately to free himself from the strangle-hold he was in. But there was nothing he could do.

Then Sasha loosened her grip.

The man sucked in air. He coughed. He passed gas.

"If you scream or yell out" Sasha whispered in the man's ear, "I will slit your throat. Just talk calmly and clearly. "Where is Ivan going to be tonight?"

The man said nothing.

The leather belt bit deeply into the man's neck, causing his eyes to almost pop out of their sockets. After one more second, Sasha relaxed her grip.

"Answer my question and you live."

The man knew that he couldn't take much more of this. He whispered. "At The Blumenthal."

Very much aware of the startling reality that this was it, her do-or-die moment, Sasha knew she had to perform the kill tonight. No ifs, ands, or buts about it. Tonight was the night!

Going into her zen-like zone, she went over the kill in her

head. She was clearly in her element now, but still had to get closer to the main entrance of the building for a cleaner shot.

She moved fast, but the three or four steps needed to pull within a few feet of the Blumenthal's front door seemed endless. However, she was now in place.

It was almost time.

At nine o'clock, a cruising car slowed, moving east across the intersection, and then pulled up behind the SUV parked further down the block. Sasha looked away from the halogen headlights, twisting her body away from the glow.

Just then the Blumenthal's door opened and Sasha watched as the first of Ivan's goon swaggered out of the building. They were watchful, non-threatening. Then came Ivan.

Sasha didn't like it. Ivan was surrounded by too many people. Ivan was slightly west of her, but due to bad luck and bad timing, the goons herded Ivan east, away from her, towards the SUV. Sasha cursed.

Everyone seemed unaware of her as she turned on her toes and took a few steps in the other direction. She moved swiftly, attempting to close the distance between her and Ivan. For a second, she flirted with the notion to abort mission, but she couldn't. This was it, the last day of forever.

On her way across the street, she was surprised that none of the goons were monitoring her so when she made a pass between a black Chevy and a green Ford Explorer, she reached into her jacket for the gun. At this distance, she couldn't miss.

She let three more goons pass by, then felt someone at her side.

"What is it, kid?" Sasha was annoyed.

"For you," the boy announced. "A gift," he added, pushing a package into her hands. "From Ivan."

"From who?" Sasha looked away from Ivan to the boy. "From who!?" she repeated.

"It's for you, Sasha, from Ivan." The boy ran off.

How did the kid know who she was, she thought as she stared at the book in her hands. Only it wasn't a book. It was the thick photo album that she always kept on her bedroom nightstand.

When she looked back for Ivan, he and his goons were speeding rapidly towards Trade Street.

At first, the photo album only seemed to twitch a little in her hands, only a slight vibration. Yet what followed next was what really got her attention. The photo album pulsed with a tremendous burst of energy, then exploded. The violent intensity ripped off both of Sasha's arms, her head, and stripped the flesh from her bones.

And so ended the night.

Chapter 41

Sunday

Just as soon as Blackmon had checked back into the hotel, it finally stopped raining. He went to look out of the big, picture glass window, and saw that the sun was trying to peek through. His spirits somewhat lifted by the promise of sunshine, he strode over to the bed where he had tossed his cell phone. He had a message. Sasha. Blackmon sported a wide grin as he picked up the phone. It was a video message. His grin grew even more. Maybe Sasha had sex-texted him a naughty video of her. That would mean that she had completed her mission. Blackmon felt that a celebration would soon be in order.

Whoooee!

Walking back over to the window to bask in the sunshine now pouring in through the window, Blackmon ginned happily in anticipation as he hit the download button on his phone. At the beginning, everything on the screen of his smartphone was dragging by slowly in a jumbled maze of colorful abstract images until the camera's angle seemed to backfire and pan diagonally across a wide street. It stopped over a passers-by left shoulder.

A building popped into view. The Blumenthal.

For some reason, a sense of dread caught up with him as he followed the movement of the camera. It focused on a woman. He gasped. Sasha. Trying not to let his fear get too far ahead of him, he stumbled over to the bed to sit down.

261

For what seemed like a long time, the camera zeroed in on Sasha. Then he saw the kid. He saw him hand her something......a book. Even though he was breathing normally, his pulse was racing, and the blood vessels in his head throbbed forcefully against his temple.

By the time he had adjusted the volume on his phone, he both heard and saw what happened next. Sasha exploded.

"Sasha!"

Blackmon found himself babbling incoherently. He lurched towards the bathroom to vomit. He sounded like a wounded bear, but very soon nothing would matter. At present, only a few things did matter. Foremost was revenge. He hungered to kill Ivan and knew nothing would satisfy this diabolical desire except a killing.

"Ivan!" he screamed at the top of his lungs.

He had to leave the hotel. It was no longer safe for him to be there.

Almost immediately after turning left out of the hotel, he noticed that he had been picked up by a man in a green jacket and a brown hat. At this stage, it was simply too early for him to tell if he was being tracked singly by green jacket or by a team. Chances were good, though, that it was a team of trackers, and chances were equally good that they had him boxed in already.

At once, all of his instincts kicked in, and he instantly felt revved up. The chase was in full effect and the years away from the action had not dulled any of his razor-sharp senses.

Walking direct in a straight line, he expertly strung the trackers out of their box and then zig-zagged into a corner building. Knowing where he was, the men following him would have to regroup in order to try to box him in when he exited the building. From the vantage point of an inside window, he visually picked out his trackers, and watched them intently as they scrambled to reorganize.

Heading back out of the building a few minutes later, he again picked up a tail, however this time it not green jacket. It was a shorter, more fat fellow. The other three were still quite near.

Viewing the street he was on, Blackmon saw it was what was known in the Agency as a 'slow area', meaning that very few people were in the vicinity which would make you---the one being followed---more visible. From his knowledge of the city, he knew that a 'fast area' lie just ahead a few blocks away. In a fast area, the trackers would have to tail him more closely because of the higher number of people in the vicinity. The last thing the trackers would want to do would be to lose him in a crowd.

At around 1:45, Blackmon reached the intersection where the street where he stood crossed into a 'fast area'. Looking left, he saw no one suspicious, but glancing over his shoulder, he spied his tails, and as expected he had drawn them in closer.

Heading east across the street, he pushed himself hurriedly down the main artery of the busy commercial district. He stole a quick peek at his watch. Only a few minutes more. He walked across a second street further down the block that swerved into another boulevard at an angle. From here, he could see the fat guy. There was another tracker off to the side but he couldn't approach any closer without giving himself away. The remaining pair, green jacket, and a tall, dangerous-looking companion were yet farther back; one prepared to follow if he went left, the other, if he turned right.

Walking slowly down the street, Blackmon fished the men out since the street had angled off into a single narrow road which forced the men to almost tail him in a single line. It was now almost two o'clock, and looking up the block, he saw it. Right on time.

Breaking for the taxi at the last second, he hopped in, leaving the surprised men, wondering what to do next.

That was fun, Blackmon thought. Now, shit was getting ready to get real.

Fifteen minutes later, he was dropped off at a safe-house not too far downtown. He rushed in. He had to move fast because he intended to finish what he had started. It would end today.

He trotted to the bedroom and inspected the materials he had removed from the cabinet. He had everything he needed. With a cold calm, he leaned over the bed, and cupped the plastic bag in his hands. Once he had examined the liquid contents, he laid the harmless seawater aside.

On another section of the bed, he picked through a handful of drab silver gaskets until he found the one he required, Then, without measuring, he cut a small hole in the rubber hosing. Not quite large enough, he performed a second incision, snipping off another centimeter from around the seal before fitting the gasket in securely.

Afterwards, he squeezed a few highly compressed drops of nitrogen tetroxide down a pinhole he cut into the membrane of the rubber tube. On the top end, he affixed a tiny, headless piston, tilting it four degrees out of its original position so that the high-compression device would be harder to detonate prematurely.

He made three such devices. Next, he filled three similar rubber hoses with hydrazine, a highly volatile chemical. Once finished, he locked them in place, fitting a glass cylinder between them with the ends of the glass hinged to the mouth of each rubber tube. Later he would leak seawater into the cylinders. That would be the icing on the cake because seawater would turn this mixture into a deadly explosive.

Once he had examined each of the tubes, he checked carefully to make sure the escape hatches were sealed tight.

Blackmon began to sweat profusely now. On the desk was a leather wrap-around utility belt. It was about as wide as a pillowcase doubled over with a dozen black compartments. Without giving it a second thought, he strapped up, lashing the belt around his waist with Velcro flaps. With even less thought, he solemnly picked up the six vials and dropped one in every other slot.

It was now time to get dressed, and to get going. The house was filled with a dizzying silence as he spent the following three minutes assembling the delicate wires, but when all the wires were connected, his bowels felt loose, like he needed to shit.

Lacking emotion, he pulled on a light jacket decorated with a gold button on the lapel. Looking at himself in the mirror, he felt electric and warm. Satisfied, he phoned the local radio station. "Play some Jodeci for me."

At precisely 3:45pm, the carload of men made their way across the busy intersection, and drove around in a clumsy circle until they ground to a halt on a desolate little street that sat at the edges of a deserted park.

Blackmon grabbed the binoculars and peeked through them. He studied the painters at the house where the cars had parked. He grunted knowingly. "Goons," he whispered to himself. The men swung the paint brushes like they had never held one before. "Goons," he whispered again. He had never seen anyone handle a brush quite like that. Blackmon grunted. If the men were packing, it would be their personal weapons. Nothing heavy-duty.

The house was large and spacious with a smaller guest house out back that was hardly ever occupied. In the rear of the house, he spotted a truck which could be either for transport or a carrier of the heavy artillery. In any event, Blackmon noticed that it was too far away to be of any help. Plus, he felt it would be relatively easy to take the truck out if it started moving inbounds.

Blackmon knew his plan had struck gold when he saw a delivery truck pull up, and watched as men scrambled across the lawn to remove pizzas and soda. Blackmon didn't see any weapons. Apparently, it was lunch time. He applauded his good luck. The girls had to be here.

Out of the corner of his eye, he cast a quick glance at another pair of men who saluted each other with dizzy delight before one of them departed into the food truck. He hoped a few more of the men would leave, giving his rescue mission less resistance.

A mere second later, another car came from out of the shadows and two more goons zoomed into view. Between them, they sandwiched a hand-cuffed companion who stood in the middle, his head drooped down in humiliation. The man who emerged from the car had a severe frown on his pale face and apparently was not moved by the man's explanation of whatever it was that he had done wrong. Still, the man pleaded his case.

Wanting to hear a second side of the story, the man with the commanding presence ordered one of the other men to relate his version of events. And though Blackmon could not hear what was being discussed, he grew tense when he saw the man make the universal 'Coke bottle' gesture with his hands indicating a nice female physique, Maybe this guy was love-struck and had fallen for one of the girls. Or worse yet, maybe he had molested one of them.

Praying for the safety of the girls, Blackmon watched silently as the handcuffed man was shoved into the waiting car which zoomed down the street.

Without much warning, Blackmon felt himself slipping into the zone. He didn't fight the feeling because he knew the one thing he could always trust was his instincts. And this morning, he was certain that the girls were somewhere in the downturned stretch of the building where the massive windows were darkened, getting blacker and blacker the farther you went to the right.

Even though nothing tangible supported these suspicions, they were still commanded by something he felt deep down in his gut. Plus, where else could they be? After putting all his anger about Sasha to rest, he moved deeper into the zone.

Over the last few days of his existence, everything about him had been geared to face the challenge of this moment. Each passing hour since then until now had sharpened itself on the conclusion that he was the right man for the job. So much was at stake, and until those girls were freed and Ivan was dead, he accepted the fact that he would not rest peacefully.

At first, from where he was, it was hard for him to track the movement of the men inside the house. Blackmon was unfazed by that difficulty. It merely bothered him that he didn't precisely know just how many people he would have to kill once he did get inside. After planting some explosives near the perimeter, he said a prayer.

It was time.

Swiftly moving from the safety of his lookout post, a deadly menace seemed to pop up from nowhere, and instantly things to be aware of sprang up from everywhere. In many ways, Blackmon immediately caught on that the young man patrolling the side entrance was not well-versed in how to keep his ass alive in the event of a sneak attack. He still acknowledged the noticeable budge under the man's jacket. A gun, more than likely.

Throughout the next fifteen seconds, Blackmon observed

the way the man moved, but decided he had to get closer. Having made up his mind, he crossed behind the deserted food truck, and with a gloved hand removed the throwing knife. Wolfing down a pair of deep, calming breaths, he got busy making the proper calculations and once convinced that everything was everything, he sent the knife zinging through the air.

Bull's-eye!

Standing over the dead man's body, Blackmon derived no real pleasure over what he had done. Instead he gazed icily through a window. A man in a brown hat stood stiff as a tin soldier, listening to whatever he was being told by another man who, apparently, held more rank. A third man, dressed in fatigues, emerged from yet another room.

Blackmon returned his attention to the man in the brown hat who rushed out of view. He returned a few seconds later with five black girls. Upon seeing the girls, Blackmon swung into action.

This was it. The final play. No more.

He set the charge on the side of the house, and after the explosive had knocked a hole in the wall big enough for him to squeeze through, he was upon the jittery men who were startled by the blast.

The inside of the room was not overly huge, but everything was so color-coordinated that barely anything got noticed except the ornate, swinging doors to the left. Two men burst through, and Blackmon hit them both with head shots. He watched in dismay as the terrified girls scrambled for cover, ducking under the table. He shouted. "Run! Get to the van!"

He killed two more of the men. Another man raised his hands over his head in surrender, but Blackmon was in no mood for peace. He killed that man also.

Blackmon stood only a few feet away from the dead men. He felt good. Nothing had gone wrong. Thank God.

In the distance, a cat howled. It was a dreadful, mournful sound and a pack of wild dogs barked back in response. Even farther away, a train could be heard, whistling by, choo-chooing as it sped across the tracks. But outside, in the front of the house, cars pulled up, and goons jumped from them. They had guns.

Blackmon watched as the men moved closer, getting almost there. This was not going to end well for them, he smiled. The men crept closer. And closer.

When Blackmon stepped out on the front porch, he felt his pulse quickening, and though his stress level was at its threshold, he remained sufficiently calm. He was now a killing machine, and with his sensory perceptions on high alert, it took him only a mere second to decipher that none of the men would get out alive.

He hurled the grenade.

The four men exploded.

Then

Blackmon sensed it before he actually saw it. The transport truck he had seen earlier was now moving, picking up speed, and just as he aimed his weapon, he saw the truck abruptly switch directions. His heart beat loudly as he watched the truck barrel towards the van where the trapped girls were huddled together in fear.

Blackmon fired his weapon. The truck barreled on.

Seeing the trapped girls, he dashed towards the van and when he saw that the truck was driver-less, he knew the vehicle was rigged with explosives.

"Get out of the van!" Blackmon shouted. "Get out of the van!"

Blackmon aimed his weapon at the right front tire, flattening it. He then disabled the tire in the back. The truck, gasping for air, slowed considerably, but it didn't stop.

"Oh, my God! Blackmon put his hands up to his face to shield himself from the blast.

Shit happens.

MOTHERS, DO YOU KNOW WHERE YOUR DAUGHTERS ARE!?

BIO

For most of my life, I was the guy most wannabe thugs wished they could be. Officially declared a "menace to society", I was sentenced to 30 years in federal prison for my role as mastermind of a series of daring bank robberies in the 70s. Two involved shootouts. One with the police. The other with a citizen in a bank parking lot where I narrowly missed being killed. While confined, I took part in an even more daring prison escape.

Despite this seeming penchant for violence, I consoled myself with the notion that I was merely a poet trapped in a gangsta's body and oddly enough, this wasn't far from the truth as I had evolved from a family of teachers, four of whom taught English. As such, I learned, early on, to respect and to appreciate language since my grandmother was very strict and would not tolerate improper grammar under her roof.

From the start, there appeared to be a household conspiracy to convert me into a writer. By the time I was ten, I possessed a private library fit for a scholar, had a new typewriter, a big desk, and plenty of blank paper. By 11, I had mastered the dictionary, was a whiz at Scrabble, and was a honor roll student in school. At twelve, I had completed my first novel.

By my 13th birthday, I had discovered hustling and I immediately dropped out of school and adopted "the streets" as my home. By 14, I was in reform school for assaulting a police officer. While there, I was a star journalist, the first black deemed smart enough to work in the print shop. I served one year and a day.

Upon my release, with hardly any delays, I embarked on a personal crime spree, and at the age of 15 years-old, I was sent to prison where I was the youngest convict there.

While in the Youth Center, I acquired my high school diploma at 16 years-old, wrote my first play, turned militant, and when released at 19, went to New York to join the Black Panthers.

In New York, I discovered heroin. Writing and the revolution would both have to wait as a drug habit left little room for anything else. When I tired of being a junkie, I kicked my fascination with getting high, but years later would emerge as the "alleged" kingpin of a notorious heroin distribution ring.

Finally brought down by the FBI and DEA in 1997, I again was sent to federal prison. This time I would be gone for another decade, but once more I turned back to what I had turned my back on: writing. I studied journalism, started a writer's colony, mentored other aspiring prison writers. I edited and founded various newsletters, performed freelance editorial services for outside writers while quietly perfecting my craft.

Hailed by some as one of the greatest prison writers ever, I was interviewed by numerous TV and print outlets. My writings have even been studied in an English class at a university where I was invited to lecture.

While in the Atlanta Federal Penitentiary, I published two novels, but soured on traditional publishing after a deal gone bad with a well-known publisher. I also developed two programs. One, PROJECT UPLIFT, which deals with drug-dealer addiction. The second, GIRLSMART, a community service program concerned with at-risk, teenaged, black girls. This program is a counter to the video vixen syndrome where sistas opt to employ their booties rather than their brains.

Lastly, I have finally gone from wrong to "write!"

www.ingramcontent.com/pod-product-compliance
Lightning Source LLC
Chambersburg PA
CBHW070854250626
47159CB00003B/1058